BE A FALLING LEAF

A Tallyforth Mystery

Bob Bibby

PIERREPOINT
PRESS

First published in Great Britain by Pierrepoint Press 1998.
Copyright © Bob Bibby

Bob Bibby asserts the moral right to be identified as the author of this book.

Lyrics from *'Raglan Road'*, *'In the Days Before Rock n' Roll'* and *'Memories'* by Van Morrison, and from *'For No One'* by Lennon and McCartney, permission applied for.

Cover design by Barry Perks based on on a concept by James Torry.

A CIP record for this book is available from the British Library.

ISBN 0 9533196 01

Typeset, printed and bound in Great Britain by York Publishing Services Ltd., 64 Hallfield Road, Layerthorpe, York.

To Enid, John and Duncan
who had faith in me.

On Raglan Road on an Autumn day
I saw her first and knew
That her dark hair would weave a snare
That I might one day rue.
I saw the danger, yet I walked
Along the enchanted way
And I said let grief be a falling leaf
At the dawning of the day.

From 'Raglan Road'
Traditional, words by P.Kavanagh

ONE

The shock of greenery had surprised him. Spring's rain had forced the fresh foliage suddenly and its vivid greenness, seen from the motorway behind a hovering kestrel, had imprinted itself on his mind.

'What have we got then, Elliott?' barked Tallyforth, entering the boardroom of Æthelfleda High School in Tamworth, where the fingerprinters, the police photographer and the Mercian Police Force's forensic scientist Jake Clifford were busy at work.

Detective Sergeant Georgina Elliott, always and inevitably known as George, who was standing by the window overlooking the school's playing fields, looked up from her notebook.

'Hubert Stanton.' She indicated the body in the plastic bodybag stretched out on the floor. 'OFSTED Registered Inspector in charge of the inspection of Æthelfleda High School. Aged between fifty-five and sixty I would say. Found dead, slumped in that chair over there by the table at seven o'clock this morning.'

Tallyforth gazed blankly at the upright wooden chair and then around the sparsely-furnished room with its plain wallpapered walls, then turned towards Jake Clifford.

'Cause of death?" he demanded.

'Couldn't tell you that, Chief Inspector Tallyforth,' replied Clifford, a short dapper man in a green lightweight suit. 'Too early to say. No obvious wounding. No gunshots. No abrasions. No sign of a struggle. Just possible it was natural causes. You know, heart attack or something. He was considerably overweight. But I'll have to examine his stomach back at the lab. and find his medical history before I can give you an answer. It could be poisoning. I've taken the contents of that coffee pot from over there.'

He pointed to the coffee-making machine on a side-table at the back of the room with its now-empty coffee jug.

'Had he been drinking from that? Was there a cup?' continued Tallyforth.

Clifford sighed.

'Yes to both questions,' he replied. 'I've taken that as well. Obviously. Now I must get off, Tallyforth. I need to get into his stomach, if you know what I mean.'

'One minute, please,' said Tallyforth. 'Let the dog see the bone.'

He moved across the room to where the body lay and pulled back the plastic sheet to see the dead man's face.

'They call them Reggies, don't they?' he mused. 'Registered Inspectors. Call them Reggies. Reminds me of Reginald Maudling. You wouldn't remember him though, would you, Elliott? Before your time. Used to be Chancellor of the Exchequer. Ted Heath's government I think it was.'

He placed the plastic sheeting back over the face of the dead man and signalled that he had seen enough. George Elliott watched him expressionlessly. She was used to his history lessons.

Jake Clifford gestured to the two police officers, who had been standing at the door of the room, that the body could now be removed. Taking an end each, they lifted it between them and left the room, followed by Clifford himself.

'So, Elliott, what else do we know? Who found him?'

She consulted her notebook briefly to remind herself of a name.

'The body was discovered at seven o'clock this morning by the school's premises manager, Gideon Lashley, who was opening up the school buildings and saw that there was still a light on in this room. When he came to investigate, he found Stanton dead in that chair,' she reported.

'Wouldn't he have seen the light last night?' Tallyforth interjected.

'Apparently Stanton had arranged with the school that he would be working late here and that he was not to be disturbed. It seems he had a key to the room and to the exit door on this side of the building,' she said. 'So Lashley claims that he had no reason to suspect anything unusual at this side of the school. He did his rounds as usual at ten o'clock last night, after the evening classes had all gone, and then went for his usual pint.'

2

'And the light was on then?' quizzed Tallyforth.

'Yes, sir. But he had been told to expect that and not to disturb the inspectors.'

George Elliott paused and watched Tallyforth as he prowled around the room.

'What about this laptop computer?' he asked, pointing at the slim black Toshiba computer that sat closed on the table in front of where Hubert Stanton had been found.

'Haven't done anything with that yet, sir,' replied Elliott. 'Presumably it's what Stanton was writing his report about the school on. Thought it best to wait till someone from the computer side had a good look at it.'

'Fingerprints?' asked Tallyforth.

'Done, sir,' she answered.

'You're technologically minded, Elliott. Can you work these things?'

'I have some knowledge, sir,' she began. 'But I'm no expert.'

'Try it,' he ordered. 'Just try it. Is there some way you can find the most recent thing that was written on there?'

George Elliott sat down in the chair recently occupied by Hubert Stanton, opened up the computer and got into its system. As luck would have it, there was a facility for discovering the most recent documents produced. She ran the cursor down to the topmost of these, which was labelled Æthelfleda Report: L&M, and clicked the mouse. Immediately a section of text appeared on the screen with the heading 'Leadership and Management'. She skim-read it quickly.

'Looks fairly technical,' she said, looking up at Tallyforth. 'Details about the school's management systems, how they work, some suggestions for improved communications, that sort of thing.'

'Does it look finished?' asked Tallyforth.

'Near as,' she answered, peering closely at the screen. 'One or two typos and there's a bit of a gap after the third paragraph with just the beginning of a sentence, which reads 'The headteacher and deputy headteacher......' Presumably there was something else to go in there. But otherwise, I'd say this reads like a fairly final draft. What had you got in mind, sir?'

'Nothing in particular. Just curious,' he said, turning away as a knock came on the door and a head appeared round its edge.

'Yes?' snapped Tallyforth.

'Sorry, Chief Inspector,' said the newcomer who now joined them in the room. 'Brian Pickevance. Headteacher. Dreadful thing that's happened. I've tried to keep the lid on everything but I need your advice about closing the school and about notifying the parents. What am I to say?'

Pickevance was a tall, slightly stooping man with rugged but careworn looks. He had grey-black curly hair and a grey moustache, and eyebrows that were permanently arched behind horn-rimmed glasses. He also had the beginnings of a stomach bulge.

'Sorry, Mr Pickevance,' said Tallyforth. 'Didn't mean to be rude. Are the children still here then?'

'Yes, I felt it best to carry on,' replied Pickevance. 'I was here within five minutes of Gideon Lashley calling me first thing this morning. It was me who called the ambulance and the police. I couldn't believe it. He was such a forceful, forthright character. We had a long conversation about the school yesterday afternoon and he said he would most likely be working late on his report. He was very complimentary about what we are trying to do here.'

'What time did you last see him then, sir,' asked Tallyforth.

Pickevance looked up at the ceiling and did some rapid calculations.

'Must have been about fourish,' he replied. 'I know he had a full team meeting at four-fifteen, so yes, I'm fairly sure that he left my office at about four o'clock yesterday afternoon.'

'And you didn't see him again?' quizzed Tallyforth.

'Not until this morning, after Gideon called me. I was here at about seven fifteen. I felt his pulse and checked his breathing, as Gideon had already done. Then I dialled nine nine nine.'

George Elliott was taking notes.

'And are there other inspectors involved in this inspection?' asked Tallyforth. 'Surely Stanton wasn't on his own?'

'Oh, yes, there was a team of ten of them altogether,' replied Pickevance. 'But most of them left last night. I also telephoned Stanton's deputy, William Reynolds, at the hotel where most of them were staying, just after I phoned the police. I explained that we had found the body and that the police and ambulance were on their way and we agreed to postpone the last part of the inspection until next week. Except for the feedbacks to the English, maths and science departments, which were scheduled for this morning and which had to go ahead because those inspectors are due somewhere else next week. So we found them another room temporarily, my deputy's office actually, and those feedbacks have now taken place. Those inspectors are still, I believe, on the premises, together with William Reynolds who has taken charge temporarily. I believe he has been in touch with OFSTED about what has to be done now.'

'So do your staff know about Stanton's death?' asked Tallyforth.

'I told them first thing this morning,' replied Pickevance. 'After discussing the matter with my deputy, I felt it best that they should be told. It's been an anxious enough week already, Chief Inspector, with this OFSTED inspection. I've operated from the start of the whole process on the basis that staff must be kept informed about everything, because fear of the unknown is the greatest cause of anxiety.'

'But you haven't yet told the children?'

'We call them students here,' he answered. 'No, not yet. I wanted your advice on this matter. Obviously the students will know there is something going on because of the police and ambulance presence, but fortunately this part of the school premises is rather segregated from the main buildings. Which is why, of course, I put the inspection team in here for the week. Should I close the school at lunch time? Should I inform the students of what has happened? Should I send a letter home to their parents?'

'Are your staff very traumatised by what's happened?' queried Tallyforth.

'I would say they have been more traumatised by the experience of the inspection itself,' said Pickevance. 'They look absolutely shattered. Some more than others, inevitably, I suppose. Few of them will have had much to do with Hubert Stanton, so I don't think there will be much personal feeling there.'

'In that case, I suggest that you carry on as normal, until the end of the afternoon.'

'No letter home?' asked Pickevance, arching his eyebrows even more than usual.

'We will advise you over the weekend, sir,' said Tallyforth, turning away from the headteacher. 'We don't yet know the cause of death. If it was natural causes, then we have no problem. If, on the other hand, it was not, then we are almost certainly dealing with murder. I think for the moment, it's best to keep quiet as far as the public is concerned.'

'Murder!' squealed Pickevance. 'But how.....? And when....?'

'Sir, at the moment we don't know what caused Stanton's death,' replied Tallyforth. 'But we have to consider all possible angles. Now, can you keep the children away from this part of the school for another hour, while we finish in here? And then I'd like to talk to you further, if I may. Is that possible?'

'Yes, of course, Chief Inspector,' said the chastened Pickevance. 'I'll be in my office all afternoon. I'd kept myself free deliberately because we were to be receiving our oral feedback this afternoon.'

'Good! Then I'll see you later, sir,' said Tallyforth, turning away from Pickevance and moving across the room thoughtfully. 'Oh, is it possible for me to see this William Reynolds character?'

'Of course! Shall I send him across? He's in my deputy's office now.'

'If you wouldn't mind, sir. That would be very helpful.'

Brian Pickevance, headteacher of Æthelfleda High School, turned briskly on his heel and departed. He was followed almost immediately by the police photographer and the two police fingerprinters

Tallyforth and George Elliott were now the only people in the room. Tallyforth paced around the table, scratching the back of his neck. Elliott was checking her notes.

'What d'you think, Elliott?'

'Sir?'

'Pickevance? Any feelings?'

'Not my type, sir,' she smiled.

'But whose type is he?' asked Tallyforth.

'Sir?'

'Probably nothing. Interesting you should say he was not your type though,' he said. 'Suggests you recognise he is somebody's type. Bit of a charmer, would you say?'

'I would say definite traces, sir,' she grinned again. 'But that sort of thing doesn't work on me.'

'No! We know that!'

She looked hard at him, thought about responding, but in the end decided against it. Not worth it. They'd had spats in the past but he always pulled rank and made her feel small.

'Do you smell something wrong, Elliott?'

'Yes, sir,' she said. 'It doesn't add up that an apparently fit man should just die like that. My brother's a deputy head of a school in Portsmouth and his school was inspected last year. These inspections cause massive stress on a school, particularly when the school has problems. If there is anything wrong, these OFSTED people will pick it up and it gets highlighted publicly. And that can have a huge and negative impact on the school's future, particularly on the headteacher's future. There's a few who have been forced out as a result of bad inspection reports.'

'So you think Pickevance killed Stanton because he was going to write a bad report on the school?' he queried, largely in jest, as she knew from the lop-sided grin on his face.

'Not saying that, sir,' she replied tartly. 'And that bit of the report that I got on the laptop computer was quite complimentary. So we don't know that the school was going to receive a bad report. All I'm saying is the effect a bad inspection report can have on a school.'

'And you're saying that you don't trust Pickevance?'

'Did I say that, sir?' she sounded surprised.

'No, you didn't,' he said. 'But you have indicated that there was something about his attempted charm that didn't appeal to you. Woman's intuition, Elliott. Always worth listening to. What's the time?'

She grimaced then glanced at her white Swatch watch.

'Eleven thirty, sir.'

'Right, we'll talk to this Reynolds character, then we'll need to interview some of the staff of the school. This premises manager Lashley, the deputy head, anyone else who was in the school yesterday evening. And, of course, Pickevance. I think I need to speak with him. Don't want him trying his charms on you again, do we?'

She pulled a face at him.

....

7

William Reynolds was a tall, thin, distinguished-looking man in his early fifties, with a monkish tonsure and a short goatee beard. He was wearing a dark, pin-striped suit and a rather loud red tie when he came into the boardroom some short time later to join Elliott and Tallyforth, who were both now sitting at the long walnut table.

'Good day to you, Chief Inspector. Good day to you too, Sergeant,' he said as he entered the room. His voice was thin and reedy, rather like his person. 'You wanted to talk to me about Hubert's death.'

'Yes, sir,' began Tallyforth, gazing at Reynolds who sat himself on the opposite side of the table. 'We need to know everything about yesterday evening when I believe you had an inspection team meeting. What time did that conclude, sir? And was Hubert Stanton working alone here last night or was anyone else here with him till late?'

William Reynolds cleared his throat.

'Chief Inspector, I must tell you at the outset that Hubert Stanton was not the easiest of persons to work with. He had a deep sarcasm in his tone that rarely disappeared. He made enemies more easily than he made friends. He was very bitter about the destruction of Her Majesty's Inspectorate, a body which he always claimed it had been a privilege to belong to, as he did for fifteen years, before Kenneth Clarke introduced this OFSTED business. But he had a brilliant, incisive mind and his judgement was absolutely first-class. This was the twelfth OFSTED inspection we had done together and I have never known him get one wrong. He knew schools inside out. He could smell their distinctive smell as soon as he walked through the front doors. And he was never wrong. Believe me, I've seen the look of astonishment on the faces of headteachers and governing bodies when he has read them some part of his report into an aspect of their school they thought was buried deep and impossible for an outsider to dig up.'

'And yesterday evening, sir?' prompted Tallyforth.

'I was coming to that, Chief Inspector,' replied Reynolds, rather waspishly. 'But I needed you to know something about Hubert first of all. I would be surprised if you didn't find in your inquiries that a significant number of people might have wished him dead.'

'Sir?' Tallyforth raised an eyebrow quizzically.

'I assume that you suspect he was killed, Chief Inspector,' came the response. 'Otherwise why would you be here? If Hubert had died of what used to be known as natural causes, I doubt if they would have sent someone of chief inspector rank, don't you? Anyway, Hubert was perfectly healthy. I've known him well for the past eight years and I've never known him to have a day's illness or time off work. He was notorious for the amount of work he could undertake, he was voracious. He could manage on as little sleep as that Thatcher woman used to claim. What was it? Three hours a night? Something like that.'

'We have no way of knowing how he died, sir,' replied Tallyforth, looking sharply at George Elliott who sat beside him taking notes but who caught his glance out of the corner of her eye. 'Not until we get a report from the forensic laboratory. But it is one distinct possibility, yes. We're here because Hubert Stanton's death occurred in suspicious and unusual circumstances. I don't suppose you have had any of your inspectors die on you mid-inspection before, have you, sir? Let along your Reggie?'

'Quite correct, Chief Inspector. Quite correct,' said Reynolds. 'Most unusual. And most distressing. Hubert was a good friend as well as an outstanding professional colleague.'

'So, last night, sir,' Tallyforth tried again.

'Ah, yes. Our team meeting yesterday evening,' Reynolds began, 'was somewhat difficult, I have to admit. You see, there had been a number of growing suspicions all week that there was something not quite right about this school. Hubert sensed it on our first visit but it took some time to find out what it was.'

'And?'

Reynolds gave Tallyforth a brief perfunctory look, as if to tell him to be patient. He was used to conducting interrogations of teachers, not to being interrogated himself. He liked to control the agenda of two-way conversations.

'It was the management. The headteacher, to be precise. He was one of this modern type who's been on all these management courses and picked up all the latest jargon about flat management structures and downsizing and empowering the workforce. But it wasn't just that. That's not unusual in itself these days. No, what was particularly unusual was that a lot of the senior staff had lost faith in him, even those whom he'd appointed some years ago and who had believed in the things he was promoting. But it took until yesterday evening to have that confirmed. At our briefing yesterday morning, Hubert asked all of the team to make informal inquiries from their respective heads of department in the school about their confidence in the direction the school was taking for the future. Some of my colleagues were unhappy about being asked to do this but it was at our meeting last night that it emerged that a good two thirds of those heads of department had expressed considerable reservations. And in every case, the head's name was mentioned.'

'Any particular reason, sir?'

'Oh, yes, one very powerful reason,' Reynolds answered, looking Tallyforth squarely in the eye. 'They did not like the influence exerted on Brian Pickevance by his deputy, Ms. Pearl Bowen.'

'Did that surprise you?' asked Tallyforth, again looking sideways at George Elliott.

'No, it did not. Ms. Bowen is a woman of strong views,' replied William Reynolds. 'It may or may not be her views that the heads of department are unhappy about. What concerns them most, however, is the reason why her views exert such an influence on Brian Pickevance.'

'And what is that reason, sir?' asked Tallyforth a little wearily, as he listened to William Reynolds's long narrative.

'Quite simple, Chief Inspector,' Reynolds smirked. 'They are having an affair!'

Tallyforth looked across at Reynolds and saw the smirk.

'Is that of some educational significance, sir? Does that make it impossible to run a school? Or is OFSTED on some kind of government-inspired moral crusade in the nation's schools?'

The smirk froze on Reynolds's face.

'It was our collective view that, whatever one's moral stance, the school could not function properly given that circumstance to which I have just alluded. It was therefore incumbent upon us to draw attention to this in our report of the inspection of Æthelfleda High School,' he said.

'You were going to state in your report that the headteacher and his deputy were having it off with each other?' Tallyforth asked incredulously.

'We would not have put it so crudely, Chief Inspector,' replied Reynolds. 'We would have merely pointed out that the close working relationship enjoyed by the headteacher and deputy headteacher jeopardised the fuller involvement of middle management in the school's development. I believe the majority of the readers of the report would have understood what was meant and would have acted accordingly.'

Tallyforth looked across at George Elliott, who returned his gaze. They both knew now what that missing sentence in the report on the laptop computer would have been.

'And that was discussed at your meeting last night?' Tallyforth queried.

'Yes. As a matter of fact, it was virtually the last item we discussed because it obviously was going to feed into one of our key issues for the school to address. As I said earlier, there was not total unanimity on this issue initially but Hubert carefully steered the meeting to ensure he got everyone's agreement eventually. The meeting finished shortly afterwards, at about eight o'clock.'

'And what happened then, sir?'

'What normally happens. The team packed up their bits and pieces and either headed back to the hotel for dinner or set off to their homes. I stayed for a quick word with Hubert, who had decided he wanted to forego dinner in order to stay here and write the draft of the main findings and key issues of the report. He planned to eat later,' Reynolds said.

'Was that unusual?' queried Tallyforth.

'A little,' replied Reynolds. 'Hubert normally does, sorry did, such work after dinner but he felt that this was a particularly tricky report to write and he wanted a clear head. I have known him do that before when the situation warranted it.'

'And what time did you personally leave, sir?'

'I would say just after eight-fifteen, Chief Inspector,' came the reply. 'I was certainly back at the hotel by eight-thirty, because I telephoned my wife before dinner, which we ate at nine.'

Tallyforth sat back, looking briefly across at George Elliott who was frantically scribbling away.

'Thank you very much, sir,' he said. 'You've been most helpful. I'd be grateful if you could let my sergeant have the details of all of the inspection team before you go. I assume you are leaving today?'

William Reynolds stood up.

'Yes, I'm going later this afternoon. I have to contact OFSTED to find out what has to be done and presumably I will have to return next week to report to the school in some fashion. I don't suppose it will be possible for me to take Hubert's computer, will it?'

'Not just at present, sir, no,' said George Elliott. 'Afraid we have to keep it for a while.'

'Any idea when I might be able to get at it?' Reynolds asked. 'I cannot give any kind of report without the information that's stored on that machine.'

'I think if you phoned us on Monday, sir, we might be able to tell you,' replied George Elliott. 'That's the best we can do.'

'Thank you, Sergeant. Thank you, Chief Inspector. No doubt we'll be in touch in the near future. Please let me know as soon as you know the cause of poor Hubert's death.'

And William Reynolds left them.

TWO

They were eating bananas in the boardroom.

'What time did you get here?' asked Tallyforth through a mouthful of squashed banana pulp.

'About thirty minutes before you,' George Elliott replied, nibbling more delicately on her fruit. 'Got held up in traffic on the M42. Some lorry had shed its load. Like they do.'

They chewed in silence for a few moments.

'I was planning on visiting my daughter this evening,' Tallyforth said at length. 'Looks like I'll have to cancel that now. Pity.'

'Your eldest?' she asked, looking in some surprise at him.

'Yes, it's her birthday tomorrow. I'd arranged with her mother to call and give her a present tonight.'

'Is that the one you've had the trouble with?'

Tallyforth nodded slowly and thoughtfully.

'Mm. That's the one. Still that's all sorted now. She's aiming for university next year, if all goes well.' He paused. 'D'you think this is a murder, Elliott? D'you think I'd better cancel this evening?'

'If you want my opinion, the answer to both your questions is yes,' she answered, looking him boldly in the eyes.

'Better phone then,' Tallyforth said. 'Can I use your mobile? Thanks. I'll have to leave a message on the answerphone. They'll all be out now'

He pressed the necessary digits, waited for the distant voice then left his message of regret, adding that he would find some way of calling the next day - the birthday itself. Then with a sigh he handed back the mobile phone to his detective sergeant.

There was a loud rap at the door.

'Come!' he commanded.

The door opened and a slim woman in her early forties, her blonde hair neatly bobbed, wearing a fashionable navy blue dress and matching high-heeled shoes, entered the room. She bore an envelope in her left hand which she held out towards Tallyforth.

'This has just arrived, Chief Inspector,' she said, handing over the sealed envelope. Her voice was clipped and precise. 'A police motorcyclist. He said it should be delivered to you personally and immediately.'

'Thank you, miss...' he began.

'Mrs Hilton. Alicia Hilton,' she said smiling. 'I'm the school's finance director. I was in the Reception area when the policeman called. I thought I ought to bring it myself.'

'Thank you, thank you,' said Tallyforth, responding to her smile with one of his own. 'Very thoughtful of you, Mrs Hilton'

He slid his finger under the flap of the envelope, opened it and took out its contents, which he studied quickly. Then he handed it to George Elliott.

'Oh, would it be possible for you to get a message to Mr Pickevance and tell him I won't be able to see him until about three o'clock?' he said to Alicia Hilton. 'And could you get your caretaker, Lashley, is that right? to come and see me as soon as possible? Thank you, Mrs Hilton.'

'Our premises manager you mean,' Alicia Hilton replied demurely. 'I'll fetch him for you. He should be helping to put the tables away after lunch.'

'Oh, and I could do with speaking to Ms. Bowen,' George Elliott butted in, putting down the envelope and its contents. 'Will she be in her office now?'

'I don't know,' came the reply, equally demurely. 'But I'll see. If she's not, I'll page her. That will bring her back to Reception within minutes.'

Alicia Hilton smiled again and swung out of the room.

'So it was poisoning then, Elliott,' said Tallyforth. 'Cyanide. Thank heavens Clifford was able to do his analysis of the coffee pot quickly enough. At least some of the possibles are still on the premises. Keep that Bowen woman talking until at least three o'clock. I need time with Lashley before I question Pickevance. Somebody spiked that coffee and Lashley will know who else was on the premises

14

last night. But I don't want Pickevance and his deputy concocting some story now. Keep them apart. See what you can get from her - about herself, about Pickevance, about the school, about the inspection, about anything. But don't at any time ask her about her affair with Pickevance. If Reynolds was right about her and the head, they could be in this deep. And what's happened to Reynolds anyway?'

William Reynolds was at that very moment in the deputy head's office debriefing the three remaining school inspectors still present in the school - the maths inspector Frances Sims, the English inspector Charles Foster, and the science inspector Valerie Potts. They had each delivered their final subject reports to their respective heads of department and were preparing to leave.

'Everything all right?' Reynolds queried, looking at each in turn. 'Any problems?'

'No, I don't think so,' said Charles Foster, a sallow-faced man with lank greying hair. He was sitting opposite Reynolds, putting his papers into his red leather briefcase. 'Ms. Bowen was there taking notes and she seemed a trifle agitated. She didn't say that much but she did query my evidence base on a couple of occasions.'

'What about?' asked Reynolds.

'Yes, I had the same,' interjected Frances Sims before Foster could answer. She was dark-haired, heavily made up and wearing what she referred to as her 'Friday suit' - a heavy black outfit with silver buttons. 'She was at my feedback too and challenged a couple of things. Wanted to know what my evidence was for the poor quantity and quality of resources in the maths department.'

'Yes, that was what she asked me too,' said Charles Foster. 'Plus she pounced on my reference for the need for the head of English to be more involved in whole-school issues.'

'Yes, I had that one too,' boomed Valerie Potts, a tall, large-bosomed lady in a tweed suit. 'I told the science woman Field she ought to get more involved in the whole school, as we agreed last night at our meeting. It was the head who sat in on my feedback and he jumped in at that point, saying there was plenty of opportunity through the Curriculum Development Group meetings.'

'So it looks like poor Hubert was right all along about the management issue?' said William Reynolds in his reedy voice.

At that moment, there came a sharp tap on the office door and, without waiting for an invitation, Tallyforth entered the room.

'I'm afraid I have to tell you that your ex-colleague, Hubert Stanton, was poisoned,' he announced. 'Someone had put cyanide in his coffee. He would have died soon after drinking it.'

The four school inspectors stared at him. Dumbfounded.

'My sergeant will need to take a statement from each of you before you leave, if you don't mind,' Tallyforth explained. 'Obviously this is a very nasty case and we are going to have to consider every possibility. We would appreciate your full co-operation.'

'Yes, of course, Chief Inspector,' replied William Reynolds. 'And I suppose, since I may have been one of the last people to see him alive, you will be wanting more of my time. Shall I book in for another night at the hotel, Chief Inspector? Would that be of assistance to you?'

Tallyforth was somewhat surprised. He had not formed the impression from their previous conversation that Reynolds would be so obliging.

'That would be extremely helpful of you, sir,' he answered. 'We obviously will need to talk to you at greater length about this inspection and about your findings, because it may very well be that they have some connection with this murder. But your three colleagues can leave shortly. If they would just each make a brief statement to my sergeant.'

'Whatever we can do to help, Chief Inspector,' said Reynolds on behalf of his colleagues. 'We are as anxious as you are that whoever perpetrated this evil deed should be apprehended as quickly as possible. It really is most extraordinary and most chastening.'

Tallyforth nodded to the four school inspectors by way of acknowledgement, then backed out of the room.

Pearl Bowen sat opposite George Elliott in the boardroom where the body of Hubert Stanton had been discovered. She was a woman in her late thirties, slim, about five foot two, with piercing blue eyes and close-cropped black hair. She was dressed in the modern style, in a short black skirt and red blouse which was buttoned to her neck. She exuded energy. Her features were always moving and she clearly had difficulty in sitting still in one position for long, as she kept shifting in her seat. Her movements were always sharp and severe.

'Ms. Bowen, as you are aware,' began George Elliott, opening her notebook in front of her on the table, 'we now know that Hubert Stanton died of cyanide poisoning. Can you tell me about the contacts you had with the deceased?'

'Call me Pearl please, Sergeant. Everyone does. D'you mind?'

Pearl Bowen's voice was as sharp as her movements but not unpleasant or strident, though there was no doubt in George Elliott's mind that it could be roused and raised to such a pitch quite quickly when required.

She continued:

'I had two interviews with Mr Stanton on Tuesday and Wednesday. The first interview was about the school's pastoral system, which I have management responsibility for; he was particularly interested in the school's attendance statistics. The second interview was about the school management system and my role in it, or rather roles because there are only two of us since the cuts of last year.'

'Tell me about the first interview,' pressed George Elliott. 'Why was Stanton concerned about the attendance statistics? Was there a problem?'

'He had clearly come with the pre-conceived notion that there was a problem,' Pearl Bowen answered quickly, crossing her hands in front of her on the table. George Elliott noted the absence of a wedding ring. 'We expected that. OFSTED tells Reggies to make inquiries about annual absence rates below ninety per cent. Ours was eighty two for last year. But I was able to show him that much of that was due to a small number of long-term absentees who had had extensive stays in hospital, to an equally small number of persistent waggers, most of whom have now been taken to court, and to the nature of our intake. I don't think he had realised how disadvantaged our intake is. The school draws from a dreadfully deprived area. You tend to think of Tamworth in middle England as being a relatively prosperous place but there are significant areas of poverty and Æthelfleda's smack in the middle of the worst of them. Too many parents had bad experiences in school themselves and they condone casual absences. But we've turned that round this year. We've instituted an electronic registration system, where the kids have to swipe their cards at the start of each lesson. It's proved remarkably successful. We can get at the casual absentees immediately and find patterns in their absence on our central computer. Then we tackle them and they know we're watching them. And it works brilliantly! We're up to eighty seven per cent attendance for the first two terms of this year.'

George Elliott noted the new note of enthusiasm that had entered Pearl Bowen's voice as she described the new system of registration.

'And the second interview?' she asked, allowing a short pause while she scribbled notes.

'That was more sketchy,' Pearl Bowen began. 'Mr Stanton kept skipping around in his questions. He did tell me at the start that he might have to, because much of what he wanted to know he had already found out elsewhere. But he said there were some bits he needed confirmation of and others he needed clarification about. I think I was able to help him.'

'What sorts of things was he asking about then, Pearl?'

Pearl Bowen flashed a quick smile of appreciation.

'Oh, things about the way senior management runs the school, about our priorities for the future, about our monitoring of teachers. You see, since I came eighteen months ago, we've developed a really powerful monitoring system in the school. Brian and I, that's Mr Pickevance and I, we have a schedule whereby we visit every teacher in their classroom twice a year, examine their lesson planning, scrutinise their marking of kids' work and observe them teaching. Then we write a short report on each of them which we discuss with them and from which we agree future priorities for action, which might include further in-service training or other opportunities for development and improvement,' she explained.

'Are the teachers happy with all this?' asked George Elliott.

'Most of them realise now that it's necessary. Especially now they've had this OFSTED inspection, because they were well prepared for being observed teaching. You know, it's one of the faults of the profession that many teachers, once they had qualified, could operate how they wished inside their own classroom for their whole careers without anyone ever coming to look at them teach,' came the reply. 'Well, that's all changed because of OFSTED. And we decided on this system because we knew we were due to be inspected. Of course, there were a few at the start who resisted. Claimed that it was too threatening. Argued that they'd always done this sort of thing but informally. Especially they didn't want me, the new deputy and a woman, coming in and passing judgement on them. But we won most of them over.'

'And those you didn't win over?'

'There were some casualties, yes,' Pearl Bowen replied, looking down at her red-painted nails. 'Because of the cuts to our budget last year, we had to lose five members of staff. One of them was the other deputy head, there were two heads of year, the head of technology, and a woman in the maths department who was only on a temporary contract. Brian managed to get fair deals for all of them.'

'And were these the teachers who had resisted your classroom monitoring methods?'

'I have to say that four of them were, yes,' Pearl Bowen sighed. 'And I also have to say that they were teachers who had become set in their ways, who did not believe that kids from Æthelfleda could ever achieve anything, and had created nice little administrative tasks for themselves which in many ways were unnecessary. The woman on the temporary contract was actually quite a good teacher but we just didn't have room in the budget.'

'Blood on the carpet then?' asked George Elliott, pausing from her note-taking to watch Pearl Bowen's face.

She reacted sharply.

'No, I wouldn't say that,' she protested. 'Brian managed it all very skilfully. Yes, it was difficult. Yes, there was some initial unhappiness in the staffroom. But in the end everyone accepted what had to happen. And the atmosphere in the school is just so different this year.'

George Elliott made a note.

'So Stanton was interested in that side of things,' she continued.

19

'Anything else?'

'He asked me about the way that money was allocated to various subject departments and how the amount kept at the centre was determined and allocated,' was the reply. 'I explained that we had a formula for allocating money to subject departments based on the number of pupil periods taught. I couldn't tell him much about the central funds. Finance is very much Brian's territory.'

'Anything else?'

Pearl Bowen sat back and looked quickly across at her interlocutor.

'Can I ask you something, Sergeant?'

'Yes, of course.'

'Are we under suspicion? I mean, us in the school?'

'Ms. Bowen, at present we know little more than you do,' replied George Elliott. 'We have been summoned here because a man was discovered dead in suspicious circumstances. We now know that he died from drinking coffee which had been laced with cyanide. We have to find everything we can about the dead man's movements in the last few days, which is why I'm talking to you. I can't tell you any more than that.'

'Aren't you going to ask me where I was last night?' Pearl Bowen asked. 'Isn't that what you detectives do?'

'And where were you?'

'I was here in school until about six-thirty. I was watching some of the rehearsals for the Offa Celebrations. D'you know about them?'

'No. Tell me.'

'Well, you may or may not know that Tamworth was supposed to have been the site of the royal palace of King Offa of the Mercians. And this July is the twelve hundredth anniversary of Offa's death, so the school is planning a big celebratory event. Norman de Courcy, our head of history, is responsible for overseeing it but I was watching Jon Mitchell with one of our school bands last night. He's our head of music - amazing man. Runs four rock bands in this school, plus he's got his own band who play in the area fairly often.'

'Interesting,' said George Elliott. 'And where did you go to after leaving the school?'

'I went for a meal with Brian,' she said. 'We were both knackered, it's been quite a bloody week, so we went for a quick Indian on the way home. At the Balti in town.'

'What time did you leave there?'

'I would say about eight o'clock to eight-fifteen. Certainly I was home by nine, if not before. Because I caught the news on BBC,' Pearl Bowen answered then stood up rather abruptly. 'Sergeant, mind if I go to the loo? I'm desperate. Shall I organise some coffee?'

George Elliott looked up a little surprised. She glanced at her watch. Two thirty. She needed to keep Pearl Bowen with her for another half hour at least.

'Sorry. Of course,' she said. 'Nothing to drink for me, though. I'm fine.'

Pearl Bowen quickly left the room.

Gideon Lashley was a broadly-built man in his late forties, with curly ginger hair that was receding so that the front part of his forehead shone. He wore a dark blue boiler suit, clean and creased. In his hand he jangled a large bunch of keys.

'Yow wanted a werd?' he asked in a broad Black Country accent.

Tallyforth looked up in surprise at the accent, which he knew well from his younger days working in the heart of the West Midlands. He had taken over Pearl Bowen's office temporarily, at Pickevance's insistence.

'You're not from this part of the world then, Gideon?' he asked.

'Naow! Oi'm from Wes' Brommidge,' came the reply. 'Ownly coom 'ere 'cos of the werk really. Got laid off from the Austin. Well, yow know, what us useta call the Austin. Till them buggers sowld it off to the Gairmuns.'

'Right, Gideon,' Tallyforth began his questioning sharply. 'Last night. I need to know what you did and did not see between the end of the school day and the time you locked up. Including who else was on the premises during that time. When you're ready. Take your time. But I need to know about everything and everyone. Right?'

'Roight, inspector,' said Gideon Lashley. 'Well, when the kids've gone 'ome, the clayners get to werk. They useta be pied boy the

Cahncil but the guvners pie them now. Berra rite 'n' all. Ennyyroadup, oi 'ave to check they'm doing things proper, loike. So oi does me rahnds then.'

'What time do they finish cleaning?'

'They 'as ter be done boy six. 'Cos that's all they gets pied fer. Ennyroad, after that there's the noight classiz.'

'So was anyone else on the premises between four and six o'clock?'

'Oh ar! Mr Mitchell, the music bloke, wuz 'ere with one of 'is bands. An' there wuz a coupla rahnders gimes, so Miss 'Adlington wuz here. And Mr de Courcy never guz 'ome till that toime ennyway.'

'Anyone else?' persisted Tallyforth.

'Mr Pickevance, of course,' said Gideon Lashley, scratching his chin ruminatively. 'An' Miss Bowen. They wuz in 'is office, till after that toime, coom to think on it.'

'So what time did they leave?'

'Must've been abaht 'arf past, oi should think, inspector. Yeah, abaht 'arf past six. 'Cos they looked in at Mr Mitchell's band whoile they wuz practising. Waved cheeriow to 'im. Yeah, that's roight. Oi remember naow.'

'And neither of them came back?'

'Nao, not as I knowed of ennyroad. Oi never seed 'em and oi never seed any loights in their offices.'

'So, at six the cleaners finished and left and by six thirty there was this Mitchell and his rock band and who else? The rounders girls and their teacher? The evening classes?'

'Nao! the girls'd gone by then, 'cos Miss 'Adlington's sardine tin'd gone. 'Er's got one of them 2CVs, we'm always pulling 'er plonker abaht it. And the evening classes doe start till 'arf seven. So, as far as oi'm aware there wuz ownly Mr Mitchell and 'is band 'ere then. Till the evening classiz, loike.'

'What were they exactly?'

'Thursday, it's just toyping 'n' naidlewerk. So they'm both in the annexe owver theer.' He pointed out of the window at a brick building that stood apart from the main school.

'And does that lead into the main school?'

'Nao.'

'And what about Mitchell and his band,' continued Tallyforth.

'What time did they leave?'

'They left abaht seven.'

'So the only people in the main school building were the school inspectors, who had their own key and who you had been told not to disturb because they would be working late?'

'That's roight, inspector. Mr Pickevance was very clear abaht that. Oi'd even offered for the woife - 'er's in charge of the kitchens 'ere - to tek 'em some grub up and a drink. But 'e said they wuzn't to be disturbed at any cost. So oi left 'em to it.'

'So where would they have got coffee from?'

'They 'ad everything in the boardroom with 'em. Coffee, tay, biscuits, cups, melk, sugar, the blooming lot. They med it theirselves.'

'Mr Reynolds says that the inspectors left just after eight, is that right? And he left about a quarter of an hour later, leaving Stanton alone?'

'Oi 'aird the cars gooing abaht eight, that's roight. An' oi sees Mr Reynolds hisself walking to 'is car a bit liter, so that would be roight, yeah. Course oi day know which 'on 'em wuz left. There moight've been more than one, but oi wouldn't know. All oi know is that the loight wuz still on in the room at ten when oi locked everything else up and it wuz still on this morning when oi opened up. That's when oi went to check and that's when oi fahnd 'im dead loike.'

'So you're sure that no-one else was in the building after eight thirty last night?' Tallyforth persisted again. He had to be absolutely sure.

'Inspector, schools ay the 'ardest places to get into, 'am they? We've bin bosted into 'ere a few toimes. They nick the videos and the computers, that sort of thing. So anyone could've got in after oi locked up, though nobody's reported any signs of a break-in. As far as oi know, there was nobody in the building except the inspectors. And, loike oi towld yow just naow, oi day know 'ow many of 'em wuz still 'ere.'

'Thank you, Gideon,' Tallyforth said, smiling at him. 'You've been most helpful. We may need to talk again but that will do for now. Thanks again.'

'Orl roight, Inspector.' Gideon Lashley stood up. He was never comfortable sitting for a lengthy period. 'Okay if oi claim the boardroom aht tomorrer? Ownly they'll be needing it again coom Monday.'

'Yes, yes,' replied Tallyforth, also standing and straightening the creases on his trousers. 'We'll be finished there this afternoon. Oh, and where does the school keep poisonous chemicals, Gideon? In the science labs?'

'Oh ar, they'm locked away safe and sahnd. Mrs Field's very strict abaht that.'

'She's responsible for the laboratories?'

'Ar, 'er's 'ead of science. 'Er keeps the key to the safe in the prep.room.'

'Well, thanks again,' smiled Tallyforth. 'Be no doubt seeing you.'

'Cheers, Inspector. I 'ope yow foind 'im quick. Nobody loikes the school inspectors, do they? But yow wouldn't wish this on anyone, would yow?'

THREE

They met briefly in the corridor outside Pickevance's office, as arranged.

'Well?' asked Tallyforth.

'She says that the two of them left the school at about six-thirty and went for a curry in town. They left there just after eight,' George Elliott said.

'Separately?'

'I presume so. She said she got home in time for the nine o'clock news. You told me not to press her about their alleged relationship. So I didn't. But I guess that, since she was so open about going for a meal with Pickevance, she had no reason to lie about going home.'

'On the other hand, she might have been covering up for him,' he said, half to himself. 'Lashley confirmed that they left the school together. And at the time she told you. The only people on the premises after that were the two night school classes, who we can rule out because they were in that annexe building, the music teacher Mitchell and the school inspectors. Reynolds says that he left Stanton alone a few minutes after the others had left and Lashley confirmed that too.'

'Oh, and by the way, sir,' she said, interrupting his train of thought. 'The school had to lose five teachers last year. And it wasn't easy. Redundancy because of budget cuts. There may be something there. One of them was a deputy head, who hasn't been replaced.'

'Really?' Tallyforth said. 'That is interesting.'

Tallyforth ran his fingers through his hair thoughtfully. George Elliott watched him, waiting for guidance on what she should do next.

'Pickevance is in there,' Tallyforth said, indicating the

headteacher's office behind him. 'I'll grill him in a minute or two. I think you might try talking to Reynolds again. Ask him about the inspection and what they found. See if he can show you anything that might be important on that computer of Stanton's. Okay?'

She nodded then turned away.

'Oh, by the way, what was the name of that rock singer you were telling me about last week? The Irish one?' he asked.

'You mean Van Morrison?' she returned.

'That's the one. Where did you say he was performing?'

'At the NEC in June,' she answered, curious at this turn in the conversation. 'Why?'

'D'you think my daughter might like him?' he asked. 'I'd thought about getting a couple of tickets.'

'Couldn't say, sir. Most of his audience are a bit older than your daughter's generation. He's been on the scene since the late sixties, you know. But there is a bit of a boom in nostalgia for the sixties just now, so she might like him.'

'Thanks,' said Tallyforth, reaching into his pocket for a handkerchief with which he proceeded to blow his nose. 'Maybe I'll do that.'

He turned away from her and reached out for the door handle to Brian Pickevance's office.

'Coffee, Chief Inspector?' asked Brian Pickevance, smiling. He was standing beside the coffee-making machine on the small table in his office.

'Hardly appropriate, sir,' replied Tallyforth dryly, looking around him.

Pickevance's office had been recently and expensively decorated in a rich maroon flock wallpaper. There were two pictures on the walls, reproductions of Van Gogh's 'Sunflowers' and of Frans Hals's 'Laughing Cavalier.' There was also an illuminated script version of Kipling's 'If' in a wooden frame on a third wall. There was a large solid-looking desk with a mahogany veneer and behind it a black executive chair on castors. There were four severe armchairs with no arm-rests, two each against two of the walls. Two black filing cabinets completed the furniture in the room.

'Sorry, Chief Inspector, I didn't think,' said Pickevance ruefully as he sat down. 'Don't mind if I do?'

'Of course,' Tallyforth said, waving a hand dismissively and sitting down on one of the armchairs to the side of the desk.

On Pickevance's desk he could see a framed photograph of a family group.

'Your children, sir?' he asked, pointing at the photograph.

'Yes,' said Pickevance, a little surprised. He lifted the photograph off the desk, stared at it for a few seconds then held it towards Tallyforth.

'As you see, I have four. Nick's eighteen and at Keele studying media, Pam's seventeen and at Tamworth College doing A levels in English, history and German, Becky's twelve and she's a pupil here, and James is nine and at the local primary school. You have children, Chief Inspector?'

'Yes, two,' replied Tallyforth, not volunteering any further information.

There was an awkward pause. Pickevance raised the cup of coffee to his mouth. Tallyforth crossed his legs.

'Would you like to tell me something about yourself and about your time here as headteacher, Mr Pickevance?' Tallyforth began again.

'Certainly, Chief Inspector,' Pickevance said, leaning back in his chair and swinging slightly away from Tallyforth so that he could gaze through his horn-rimmed glasses out of the window as he spoke. 'I was appointed here five days after the nineteen eighty-seven General Election. It was a time of great excitement in education, as the Conservatives had promised to introduce their Education Reform Bill within months of the sitting of the new parliament. That was known at the time of my appointment and I was appointed by the then-governing body to implement the changes that were about to be legislated for. No-one knew quite at that stage what exactly these might entail, but we knew there was to be a National Curriculum, we knew there was to be the Local Management of Schools scheme whereby funding would be managed by schools rather than by Local Education Authorities and we knew there was to be the option of Grant Maintained status.'

'What does that precisely mean, sir?' asked Tallyforth.

'Grant Maintained status? Well, it means that a school, through the decision of its governors, can request a vote by its parents to decide whether it should opt out of Local Authority control and receive its funding directly from central government. It also meant in the early years of the scheme that generous capital funding was made available to such schools to enable them to develop their facilities.'

'And when did Æthelfleda High School become grant maintained?' asked Tallyforth.

'Not until nineteen eighty-nine,' came Pickevance's reply. 'I tried....er....the governors discussed the matter in nineteen eighty-eight but decided against it. But by the following year, the composition of the governing body had changed somewhat and, shall we say, a different view was taken?'

'So then there was a vote by the parents?'

'Yes. It wasn't straightforward by any means. The Local Education Authority tried very hard to convince parents that the school should not go grant-maintained and there was quite a lot of bad feeling generated. There was some unfortunate misinformation put about. In fact, we do not buy any of our services from the Local Education Authority now that we are grant-maintained. We feel we can get better value for money elsewhere.'

Pickevance smirked in Tallyforth's direction. He was clearly proud of the actions taken.

'And you, sir, were obviously very much in favour of the changes?' asked Tallyforth.

'Yes, of course,' agreed Pickevance. 'I agreed wholeheartedly with the government's philosophy of schools taking greater responsibility for their own direction. We've made major improvements to this school since we had control over our own funding.'

'Such as, sir?'

'The physical condition of the buildings, for instance. We've carpeted every classroom. For our students, that makes a significant difference to their behaviour. They tend to be a bit noisy and boisterous at times coming from the homes they do but the carpeting deadens much of that noise and produces a much calmer

28

working atmosphere. Also we now have over one hundred state-of-the-art computers. That's roughly one for every six students - one of the best ratios in the country. And every member of staff has their own laptop as well. And, of course, we've had our new music and drama suite and been able to adapt a number of other rooms to make them more suitable. The boardroom, for instance, used to be a special needs classroom, but we've integrated all the special needs students into the mainstream classrooms so we did not need a separate base for them. What we did need was a room where meetings could be held, which had the professional atmosphere you would find in any decent-sized business. Remember, Chief Inspector, a secondary school such as Æthelfleda High School is a one and a half million pound business. It has to be managed according to business principles. That has been the lesson of the eighties and nineties.'

'What about your teachers, sir?' queried Tallyforth. 'Were they all in favour of the changes?'

Pickevance removed his spectacles and placed them on the desk in front of him before swivelling round to gaze again out of the window.

'I have to admit that not everyone saw things as I did,' he began. 'Not too surprising really, is it? New head, new broom, that sort of thing. My predecessor had been head of Æthelfleda for seventeen years. When I came here, I was aware that a number of staff had been here for most of their teaching careers. Some of them had never taught in another school. And I have to say that a significant number of them, in my opinion, had low expectations of the students. And I challenged those expectations. I believe that schools can make a difference. I come from a very humble background myself, Chief Inspector, but I succeeded in overcoming that background. I went to the local grammar school and then on to teacher training college. And I now have a M.B.A. I want students from Æthelfleda to have the same opportunities as I had.'

'So did you win over the doubters?'

'Some, yes,' he replied. 'But not all. Two of my biggest problems were the head of year eleven and one of my deputy heads. Fortunately, because of budget cuts last year, I was able to arrange satisfactory redundancy terms for those two, plus three others, and I persuaded them to go. It wasn't easy, believe me, but I am convinced it was in the best interests of the school and the students.'

'So there's no doubt quite a bit of animosity towards you in the staffroom?' Tallyforth asked.

'I don't believe so,' came the reply. 'I have my allies too, Chief Inspector. Jack Parry, our head of maths, has also been at the school a long time but he's the exception. Very able man. And he expects the students to achieve. He keeps me informed about staffroom feeling. Funnily enough, this inspection has drawn the staff more closely together.'

'So you had nothing to fear from this inspection?' asked Tallyforth.

'I took a positive attitude to it from the start,' said Pickevance, replacing his spectacles. 'And I insisted the staff should do the same. I said to Hubert Stanton on his very first visit here that I knew our exam results weren't brilliant and that our attendance rate was low but I could show him and his team evidence that things were definitely on the up. Yes, I was anxious about the composition of the inspection team before we knew it, because I was afraid we would get people who had no knowledge or experience of schools such as Æthelfleda. But I was more than happy in the event, after Hubert Stanton had told me about the backgrounds of his team.'

'You seem to have warmed to Stanton, would that be correct?'

Pickevance looked quickly at Tallyforth.

'I came very quickly to respect him,' he said guardedly. 'A headteacher has to manage an inspection of his school just as he has to manage any other aspect of it. Hubert Stanton was, I believe, a man of integrity and fairness. I couldn't ask for more than that.'

'So would it have surprised you if the inspection report were to be critical of yourself?' asked Tallyforth.

'What do you mean, Chief Inspector?' he asked, struggling to keep his composure.

'If there were any criticism of the management of the school you would have been surprised, yes?'

'Yes, very.'

'So Stanton did not indicate any such criticism to you personally, sir?' pressed Tallyforth.

'No.'

'And it is your belief that your staff are completely behind you?'

'As far as I am aware, Chief Inspector. As I've said, there were some who did not support the direction I was proposing for the school but they have now left. I believe my staff to be completely loyal. Where is all this leading, Chief Inspector? Are you suggesting something?'

'Sir, I have to remind you,' began Tallyforth in magisterial style, 'that we are investigating the death on your school's premises of the person who has been leading the inspection of your school for the past four days. I have to follow every lead to find out why Hubert Stanton died. And that sometimes means asking questions that some people would prefer I didn't ask. If you suspect there are tensions within this school between yourself and some staff, it's best that I know as soon as possible. Because when we start interviewing teachers and they say something different, then I have to ask why you didn't tell me about that in the first place.'

Pickevance removed his spectacles again and sat forward in his chair, his elbows resting on the desk and with his head in his hands. He took another sip of coffee.

'If there is resentment of management, it is most likely aimed at Pearl,' he began. 'Pearl Bowen, my deputy. She is a person of strong views, strongly expressed. I have spoken with her about it on a number of occasions. She is an extraordinarily capable person but she has not yet learned the skill of taking people with her. She does, at times, cause some resentment, particularly amongst some of the male staff.'

'The usual anti-female thing?' queried Tallyforth.

'Partly that, yes,' replied Pickevance, sitting back in his chair again. 'But more than that. I think there was a feeling amongst some of the staff that the governors should have appointed a strong disciplinarian. That's what her predecessor was. But it wasn't what I believed a modern deputy head should be. I wanted someone with ideas and flair and drive. That's why I pushed for Pearl's appointment. She's only been here eighteen months but she is already making a significant impact, although, as I have just said,

31

there is a downside to that in that she hasn't carried everyone with her.'

'So, if there had been criticism of the school's management in the inspection report, it would have been directed at her, not at you,' asked Tallyforth. 'Is that what you are saying, sir?'

'I suppose so. Though I would have to take the blame ultimately for not helping Pearl to carry people with her. But where is this line of questioning leading to, Chief Inspector? I really don't understand.'

'As I said just now, sir, I am investigating a case of murder,' replied Tallyforth patiently. 'It seems quite likely to me, given the timing and place of Stanton's murder, that there is a connection between his death and the inspection of this school. Therefore it is important that I get to know all I can about the school and its personnel. I need to know about the animosities within this institution, about who's in and who's out, because that's where I might find some clue to Stanton's murder.'

'And staff reaction to Pearl Bowen might lead you in that direction?' quizzed Pickevance, arching his eyebrows precipitately.

'It could, sir. It could,' answered Tallyforth. 'No stone unturned and that sort of thing. D'you mind telling me your movements last night?'

'I was here in school until about six-thirty. Pearl and I were discussing the subject reports we had already heard. As you know, a number of the inspectors left last night. Then Pearl and I had an Indian meal in town. We left there at about eight-fifteen to eight-thirty and then I went home,' Pickevance replied.

'You didn't call back at the school for anything then?'

'No.'

'So you couldn't have known if the inspectors were still here or not?'

'No. I had arranged for them not to be disturbed. Hubert Stanton had keys to the boardroom and to the rear door of the building. I knew they would be working late.'

Tallyforth suddenly stood up.

'Thank you, Mr Pickevance. I think that will be all for now. I expect you'll be wanting to get home. If I need to speak to you again tonight, where can I reach you?' he said.

'There's a sort of party at the Conservative Club tonight,' replied Pickevance, also standing and coming round his desk. 'My chairman of governors, Perry Stevens, thought it would be a good opportunity for the governors to thank the staff after the rigours of the inspection. Despite what's happened, we've decided to go ahead with it, though I'm not sure how many staff will attend. As I said, a lot of them look very tired. But I shall be there later on. It could be a late finish.'

'Thank you, sir,' said Tallyforth. 'It's unlikely that we'll need to disturb you but just in case. And over the weekend?'

'At home. Here's my address and phone number.' Pickevance took a card from the breast pocket of his suit and passed it over to Tallyforth.

'Thank you again,' said Tallyforth. 'I hope to have some clearer news for you in the near future.'

'Amazing machines, aren't they, Sergeant?' said William Reynolds, giving George Elliott a thin smile.

They were in the boardroom and he was opening up Hubert Stanton's Toshiba computer as she had asked him to do. She sat next to him and watched his thin fingers as they danced across the computer's keyboard.

'I would never have believed five years ago that I would find them indispensable. It was Hubert's idea that all of the team should have one, so that we could each send him our copy on disk within three days of the end of the inspection. I don't know if you realise but there is an amazingly tight schedule for getting the report written and presented. Hubert and I were due back at the school a week today, next Friday, to go through the first draft with the headteacher and his deputy. Hubert would have spent the whole of Monday, Tuesday and Wednesday putting the report together from what we sent him on disk, then he and I would have met on Thursday to edit that version. So you can see why he thought it important that we should each be able to complete our work on disk. If he'd had to type text in as well as work on it, it really would have been next to impossible, even for Hubert.'

'Don't you have any secretarial help, sir?' she asked, surprised at what Reynolds was telling her.

'Good heavens, no, Sergeant! Market forces have driven the price of inspections down, so we can no longer afford clerical assistance,' Reynolds replied, simultaneously opening the file marked Æthelfleda High School and waiting for it to appear. 'We wouldn't win contracts if we included the costs of a secretary. No, Sergeant, this whole almighty school inspection system is being run on a DIY basis. God help OFSTED when it runs out of people prepared to do this work for peanuts.'

'Are you poorly paid, sir?'

'By comparison with what I earned when I was an HMI, yes, Sergeant,' he answered sharply. 'If it weren't for the fact that I was fifty and therefore eligible for my pension, I would not have left. But with the pension, I manage. I have to remind myself that, when this government closed the mining industry down because of its dislike of the trade unions, it didn't set up immediately an alternative source of work for those poor miners who got their redundancy payments, as it did for us. Things could be worse, I suppose.'

She looked at him, surprised again. She had not expected a tinge of social conscience. Her brother had told her that the inspectors involved at his school had appeared quite heartless.

'Ah, here we are, Sergeant,' said William Reynolds, peering at the computer screen. 'Here are the key issues that we agreed last night at our meeting.'

She looked over his shoulder at the screen and read:

Key issues for action
To raise further the standards of work and the quality of learning and provision, the governors and senior management should:
- improve examination results in English and science;
- improve attendance rates;
- provide greater In-service opportunities for all staff;
- ensure better provision for religious education;
- develop better links with feeder primary schools.

'Just a minute, sergeant,' said Reynolds suddenly, focusing

closely on the screen. 'There's something missing. There's no criticism of the school's management! I told you earlier that there would be. We agreed it last night. It would be most unlike Hubert to take out anything that had received common agreement, especially when it was the issue he was most insistent upon himself.'

'Are you saying that someone else might have got at this machine and removed that part?' George Elliott asked.

'It is possible, Sergeant,' replied Reynolds. 'I really find it impossible to believe that Hubert would have removed that criticism of management, certainly without consulting me. Let me just check. The original comments came in the management section - Hubert read us his draft last night. Let me just find that section.'

And Reynolds clicked on to the appropriate menus until he found the relevant section, the one that Elliott had found when she first got into the programme earlier that day.

'Why! This is ridiculous,' he cried after a moment. 'This is a lot less critical than it was. And there's a whole paragraph that has gone. Look! That one beginning "The headteacher and deputy headteacher...." When Hubert read that to us last night it contained phrases like "....enjoy a very close working relationship" and about the need for that not to "jeopardise the fuller involvement of middle management in the school's development". I remember Hubert's phrasing quite distinctly. He was very skilful in the way he worded things. Philosophy man, you know. Emmanuel College, Cambridge. It is impossible that he would have taken that out, Sergeant. Someone has been tampering with this computer! Find that person, Sergeant, and you will have found your murderer, mark my words!'

'Thank you, sir,' she replied, rather dryly. 'We'll do our best. We are the detectives after all. But is there anything else that Stanton would have written last night that might be of interest?'

'Apart from the main synthesis which he had to do, Hubert always did the sections on management and on efficiency,' explained William Reynolds, turning towards her. 'He wasn't a natural with financial matters but he taught himself how to look at school budgets and spending patterns. He used to argue that under the new dispensation, there were likely to be more financial irregularities in schools than beforehand. And it was therefore necessary for him to get a sense of where to look for such irregularities. I'll find his draft of the efficiency section if you like.'

Reynolds turned back to the machine and rapidly found the relevant section, which they quickly scanned together.

'What does that bit mean?' asked George Elliott. 'Where it says "Governors need to ensure that better internal auditing procedures are put in place"? What's that all about?'

'To tell you the truth, sergeant, I really don't know,' answered Reynolds. 'I'm not especially good at that side of things myself. I don't remember Hubert mentioning anything untoward. Maybe he found something out after we'd all gone. Though it would be most unusual. We could try the School Profile to see if he's recorded any evidence there.'

There was a further scrambling of menus.

'Look, Sergeant! There you have it!' Reynolds pointed excitedly at the screen. 'Hubert must have discovered that last night. Fifty thousand pounds unaccounted for! That's a hanging matter!'

'What does that mean, sir?' she asked, straightening up.

'Sergeant, it means that someone who has access to the school's money has been helping themselves to a substantial amount of it. And, until Hubert found out, no-one had noticed! I think the finger of suspicion points, don't you, Sergeant?'

'Sir?'

'Why, Pickevance of course!' he cried. 'He had access to the school's finances. He was going to be criticised for his management of the school. There's two good reasons for suspecting him. And who else could have a possible motive for killing an OFSTED Registered Inspector?'

'Thank you, Mr Reynolds,' she said. 'But please remember who are the police officers here. I must ask you not to breathe a word of your suspicions to anyone. I need to tell my chief - he may want to talk to you later at the hotel. Thank you again. If you would just close down the programme, I'll take charge of that again.'

And she held her hand out, waiting for Reynolds to close down the computer and pass it over to her, which he did in seconds.

She watched him as he stood up and then exited.

Was he right? she wondered. As he had said, the finger of suspicion was certainly pointing strongly in one direction.

FOUR

By eight o'clock that same evening, several members of the staff from Æthelfleda High School had already arrived at the Tamworth Conservative Club. They had been welcomed in by Perry Stevens, the school's Chairman of Governors, who had stationed himself by the entrance to greet them as they arrived and to congratulate them personally for their hard work and efforts in securing a good report for the school from its inspection. Perry Stevens knew from his long years as senior partner in Stevens, Stevens and Ferris Chartered Accountants the importance of making people feel that he personally was interested in them. That had been the basis of the success of his business and that had been the quality that had led him to succeed in local politics, where he had been the Leader of the Conservative group on the Borough Council for several years. He prided himself on the fact that he knew the first names of every member of staff, teaching and non-teaching, that had ever worked at Æthelfleda High School during his time as Chair of Governors, which went back to the mid-nineteen-eighties.

So Perry Stevens, in dark blue blazer and grey flannels, his white hair carefully groomed, was delighted that by eight o'clock there were already so many of the school's staff present in the Conservative Club. Brian Pickevance had phoned and told him about the awful tragedy of Registered Inspector Hubert Stanton's death and that the police were treating it as a matter of murder and that the staff were looking pretty tired out and so might not feel up to coming to the governors' party for them. Stevens wasn't sure whether all the staff knew about the fact that the police were treating Stanton's death as murder but decided that there was no point in raising the issue with individuals. After all, the purpose of the evening was to celebrate the end of the school's inspection, not to hold a wake.

'Delighted to see you, Norman!' he beamed, holding out his hand to the short, bald-headed man who entered the building.

The man spoken to, who wore a tweed jacket and sported a green bow-tie, grimaced and, for a second, considered not taking the proffered hand, but in the end relented and allowed his hand to be shaken.

'It grieves me mightily,' he began, 'that after living peacefully in this historic town for over three decades I have to spend some hours of my time in a place where those responsible for creating the me-society of our time assemble. Were it not for my colleagues from school, I would not be here, Stevens, and you know that. But I cannot let them down, because of my personal prejudices against your political views.'

And Norman de Courcy, head of history at Æthelfleda High School and the sole remaining Liberal Democrat councillor on the Tamworth Borough Council, withdrew his hand from Perry Stevens's firm grasp.

'Now, now, Norman,' said Stevens. 'This is not a council meeting and you know that. The governors merely wished to say thank you to the staff and I was able to secure the Conservative Club for the purpose.'

Before de Courcy could engage Stevens any further, however, there was a shout from behind him.

'Norman! Wait for me, will you?'

Norman de Courcy glanced down the steps to the building and saw the pony-tailed head of Jon Mitchell, the school's music teacher, emerging from a taxi that had just pulled up in the street.

Having paid the taxi-driver, Mitchell, in Levi jeans and black leather jacket, leapt up the steps two at a time till he was at Norman de Courcy's side and facing Perry Stevens.

'Like the bow-tie, Norman! Proper Jeremy Thorpe, eh?' chuckled Mitchell. Then, without giving the other man chance to reply, he asked:

'What guest beers you got here, Mr Stevens, eh? Bet you serve

Burton, am I right?'

Stevens smiled a wan smile. He had had many discussions with Pickevance about the suitability of Jon Mitchell for the staff of Æthelfleda High School. Yes, he was aware that the man had a unique talent for encouraging youngsters to participate in music-making and it was remarkable that the school had four rock and roll bands. However, he did not approve of the pony-tail and the ear-ring that Mitchell insisted on wearing but it was the morality of the man that Stevens disliked most. Jon Mitchell, though only thirty-four, had been twice-married and twice-divorced, and now lived with the singer from his own band, the Falling Leaves; he had four children, two from each of his marriages but none lived with him, and he was widely believed to smoke marijuana. Pickevance's argument was that Mitchell's work and reputation were responsible for attracting pupils to the school and, in this age of consumer-led education, money followed pupils. To lose Mitchell brought the concomitant risk of losing pupils, and therefore money, claimed Pickevance. Stevens's view was that the sort of pupils Mitchell attracted to the school were not necessarily the sort of pupils that the school wanted.

'Naturally we have Burton ale,' he replied haughtily. 'And I think you'll find we have a good range of other guest beers. Please do go through and sample them!'

And Perry Stevens stood aside to allow Norman de Courcy and Jon Mitchell to enter the Conservative Club and head for the bar.

'How could anyone salt away fifty thousand quid from a school?' mused Tallyforth. 'I mean, it's public money, isn't it? Surely there are checks and balances on schools' spending, aren't there? Surely they can't give schools thousands of pounds of actual cash to spend as they please?'

George Elliott looked over at him. They were sitting at a table in Armando's Italian restaurant in the centre of Tamworth awaiting their meals. After William Reynolds's revelation to George Elliott about the financial irregularity uncovered by Hubert Stanton and entered on to his laptop computer, she had hastily found Tallyforth and demonstrated to him on the machine this new and crucial piece of evidence. He had ordered her to keep this information to herself and to ensure they had a complete list of all the school staff and of the inspection team, together with addresses and telephone numbers, before they left the premises of Æthelfleda High School. Tallyforth had been summoned back to headquarters in Birmingham by Superintendent 'Nobby' Clarke to brief his boss on what had happened and on the progress of their investigations.

'Are you absolutely sure it was poisoning?' Clarke had asked him, with that quizzical look he favoured whenever Tallyforth seemed launched on a particular line of enquiry.

Tallyforth had nodded affirmatively and showed his superior the note from Jake Clifford.

'But all it says here, Tallyforth,' Clarke had riposted, after reading the slip of paper, 'is that Clifford found traces of cyanide in the coffee pot. He could not have had time to examine the contents of the dead man's stomach to find out if there are signs of cyanide poisoning there. I agree it looks strong but we must be absolutely sure.'

Tallyforth had protested that there was no other logical explanation and then had told Clarke about the missing fifty thousand pounds and about the missing criticism of the school's headteacher and deputy headteacher from the inspectors' findings.

'Not saying there isn't something fishy, Tallyforth,' Clarke had said. 'I know your instincts often prove right but just be careful. We don't want a full-blown murder investigation before we know for sure that the man was killed by cyanide. It is just possible that he died otherwise and that somebody, for reasons known only to them, subsequently put cyanide into that coffee pot. It is also possible that the deceased, again for reasons known only to himself, committed suicide. Have you got a full dossier on this Stanton yet?'

Tallyforth had mumbled that they were working on that. And that part of the conversation now came back to him.

'What do we know about this Stanton, sergeant?' he queried. 'Have you managed to get any further information?'

'I took the liberty, sir,' she replied, a ghost of a smile flickering across her face, 'while you were gone, of making a few enquiries about some of the key players in this case.'

'So?'

But before she could reply, a moustachioed waiter appeared with their meals - a *tagliatelle carbonara* with cream and mushroom sauce for her and a *spaghetti bolognaise* for him.

'Is alright?' queried the waiter, when he had deposited the dishes.

'Yes, fine,' answered Tallyforth.

'Could you leave the parmesan on the table?' George Elliott asked, smiling, 'I'm rather fond of a lot, I'm afraid.'

'Si, signora,' came the reply. 'Is no problem.'

The waiter placed a small bowl of grated parmesan cheese on the table by George Elliott and left them.

'You remember I told you my brother's school was inspected last year, sir? Well, I rang him to see if he knew anything about Æthelfleda High School or Brian Pickevance or Pearl Bowen. Well, not surprisingly he didn't. Portsmouth is a bit of a distance from Tamworth after all. But Philip is quite heavily involved in the Secondary Headteachers' Association - I believe he's currently on their Executive - and he offered to contact a colleague of his in the Midlands to see what he could find out. When he called me back, he told me that Pickevance is perceived as a bit of a Flash Harry, because of his embracing of the enterprise culture, that he and Pearl Bowen are always together at conferences and always taking the same line on the need for schools to be more entrepreneurial.'

'That doesn't tell us much then,' said Tallyforth, winding spaghetti around his fork. 'What about Stanton? Anything on him?'

George Elliott carefully forked another portion of pasta into her mouth and chewed.

'I had to speak to Steve Anthony.'

Tallyforth put down his fork, leaned back in his chair, and grimaced at the ceiling.

'Not that little rat again!' he said through clenched teeth. 'Do you always have to bring him in?'

Tallyforth's aversion to Steve Anthony, her fellow-student from Swansea University who was now a high-flying civil servant in the Home Office, was well-known to her. The aversion seemed to arise not just from Tallyforth's homophobia, which was fairly commonplace in the police force, but also from his reluctance to accept that anyone other than the police should have information about people that they might want to know about.

So she refused to rise to his bait.

'Steve has access to the files of all those people who used to belong to Her Majesty's Inspectorate of schools, because they all had to sign the Official Secrets Act,' she began. 'Hubert Stanton was in the inspectorate for over twenty years and there is a lot of information on file about him.'

'Go on,' said Tallyforth, resuming his meal.

'Do you want it all?'

'Just the relevant bits, Elliott. Spare me the full detail'

'I think you ought to know just a little of the general stuff, sir. I think it informs us of what sort of a person Stanton was.'

'Press on, Elliott,' Tallyforth urged. 'Spill the beans.'

'Well, sir, Hubert Stanton joined the inspectorate in nineteen seventy-five, initially as a mathematics specialist though he later took on a wider role. It is believed that he wrote a large amount of the mathematics section of the influential *Aspects of Secondary Education*, which appeared in the late nineteen seventies. He was certainly one of those involved in advising the Cockcroft Committee which produced its important report on the teaching of mathematics in 1982. He also advised several Secretaries of State for Education, notably Sir Keith Joseph over the development of the GCSE examination and Kenneth Baker over the National Curriculum.'

'And how does all this help us, Sergeant?' Tallyforth asked dryly, as he sucked a strand of spaghetti into his mouth.

'Just a moment, sir,' she answered, taking a forkful herself. 'I believe it is helpful for us to know that Hubert Stanton was once a man of considerable influence in the world of education. You remember that Reynolds said he was very bitter about the destruction of the inspectorate? Well, you can see why, can't you?'

'You mean, because he was no longer as powerful or influential as he had once been?'

She reached across the table for a piece of bread, which she then used to mop up the remains of the sauce on her plate.

'It might suggest that Stanton was not a happy man,' she

43

answered.

Tallyforth put down his fork and sighed.

'Sergeant, are you getting at something?'

'Sir, we have made the assumption up to now that Stanton was murdered by someone who put cyanide into his coffee. But what if he had laced the coffee himself?'

He shook his curling grey locks.

'Elliott, you're beginning to sound uncannily like Superintendent Clarke. That was one of the scenarios he presented me with earlier. But I'm not convinced,' he said. 'Why would Stanton want to do that? People don't tend generally commit acts of *auto da fe* because of some change in government policy, do they? Do we know anything about his personal life?'

'Yes, sir. His wife died of cancer of the oesophagus twelve months ago. One of Steve's colleagues was in Stanton's club and, when he saw Steve with the file on him, he volunteered that information.'

'Anything else?'

'Not as far as we know, sir,' she said.

Tallyforth drew a notebook from his inside pocket and quickly wrote down the substance of what she had told him, while she finished her meal and sipped from her glass of iced Perrier.

'So, Stanton had every reason to be, as you put it, not a happy man,' he mused aloud. 'But that hardly leads us to the suspicion that he might have killed himself on the final evening of the inspection of Æthelfleda High School. Especially when we have strong evidence suggesting that he had discovered some financial malpractice in the school and was convinced that the liaison between Pickevance and Bowen was detrimental to the running of the school. I think we'd be better off clarifying all the issues there, so let's start with the money business. We need to find out how school finances are managed and who has access to them. Any ideas?'

'I could ring my brother in Portsmouth,' she volunteered.

'Right, do that,' he said firmly. 'Can you get him now? I want to call at the Conservative Club where the staff post-inspection party is taking place before we finish for tonight.'

'I'll try him on my mobile,' she said. 'Just let me ask the manager here for the use of his office.

George Elliott pushed her chair back and stood up, brushing the creases from her tartan skirt as she did so. Then looking around the room she caught the waiter's eye and indicated for him to come over.

It was nine thirty that same evening. In the Conservative Club, the disc jockey was playing the Rolling Stones' *Get Off My Cloud* and several of the staff were dancing.

'How's the Offa celebrations going then, Norman?' asked Jack Parry, carefully placing his full pint of bitter on the table where Norman de Courcy sat. 'Still on schedule after the week's excitements?'

De Courcy gave him a condescending smile. The two of them had been at the school together for thirty years, de Courcy predating Parry by two years. Jack Parry had come to the school in the mid nineteen-sixties straight from Teacher Training College in Worcester, which was his home town. He was initially appointed to teach mathematics and physics but by his third year in the school had quite clearly established himself as a full-time member of the mathematics department, as well as coach to the chess team and treasurer of the Parent Teacher Association. As the years passed, other more ambitious colleagues moved on to further their careers while Jack Parry settled himself in Tamworth, married the domestic science teacher Maureen who bore him three children, and became head of mathematics and later, in addition, examinations secretary.

Norman de Courcy had been appointed as head of the history department two years before Jack Parry arrived. He was a graduate of Oxford University, with a third-class degree in Politics, Philosophy and Economics, who openly admitted that he had entered teaching because it would give him time to pursue his political ambitions. Those ambitions had led him only as far as the Tamworth Borough Council. This was partly because his interests had been diverted by his enthusiastic embracing of all things relating to the study of Offa, King of the Mercians, who had had his royal palace in Tamworth. But it was also partly, and more significantly, because his first wife Ethel had developed muscular sclerosis at the young age of twenty-seven, which had put her in a wheelchair from the age of thirty and led to her premature death at the age of thirty-nine. The long years of having to give loving care and attention to Ethel had prevented de Courcy from seeking to enhance his political ambitions and, although he himself was only forty-two when she died, he no longer felt that strength of will that he knew was necessary and he had decided to content himself with seeking to contain the worst excesses of the then Tory majority in Tamworth. At the age of fifty he got married again to Mavis, the secretary of the Mercian Society of which he had been a founder-member.

Æthelfleda High School had been called Lud Lane Secondary Modern School when the two of them were appointed. It was only in the nineteen-seventies that it had become Æthelfleda High School, under the rush towards comprehensive schooling ushered in by the Labour government of that time, first of all on the old school site in Lud Lane and then some three years later moving to its new purpose-built premises on the edge of the town.

The two men had never got on. De Courcy regarded Parry as a creep, because he had always pandered to the wishes of the headmaster of the day and, on the appointment of Brian Pickevance, had simply transferred his sycophantic pandering to the new man. Parry regarded de Courcy as an out-of-touch intellectual, who chose to flout his liberal [and Liberal!] heart while drawing a salary from the public purse without regard to where that salary came from. Jack Parry, though not active politically, was a great admirer of Margaret Thatcher and believed strongly with her that the country had to earn its living before it could afford to spend.

'1996, the Twelve Hundredth Anniversary of Offa's death will be well and truly marked,' de Courcy replied. 'I shall be outlining the details to the staff sub-committee next week. The focus of it all, of course, will be the re-creation of the Boxing Day feast of 781 *anno domini*. Present at that feast was the most powerful group of people in England at the time - King Offa, his Queen Cynethryth, Bishop Eadberht of Leicester, Bishop Hygeberht of Lichfield, Bishop Hathored of Worcester, and the Mercian chiefs Brorda, Berhtwald, and Eadbald, plus several thegns, a number of royal

46

officials, and abbots from nearby Mercian monasteries. Altogether there would have been between twenty and thirty present, with the feast supervised by Offa's steward and served by the royal staff who lived and worked permanently at the residence or its attached farms.'

'Sounds like a pretty massive undertaking, Norman, if I may say so,' retorted Jack Parry, raising his beer to his lips and half-smiling at Denise Hadlington, the girls' physical education teacher, who passed by the table as they were speaking. 'Are we really going to be able to do anything on that scale by the end of term? You can see how exhausted everyone is after this OFSTED business.'

'It will happen!' expostulated de Courcy, his bald head gleaming under the phosphorescent lights. 'If we are going to allow this Conservative-inspired bash-the-teachers brigade to interfere with the proper business of educating our children to understand and appreciate their roots, then there is very little hope for this country. The children of Tamworth need to know that this was once the royal seat of one of the most powerful kings in the history of this country and that Mercia, stretching from the Rivers Trent and Don in the north-east, the Mersey in the north-west, with the Wye and the Powys hills to the west, to the Thames and the Fens in the south, was the dominant force in England in the eighth century. If it's the last thing I do in this school, I will give them a day to remember this summer, when the full glory of Offa's court will be brought to life to celebrate the twelve hundredth anniversary of his death.'

Before Jack Parry could say any more, they were disturbed by the arrival of another of their staff colleagues, Gideon Lashley, the premises manager.

''Ave yow 'eard?' he began, standing over them, holding a freshly-pulled pint of mild ale in his right hand. 'They think 'e wus murdered, that Stanton blowk. Pisoned, oi 'eard. In 'is coffee. Cyanide. What d'yow mek on that then?'

'Where did you get that from, Gideon?' asked Jack Parry, while Norman de Courcy looked on, apparently unperturbed.

'One of moy lidies 'eard that inspector talking to the 'eadmaster when 'er wus clayning outside 'is office this evening,' came the reply.

'So it's not definite then,' said Parry.

'Well, oi should say it wus,' answered Gideon Lashley. 'They wouldn't be saying that if they day suspect summat, would they? And anyroad up, Mrs 'Ilton took a message from a police mowtorcoiclist to that inspector and 'e told 'er, the mowtorcoiclist loik, that it wus from the forensic lab. So it all meks sense to me.'

'Well, gentlemen,' interjected Norman de Courcy,' you'll be able to ask for yourselves now, won't you? Because I spy the police inspector over there near the door talking to our dearly-loved Chairman of Governors, Mr Peregrine Stevens. Shall we invite him over?'

The other two looked over in the direction he was indicating.

'How do you know that's the policeman in charge?' asked Jack Parry. 'You didn't meet him, did you?'

'I had occasion to pass the boardroom, as we must now call it, late this morning and spotted a strange man in the gents' toilet over there. When I asked him if I could help him, he told me who he was,' replied de Courcy. 'I surmise, therefore, that he is the officer in charge of this investigation into the death of that inspector Stanton. No doubt we shall discover soon if he died of natural causes or not. And if not, in which direction points the finger of suspicion. Though I know where I would start looking!'

He ended triumphantly, beaming in the direction of Jack Parry.

'Can I replenish your glass, Jack?' he asked, stretching forward in the direction of Jack Parry's almost-empty glass.

FIVE

By ten o'clock on the Saturday morning, Tallyforth had a complete dossier on all the teaching and non-teaching staff of Æthelfleda High School and of all the members of the OFSTED inspection team. When Brian Pickevance had failed to put in an appearance at the Conservative Club the previous evening, Tallyforth had contacted him at his home and got him to arrange for the files on the school's staff to be sent by taxi to Birmingham. George Elliott meanwhile had contacted William Reynolds, who was staying as he had promised for an extra night at the Granada Lodge Motel close to Junction 10 on the M42 motorway. From him she had gained all the necessary background information about the school inspection team.

They were in Tallyforth's office at police headquarters of the Mercian Police Force in Birmingham, comparing notes.

'Anything from Reynolds then?' asked Tallyforth, scratching his head and flicking through one of the files in his hand.

George Elliott glanced up from her own reading.

'Nothing special,' she said. 'He didn't know much about the rest of the inspection team. He had only worked with one of them before - the Potts woman, who's a retired headteacher apparently. Used to run a private girls' boarding school. The rest of them he'd met for the first time on Monday of this week. That's normal apparently. They're all signed up with some agency who tell them where to go and when and that's it. Apart from a few bits of correspondence beforehand, they don't have any contact with each other until the actual first day in the school they're inspecting.'

'That's what the police force will be like if this lot continue their privatisation scams, Elliott,' moaned Tallyforth. 'So Reynolds wasn't dropping any hints about any of them?'

'No. Except that he repeated what he told us initially about Stanton not being an easy person to work with. But that's hardly a reason for murdering him.'

Tallyforth sighed.

'Have we tried them through the police computer?' he asked.

'Yes. Nothing there at all.'

'And the staff of the school?' he asked again.

'Mm. The same,' she replied, 'There's nothing on the police computer about any of them, as you might expect, other than that Pickevance has a speeding offence against his name, but who hasn't?'

'What about that music bloke who was there with his rock band till quite late on the Thursday evening? He's apparently got a band of his own, you know, as well as the four kids' bands. Some of these rock people have murky pasts.'

'You mean Jon Mitchell? Nothing so far, sir,' she mumbled. 'Unless he's changed his name!'

'Elliott, you just might be on to something there,' he said. 'Just check that one out, will you? After all, Cliff Richard was once Harry Webb. You never know!'

She looked across at him to see if he was joking, but saw from the studied look on his face as he read the papers in front of him on his desk that he was not. She looked down at the notes she had made the previous evening.

There was a lengthy silence as they both read.

'So, let's concentrate on Pickevance and Bowen,' he said suddenly, standing up and moving across the room to look out of the window. 'I want to get as full a picture as we can of them. We've got some information from what they told us yesterday and from the staff files that Pickevance gave me last night. But what about their affair? Who knew about that? Where do they meet? What's her personal situation? Do we know? Married? Divorced? What? Are they taking expensive trips together? Does she have expensive tastes? Have they got some love-nest somewhere? How might they have spent this missing money? If, that is, they are responsible for embezzling it, and we don't know that yet. And if it wasn't them, who else had access to the school finances? There's that finance director woman for one - what do we know about her? And that Parry bloke who's treasurer of the Parent Teachers' thing, doesn't he have something to do with them? And is there anyone else? Did your brother come up with any other suggestions?'

'That's about it, as far as the school is concerned,' she said, chewing on the end of a pencil ruminatively. 'Though he did say that the school's auditors should have picked up any discrepancy.'

'And who would they have been?'

'Most likely a local firm of accountants.'

'Find that out, will you? It might lead us somewhere. If that money really has gone missing, it amazes me that no-one had noticed before Stanton did.'

'Sir?' she quizzed.

'Mm?'

'How do you suggest we find out about Pearl Bowen? Do you want me to quiz her about the affair? You told me yesterday to say nothing.'

Tallyforth swung round from the window where he had been watching the traffic speeding below.

'I think it's time we upped the stakes, Elliott,' he replied determinedly. 'Yes, I think Ms. Pearl Bowen needs to be shaken up a little bit. Go and see her. See what you can get from her. I think I could do with seeing William Reynolds and the computer again. Where is it?'

'It's downstairs, sir,' she answered. 'And Reynolds said he was going to phone in this morning to see if there was anything more he could do before he went home.'

Tallyforth beamed.

'Excellent, Sergeant,' he said. ' I just might go and visit our Mr Reynolds. Where did you say he was staying?'

'I didn't, sir,' she replied. 'He told you himself. The Granada Lodge. By the motorway.'

'Right, let's get on with it, Sergeant. Who knows? With a bit of luck, I'll have cracked this case by tea-time. Keep me posted on the Bowen woman.'

George Elliott stood, opened her mouth to speak, then closed it again. If he wanted to play the great detective, let him, she thought.

No skin off her nose.

She headed towards the door.

Saturday morning in the Granada Lodge is always quiet. The tables in the lounge which are daily hosts to deals between similarly-suited businessmen and businesswomen, armed with their mobile phones and mobile lap-top computers, are deserted. The air that on week days is full of chirruping phones, the smell of cheroots, and talk of deals is full only of the aroma of furniture polish and carpet shampoo on Saturday.

It was into this hushed atmosphere that Tallyforth entered, with Hubert Stanton's lap-top computer clutched to him, to meet William Reynolds. He selected a table, ordered coffee, and asked for Reynolds to be told he was waiting for him.

But the planned route of interrogation which Tallyforth intended to pursue was disrupted by the sharp outburst of words that accompanied Reynolds's sudden appearance.

'Have you see this, Chief Inspector?' he said, waving a newspaper in front of him as he approached Tallyforth's table.

'And what would that be, sir?' enquired Tallyforth gently, looking up at Reynolds, who was wearing a yellow Pringle sweater and fawn-coloured slacks. 'Coffee?'

'Thanks but no. I've just had some,' came the reply. 'I mean this letter in the *Tamworth Herald*. Have you seen it? This week's local paper. From an Alfred Pugh. Accusing Pickevance of disregard for what was best for children's learning by getting rid of experienced staff simply to cover up for poor financial management.'

'So?' queried Tallyforth, a puzzled frown creasing his forehead. 'Who is this Alfred Pugh?'

'Don't you know, Chief Inspector?' yelped William Reynolds. 'He's the year head who was made redundant last year!'

Tallyforth looked across at his interlocutor, who had now seated himself opposite.

'And you think this Pugh might know something about the missing fifty grand?'

'Chief Inspector, I think it is too great a coincidence that this letter should appear in the local newspaper on the very last day of the school's OFSTED inspection, don't you?' replied Reynolds sharply. 'Tamworth is a small town. Pugh was bound to have known about the inspection. He could have written directly to Hubert beforehand but he chose to seek publication in the local weekly. Odd, don't you think? Of course, the paper would have been printed before poor Hubert's death was known about.'

'Let me see the letter, will you?' And Tallyforth reached across to take the proffered newspaper.

He read:

Sir,

Many of your readers will be unsurprised to learn of further evidence of financial mismanagement at Æthelfleda High School. It is my understanding that three experienced teachers are seeking to leave the troubled school on ill-health grounds, brought on by the stress of dealing with some increasingly unmanageable groups of pupils. The expulsion of three pupils for drug-dealing in February is just the tip of the iceberg! Several teachers of my acquaintance have spoken of verbal abuse from children which has gone unpunished and of an increasingly hostile and frightening atmosphere in the school. Much of this is directly attributable to the loss through compulsory redundancy of four very experienced and well-respected teachers last year, who knew the children well and knew how to enforce discipline firmly but fairly. Those four teachers were sacrificed to the financial mismanagement of the current headteacher of the school, who chose to spend the money allocated to the school in such a way that he could only afford young inexperienced teachers. The children of Tamworth deserve better. The sooner that someone investigates this blatant abuse of public funds, the better.

Yours etc.,

Alfred Pugh

Tallyforth drew in his breath as he read.

'Strong stuff, sir,' he said. 'Do we know anything of this Pugh?'

'Only that he was the head of year eleven and was made redundant last year after working in the school for the past twenty years. Began as the boys' P.E. teacher and apparently had a reputation for tough discipline. Used to have a row of desks outside his office where the troublemakers were made to work in silence under his supervision. Known as the sin bin.'

'Bit of a hard-liner, then, sir?'

'Definitely,' replied Reynolds, crossing his legs and hitching his trousers so that the creases remained clear.

'What about this bit about the poor behaviour of pupils? Did you find out about the drug-dealing?'

'Chief Inspector, we made appropriate enquiries into the incidents of exclusions and were satisfied with what we discovered. The behaviour of pupils during our inspection of the school was not generally such that we considered it a major problem, though there were examples of unruly behaviour.'

'And you think Pugh might have some knowledge about the missing money?'

'You read the letter, Chief Inspector. Don't you think it's likely?'

'It may just be sour grapes, sir,' said Tallyforth, sipping from his coffee. 'But may I keep this?'

'Of course,' replied Reynolds. 'Chief Inspector, I really would like to get home this afternoon. It looks like I'm going to have one hell of a week next week. And I need some rest. Is there anything else you need me for now? You have my home address and telephone, so you can reach me at any time.'

'No, I don't think so,' Tallyforth began. 'Oh, there was just one thing, sir. I nearly forgot. If you wouldn't mind. It really would be most helpful to us if we could get access to all the relevant information about this school's inspection that's on this computer. Is there some way that you could show me where everything is that matters?'

William Reynolds momentarily narrowed his eyes, as if in exasperation. But he knew that he had to help the police to find out who had murdered his old friend Hubert Stanton, so he would do what he could.

'Of course, Chief Inspector,' he answered with a sigh. 'What I'll do is transfer everything about Æthelfleda High School from the computer on to a disk, so that you can read it all on any computer. I have a spare disk in my pocket.'

'You won't wipe anything off the computer, sir, will you? That is still evidence and may be important.'

'No, no! This will just be a copy so you can read it all easily. All you'll need to do is ask someone at your headquarters to load it on to any computer and you can scroll through the text at your own speed. Will that help?'

'Thank you, Mr Reynolds,' replied Tallyforth, pouring himself another cup of coffee as Reynolds opened up the Toshiba lap-top. 'That will be most helpful.'

Norman de Courcy cleared his throat as he prepared to speak. It was Saturday afternoon and the monthly meeting of the Mercian Society, held in the Tamworth Assembly Rooms. Present were a scattering of the society's members, mostly retired schoolteachers and local government officers, including two former town librarians.

'As you know, ladies and gentlemen,' de Courcy began, smiling benignly at his audience across the table at which he sat, 'this year, nineteen ninety-six *anno domini* is the twelve hundredth anniversary of the death of King Offa. And Tomtun, the seat of Offa's royal palace, will mark that anniversary even though the rest of England ignores it. However, thanks to the unsurprising lack of generosity of the town council, no grants have been given to support these celebrations and we have to consider how we might raise funds to ensure that Offa, whom many of us consider the founder of the English nation, is not neglected.'

'You mean we have no funds at all?' asked one of his audience, a tall weedy man, with a heavily-lined face and eyes sunk behind folds of skin.

'Not quite true, Horace,' replied de Courcy. 'We do have the money that we have collected in the past five years from our various fund-raising events. As you know, I am also hopeful that our bid for support from the National Lottery may come to fruition, though we must not count on that. And I am pleased to report that your successor at the town library has indicated that a small portion of his budget can be made available to support the exhibition that we want to mount in the Old Town Hall.'

'Who is going to do the work?' asked his interlocutor again.

'Exactly my point, Horace,' said de Courcy. 'The library will provide us with the facilities to prepare the exhibition but it does not have the manpower to spare. Any suggestions?'

'Couldn't we get one of the schools to help out?' came another voice from the audience.

'Æthelfleda High School is already totally committed to the re-enactment of the Boxing Day feast, as you know,' said de Courcy, 'and given current events, I somehow doubt whether we could get any more support there. And none of the other schools has shown the slightest interest. You know the problem, Horace - people simply aren't interested in their history, certainly not when it goes back so far. And we all know that the neglect of Offa, the greatest of the Mercian *bretwaldas* who did so much to weld together the subject provinces to form a unified English state and to develop many of the features that were to characterise royal administration in England during the succeeding centuries, is a crime. That is why we formed this society thirty years ago. That is why we're organising these celebrations, to show the people of Tamworth where they came from and how proud they should be to know that this town, Tomtun as it then was, was once the centre of England.'

'So where are we going to put the coin collection?' asked another member of the audience, a frail elderly lady who sat leaning on her walking sick.

'In the Town Hall as we planned, Mrs Atkins. As part of the exhibition,' answered de Courcy. 'The gathering together of *sceattas* and pennies proceeds apace, under the scrupulous guidance of the curator of Mercian artefacts at the British Museum. I am in touch with him regularly and he tells me that he has persuaded the owners of a number of significant private collections, including some in the United States, to loan their coinage for the duration of the exhibition.'

'And the security?' she queried. 'How are we going to guarantee the security of those coins? They're worth thousands of pounds, you know, Norman. They'll need round-the-clock surveillance with all these criminals around nowadays. It almost makes you long for the Mercian days. At least robbers would know what short shrift they would get in those days if they were caught.'

'I'm investigating a way in which the display cases can be electronically monitored day and night,' replied de Courcy. 'And I'm also in negotiations with the curator at the British Museum, where some of these coins will be borrowed from, to see if they will help us. Their expertise in these matters is extensive. I think we can rely on them.'

Norman de Courcy looked down at the notes he had prepared for this meeting, which he had spread out on the table in front of him. He cleared his throat again.

'So, ladies and gentlemen, I believe that the two major events, that is the Boxing Day feast to be held at Æthelfleda High School and the Offa Exhibition to be held in the Old Town Hall are well on the way. However, as I said earlier, we are woefully short of funds to ensure the success of the latter and the other tentative plans we discussed, such as the reconstruction of the Battle of Benson between the armies of Cynewulf of Wessex and Offa or of the building of a section of Offa's Dyke, will have to be deferred, I fear.'

The elderly lady who had spoken earlier leaned sideways to mutter something to the short squat man with the ruddy face who sat next to her.

'Can't we get the Offa's Dyke lot to do something?' the latter asked. 'Isn't there some kind of an Association? I'm sure when Edith and I walked the Dyke fifteen years ago there was some sort of an Association looking after it. Have you tried them, Norman? Couldn't they help?'

Norman de Courcy smiled resignedly.

'Same problem there, I'm afraid,' he said. 'They would love to help but they have had their budget from the Countryside Commission cut and they just can't offer anything other than moral support. Mind you, they will be sending us maps and photographs for the exhibition. And, if we could find some way of funding the construction of a section of the Dyke, as we had originally planned, they would be happy to loan us their expertise. But we can't afford it.'

There was a slight commotion at the back of the room which attracted de Courcy's attention and caused him to pause. The other

Mercian Society members also looked round.

Someone else had just arrived. Someone else who was not a member of the Society. Someone who was not even a resident of Tamworth, their beloved and revered Tomtun. Someone whose thoughts were not on the death of Offa, king of the Mercians and *bretwalda* of the English nation but on the death of Hubert Stanton, OFSTED Registered Inspector and an official of quite a different court.

Chief Inspector Tallyforth, in a blue cotton windcheater and grey flannels, nodded curtly to Norman de Courcy, then sat down on one of the empty chairs at the back of the Assembly Rooms, waiting.

It was a sunny day and he had been walking alongside the River Anker, watching the mute swans with their arched necks and wings held slightly raised as they swam. Wonderfully graceful birds, he thought to himself, sailing their stately passage through the water, their orange black-tipped bills and the black patches around their eyes making them instantly distinguishable and reminding him of bloody daggers. But he knew that those gentle snorting calls they made to each other across the water could turn into aggressive hisses for no apparent reason when they were disturbed by humans. He had read before of how the herd of mute swans on the Rivers Anker and Tame could reach over one hundred birds during the winter and how the townsfolk had been known to supplement the birds' diet of aquatic vegetation and grass when the winter was particularly severe and prevented them from easily accessing their regular sources of food.

What had her reaction been again? He mused. Gratitude? She rarely let herself reveal that. In the ten years since the divorce he had never had more than what seemed to him cursory thanks - no excited hugs, no twinkling eyes, like he remembered from when she was a little girl. Maybe that was just growing up. Disdain then? But not really, not if he truthfully looked in his soul. She may not have been a great fan of this Van Morrison character whose concert in June he'd been able to get tickets for but she hadn't refused them. And, even though she would probably have preferred to go to the event with one of her own friends of her own age, she had agreed happily enough to go with him. So he shouldn't complain really - she was trying.

Tallyforth's thoughts turned away from the pain he always felt on contemplating his children and the regret he had for ever having left them, and turned instead to the case that he and George Elliott were engaged on.

A pair of mute swans grazing on the river bank hissed in his direction as he passed, as if to warn him against the mistake of getting too close. And there was something about this case that felt the same way. All the clues, both circumstantial and almost certainly substantial, seemed to point in one direction - at Brian Pickevance. He had the motive, because his affair with the Bowen woman, if true and that seemed very likely, had probably caused the staff of the school to lose confidence in him and because he certainly had access to the school funds from which this fifty thousand pounds had apparently gone missing. And all of that had been discovered by Stanton who had been on the point of revealing all in his inspection report on the school. And the result of that, without a doubt, would have been the sacking of Pickevance and probably of the Bowen woman as well. Followed by criminal investigations of Pickevance into the embezzlement of the school funds. Followed by a term in prison. In other words, a man's life and career about to be ruined. And a desperate man, as Tallyforth knew only too well from all his detective work over the years, will do desperate things to try to stave off the inevitable, even though he suspects that all he is doing is putting off the day of reckoning.

So why was he hesitating? Why didn't he just arrest Pickevance straightaway and bring him in for questioning? The man was a schoolteacher, he had no criminal record, he would break quickly enough, reasoned Tallyforth. If, that is, he was guilty, as looked so likely. But what if he protested his innocence, what then?

And what was that little seed of doubt that was nagging away at the back of Tallyforth's head? Whence did it come? And should he listen to it? Or was he just being over-cautious?

As his thoughts had led him in these directions, his footsteps had led him back into the town centre and he had found himself standing outside the Assembly Rooms, where he had seen the notice for the meeting of the Mercian Society.

59

SIX

George Elliott pulled on the hand brake of her powder blue Renault Clio and looked out of the side window at the row of Victorian terraced houses in Church Lane. The end house was the one where Pearl Bowen lived. It had two flower baskets, dripping with yellow and purple, hanging on either side of the front door. The sunshine made it look very attractive.

She locked the Clio, walked over to the door of the end house and knocked.

'Oh, hello!' Pearl Bowen's face lit up as she recognised the sergeant, then immediately darkened as she realised that this wasn't a social call. 'You'd better come in. Can I get you a drink of something? Tea? Coffee? Or would you prefer something stronger?'

'Tea will be fine, thanks,' replied George Elliott. 'Milk. No sugar.'

And she followed Pearl Bowen into the house, noting that even on Saturday afternoon the deputy headteacher of Æthelfleda High School was fully made up and wearing the obligatory tight-fitting mini-skirt and figure-hugging salmon pink cotton body. Was she expecting someone? she wondered.

The room she entered, however, was one she felt immediately at home in, with its cottage suite, its carefully-chosen bric-a-brac, its scattered cushions. She noticed a copy of Margaret Attwood's *A Handmaid's Tale* open on one armchair and books about vegetarian cookery on a bookshelf. Sting's *Fields of Gold* was playing quietly in the background. She selected a comfortable-looking armchair and sat down.

'Nice place,' she said out loud.

'You like it?' came the voice from the small kitchen in the back. 'Jim and I bought it ten years ago. We were both working in

Lichfield at the time and this was just about the right distance from work. I didn't think then I'd end up working in Tamworth itself but there you go. The strangest things, you know!'

'Is Jim your husband?' George Elliott asked, trying to sound as casual as she could.

'My partner,' came the reply. 'We've been together for the last twelve years but neither of us believed in marriage. Thought it was medieval. Still do, I suppose.'

Pearl Bowen re-appeared, carrying two mugs of tea.

'Afraid they're not very delicate,' she said, passing one mug over to George Elliott before sitting down opposite. 'What were you saying?'

George Elliott smiled. The woman was very clever, she could see, from the way she played for time with such apparent innocence.

'Your partner,' she reminded. 'You were telling me about him.'

'Jim! Oh, he's a financial adviser. Spends most of his time in London these days. Comes home at weekends. Though he's had to stay down this weekend because of some conference or other. But that's OK. We're both very busy people, always have been. It's not possible to be deputy head of a comprehensive school without giving up a lot of your time to it. And Jim's work has just boomed over the past few years - the City, you know. Can't say I fully understand, though I've tried. But he does do very well - well enough for us to holiday in the Seychelles or Mauritius or Java every year, as well as go skiing every Christmas.'

Pearl Bowen sipped her tea. George Elliott watched. There was no hint of boastfulness in what had just been said. It was matter-of fact and unadorned. But was this woman dissembling?

'So, a weekend on your own, then?' she said smiling.

'Yes, and don't I just need it after the week I've had! You've no idea, Sergeant, how stressful these school inspections are. This is my second. I had the bad luck to be in my last school in the first year of this new system when we were inspected. So you can imagine my feelings when Brian showed me the letter earlier this year that said that Æthelfleda High School was to be done. And then, to cap it all, this dreadful situation with poor Mr Stanton. Have you found any more?'

'Not an awful lot yet, no,' George Elliott admitted, 'but we have a number of leads we're following up. You know, the usual police work.'

'Mm, yes, I suppose so. I guess you have to look at every angle. I just can't believe it. Who would have wanted to kill him? Who could have done it? It's all very upsetting.'

George Elliott looked across at her again. If she was dissembling, she was very good at it. There wasn't a hint of anything in her voice which might suggest more knowledge than she was currently admitting. Time to probe a little.

'Where was your previous school?' she asked.

'Oh, that was in Lichfield. It was the school I started teaching in actually. I did three years there, then I got promoted to a head of department job in a school in Burton, then I went back to my first school as senior teacher, responsible for staff development and appraisal. I was there five years before this job came up and I got it. Of course, I'd applied for other deputy headships but this was the one I got. I think my age may have gone against me before.'

'And male chauvinism?'

'Possibly, though I don't think so. There's still a lot of governing bodies who think there ought to be a woman in the senior management of a school. You know, to dole out the Tampax and deal with the unexpected pregnancies, that sort of thing. Though how they're going to manage that when all these budget cuts are reducing the number of deputy heads, I do not know!'

'So Brian Pickevance picked you,' asked George Elliott smiling.

Pearl Bowen returned her smile.

'You could say that,' she began. 'Although technically speaking, it's the governors who make the appointments. Though I know Brian wanted me because he's told me since.'

'You seem very close,' she tried.

'Yes, we are,' replied Pearl Bowen, her skin colour not changing one iota. 'Brian inherited two deputies who had been appointed by his predecessor, basically because of their long service in the school and because they were yes-men. One of them was part of the Rugby Club mafia. Alf Pugh was part of that lot too. They used to rule with a rod of iron. Used to put the fear of God into little kids. They were both renowned thrashers and bashers. When the cane was allowed, that is. Though I'm pretty sure they still used

62

physical violence when they thought they could get away with it. And on the estate round the school there's still too many homes where male violence is regarded as normal behaviour.'

'Was Alf Pugh the year head who was made redundant last year?' asked George Elliott.

'Yes, that's him. Nasty piece of work,' came the reply. 'Thought he was God's gift as well. Always trying to stare up my legs and ogling my breasts. Though how he thought anyone could fancy him, I do not know, the fat toe-rag!'

'So, you were saying about you and Brian Pickevance working closely together?'

'Well, Brian is a man with a vision,' began Pearl Bowen, placing her empty cup on a side-table and stretching back in her chair. 'He believes that these children need to be shown that life is possible without violence, without constant argument, without confrontation. And he desperately wants them to succeed. Despite their backgrounds, despite their poverty, despite their low self-esteem, Brian believes they can do well. And he burns for them. He has given his life to the children of Æthelfleda High School.'

Her eyes were burning with excitement. And it was not put on for her benefit, George Elliott realised. It was totally genuine. No doubt about it, Pearl Bowen was besotted with Pickevance. Whatever else had happened, there was no doubting that. But would she admit there was more to their relationship than professional closeness?

'Are you sleeping with him?'

Pearl Bowen looked suddenly startled. She sat upright in her chair. Her eyes stared fiercely at George Elliott. But she gave no reply.

'You are, aren't you, Pearl?' George Elliott said gently. 'It's alright. It's not a crime.'

'Do you sleep with your chief inspector, Sergeant? Tallyforth, or whatever his name is? Do you?'

'That's neither here nor there, Pearl,' she answered. 'But your relationship with Brian Pickevance, both professional and personal, may have a bearing on the murder of Hubert Stanton. It has been alleged that staff knew of your affair and that some at least were unhappy about the unhealthy influence it was having on the management of the school.'

'No one has the right to say that,' Pear Bowen expostulated. 'The school has probably been managed better in the last year since.....'

'That long then?'

'Yes,' Pear Bowen looked down at her brightly-painted finger nails. 'It started at the Abbey Hotel in Malvern at a conference on School Effectiveness a year last Easter.'

'Jim?'

'He doesn't know.'

'Pickevance's wife?'

'Sarah doesn't know either. We thought we'd been very discreet. Who told you?'

Pearl Bowen looked pleadingly up at George Elliott. Her world had suddenly crashed around her.

'It was actually William Reynolds, the inspector. Apparently Stanton had found out from somewhere and asked all his team to check out if the department heads had total confidence in the directions that Pickevance was leading the school. They confirmed what he had found out. Did he used to come here?'

'Yes. Very occasionally, though,' came Pearl Bowen's reply. The warmth and excitement had gone out of her voice, which was now little more than a whisper. 'But we had a place in Lichfield. Belongs to a friend of mine. She was renting it to us. We'd half-thought of going to live there when.....'

'When you'd each told your respective partners?' Elliott's voice was tinged with sarcasm. She'd heard all this sort of thing before.

'Yes,' came the whispered answer. 'We'd decided to get through this inspection first and Brian's daughter Pam was doing her A levels this summer. After that, we'd thought we might.'

'Might?'

'Would! I mean, would. Sergeant, what happens now? I haven't committed a crime.'

'Pearl, just tell me honestly about your movements on the evening of the Thursday when Hubert Stanton was poisoned.'

Sergeant George Elliott reached into the pocket of her jeans for her notebook and pencil.

'Good evening, ladies and gentlemen. And members of Tamworth Rugby Football Club! No, only joking! It really is a pleasure to see so many of you here tonight and I know you're going to have a really good time. So I won't waste any more of it, because you haven't come here to listen to me. Please welcome back to Tamworth Rugby Club Jon Mitchell and the Falling Leaves!'

The dinner-suited compere walked backwards to the edge of the small stage, leading the applause as the curtains opened and the five-piece rock band began their first set with a rendition of their theme song *Raglan Road*.

Jon Mitchell launched into the song's opening chorus of:

> *On Raglan Road on an Autumn day*
> *I saw her first and knew*
> *That her dark hair would weave a snare*
> *That I might one day rue.*
> *I saw the danger, yet I walked*
> *Along the enchanted way*
> *And I said let grief be a falling leaf*
> *At the dawning of the day.*

Alf Pugh turned to his companions sitting at a table half way back on the lounge floor and leered:

'Like Jon Mitchell's latest bit of stuff,' he said, 'How about you, Frank? Alright, eh, Clive? Not your type though eh, Den?'

'Piss off, Pugwash,' hissed Denise Hadlington, head of girls' physical education at Æthelfleda High School and long-time colleague of Alfred Pugh. 'I'm gay and proud of it. You never could cope with anything other than one type of sexuality, could you? And in your case, that was fat farting men lusting after anorexic little girls, wasn't it?'

'Ooh, who squeezed her tits then?' mocked Al Pugh, laughing in the direction of his other companions.

'Lay off, Alf,' protested Frank O'Donnell, who was head of geography at Æthelfleda High School, looking to his art colleague, Clive Barnsley, for support. 'You're always winding Den up. It gets boring. Give it a rest.'

Clive Barnsley, handsome with black hair and black Errol Flynn moustache, sat back, drumming his fingers on the table in time to the music.

'I like Margi,' he said at last. 'I think she and Jon have a real good thing going for them. I go and visit them occasionally. We have a real cool time.'

'What? Smoking dope and then three-in-a-bed stuff, eh, Clive?' interjected Alf Pugh, with a lecherous look in his eyes.

Clive Barnsley closed his eyes momentarily; when he opened them, they were fixed coolly on Pugh.

'What's your problem, man?' he began. 'Have you ever smoked dope? Have you ever done anything to enhance your mood other than pour large amounts of crude alcohol into your blood-stream and then puke it all up? Is that really the height of your enjoyment? I pity you.'

'Tell him, Clive', interrupted Denise Hadlington. 'He's just a sad prick.'

Alf Pugh turned back towards the stage, ignoring the ribald comments which he had initiated and which for him were just part of the mindless banter that he felt it was necessary to engage in at the rugby club, where he came every Tuesday and Saturday evening throughout the year. He had once been captain of the club, in his day a nippy fly half, but age and alcohol had caught up with him and the sleek ten-stone athlete of yesteryear had ballooned into a sixteen-stone, rotund, balding fifty-year-old.

Margi Benetti, the singer with the Falling Leaves band and partner of Jon Mitchell, was beginning the group's second number. Dressed in a green lycra skirt and a dazzling white tee-shirt, she clasped the microphone in both hands up to her lips and started to croon the Beatles' *For No One*:

> *The day breaks, your mind aches,*
> *You find that all her words of kindness linger on*
> *She no longer needs you*
> *She wakes up, she makes up,*
> *She takes her time and doesn't feel she has to hurry*
> *She no longer needs you*

Alf Pugh's eyes were closed as he silently mouthed the words in time with the singer. Denise Hadlington nudged Frank O'Donnell to draw his attention. O'Donnell smiled, then reached into his trouser pocket and pulled out a piece of paper. Carefully and silently he manoeuvred himself out of his seat to lean across the table until his hand, with the piece of paper, was only inches from Alf Pugh's mouth. Then, as Margi Bennetti's powerful voice sang out the dying fall of:

......a love that should have lasted years.

he slipped the paper between Alf Pugh's lips and abruptly sat back.

'What the bloody...!'

Alf Pugh's eyes opened at once, his right hand tore the offending piece of paper from his mouth, and he glared round at his companions angrily.

'Who the hell?'

'Aren't you going to read it, then, Pugwash?' laughed Denise Hadlington, as she raised her bottle of Stella Artois to her lips.

Pugh glanced at the paper, which he now saw had been ripped from a newspaper, and, as he read, his anger gave way to amusement.

'So, you all saw my letter in the *Herald*? Thought it was a good time to get at that bastard Pickisnose, eh! Bet he's been shitting himself this week with the inspection crew in, eh?'

'No, I haven't seen anything,' said Clive Barnsley. 'Give it here! What is it?'

Denise Hadlington leaned sideways at him to explain.

'Only old Pugwash here having a moan about being made redundant last summer. As per usual,' she answered, as Barnsley read the newspaper cutting. 'You'd think he hadn't got a good pay-off, wouldn't you? Wish I could get the enhancement deal you got, mate.'

'You're still too young and beautiful, sweetheart,' replied Pugh laughing.

'So what's all this about financial mismanagement then, Pugs?' asked Frank O'Donnell.

Alf Pugh tapped his finger against the side of his bulbous nose and grinned conspiratorially.

'Little bird told me,' he said. 'Little bird that wants to remain anonymous. But it's genuine. Story is that there's money gone missing from the school. And we're not just talking a few quid here. Somebody's had their fingers in the till in a very big way, if you ask me. More than likely gone to feathering the Pearl 'n Brian love-nest, know what I mean? And just in case the inspectors didn't find out, I made sure that complimentary copies of the *Herald* were given to certain guests at the Granada, where I heard they were staying.'

'What about the Reggie dying then, Pugs? How does that fit in then?' asked O'Donnell. 'You got a theory on that too, have you?'

'I'm not saying anything,' said Alf Pugh, 'in case any of you lot go blabbing off to the cops. But I've got my suspicions, haven't you? Who stands to gain most from the guy's death? Ask yourselves. It looks cut and dried to me.'

'You saying Pickevance murdered him?' gasped Denise Hadlington. 'Now I know you've lost your marbles. Okay, so the bloke's a bastard but that doesn't make him a killer!'

'I'm not saying anything,' replied Alf Pugh, turning back towards the stage where the Falling Leaves were just concluding their rendition of *For No One*.

Just then there was a minor commotion at the door to the lounge, where someone was clearly having difficulty in gaining entry. The two prop forwards who were on duty that evening as bouncers were being very insistent that a woman in a fawn raincoat could not come in because she did not have a ticket.

'It's alright, boys,' called out Alf Pugh, as he recognised who it was and moved over towards the door to rescue her. 'The lady's with my party. Let her through.'

As she pushed quickly past the two bemused prop forwards, Pugh took her arm and led her towards the table where the others were sitting.

'What you having, Alicia?' he asked. 'Here, Frank, take Alicia's coat, will you? What's it to be then?'

Alicia Hilton, the school's finance director, rather flustered from the bother at the door, undid her coat and passed it to Frank O'Donnell then sat down demurely.

'Gin and tonic, please,' she said. 'And plenty of ice please.'

'As you wish, ma'am,' replied Pugh, half-bowing in mock-courtesy as he turned towards the bar.

'Didn't think this was your sort of scene, Alicia,' began Denise Hadlington. 'Didn't have you down for a rock 'n roller!'

'I'm not really,' answered Alicia Hilton, smiling wanly at the others. 'But, now the children are more independent, I thought I ought to get out a bit more often. And Alfred kindly suggested that I spend this Saturday evening here. He said quite a few from the school were coming.'

'Afraid there's only us,' said Denise Hadlington. 'Any news on that Stanton chap's death?'

'I haven't heard anything today,' Alicia Hilton replied. 'They say he was poisoned, though. With cyanide. But I don't think the police have any ideas about who might have done it.'

'Have you heard from the boss today?' asked Clive Barnsley.

'No,' she blushed slightly.

'Pugwash reckons Pickevance was involved,' said Barnsley.

'Oh!' Alicia Hilton looked genuinely surprised.

'Apparently someone's told him that there's money missing from the school accounts, so he thinks that Pickevance had been helping himself in order to sponsor his love-life with the Bowen bitch,' continued Denise Hadlington.

'Oh!'

'But surely you'd have noticed if there was money missing, wouldn't you, Alicia? It all goes through you, doesn't it?' queried Barnsley.

'Yes,' she replied. 'No. I mean, I do handle most of the finances but Bri...Mr Pickevance has the final say. So I wouldn't really know about missing money. I'm not an accountant, you know. I'm just a glorified school secretary who's done a course in book-keeping.'

'So, you know nothing?' asked Denise Hadlington.

'Afraid not.' She looked up as Alf Pugh leaned over her shoulder to place a glass on the table in front of her. 'Thank you, Alfred.'

Alf Pugh deposited Alicia Hilton's gin and tonic on the table, nodded acknowledgement of her thanks, and turned back to the stage, where Jon Mitchell was announcing that the Falling Leaves' next number would be Eric Clapton's *Layla*.

Denise Hadlington looked at Clive Barnsley. Barnsley looked back. The same thought was forming in their heads. Was this the little bird who had informed Alf Pugh about the missing money?

SEVEN

After the Mercian Society's monthly meeting had ended, de Courcy had explained to Tallyforth about the intended twelve hundredth anniversary of King Offa's death and the celebrations that had been planned. He had also explained about the lack of financial support from the Borough Council, although he had admitted that he had not been too surprised by that, given that he was the only Liberal Democrat member of the council and had constantly battled with the administration over the years.

In answer to Tallyforth's further questions about the importance of Offa, de Courcy had described how Offa had welded together the disparate and warring tribes of Middle England in the eighth century, extending his influence westwards into Wales and southwards into Kent and Wessex, how Offa had invited the Pope's legate to England, as a result of which the new archbishopric at Lichfield had been created, and how Offa had demonstrated his gift for diplomacy in his dealings with the Emperor Charlemagne, who had sent Offa gifts which included silks, a belt and an Avar sword. According to de Courcy, Offa had been one of the founders of modern-day England and his major contribution to the unification of the country had been sadly neglected by subsequent historians. He had quoted the words of one of his contemporaries, Alcuin, who had written:

"Never forget Offa's fine character, his modest way of life, his concern to reform the life of a Christian people, but do not follow him in his cruel and greedy acts."

The sadness, according to de Courcy, was that later writers had chosen to concentrate on the 'cruel and greedy acts', such as the bloody murders of all possible rivals to his son Ecgfrith's succession, and to ignore 'his concern to reform the life of a Christian people.'

One of Offa's significant achievements, which had influenced the United Kingdom until very recently, had been the introduction of the penny coin, two hundred and forty of which made up a pound. It was only the Conservative government's decision to embrace decimilisation in nineteen seventy-one that had ended that particular historical link. The exhibition planned for the anniversary celebrations would, he explained, have a display of pennies and *sceattas* from Offa's time, with designs which included porcupines, plumed birds, a bird and branch, the king holding a bowl or chalice, a wolf, a hound and tree, runes, as well as the bust of Offa himself and of his queen Cynethryth.

'Was that when Maudling was Chancellor of the Exchequer?' Tallyforth had queried, musing aloud almost. 'Odd if it was, don't you think? Him being Reggie, I mean. Curious coincidence. But maybe I'm wrong.'

De Courcy had also explained where Æthelfleda High School had got its name from. Tamworth had also been the royal residence, he had explained, of Æthelfleda, the eldest daughter of King Alfred, whose husband was the king's representative - the ealdorman - in Mercia till his death in 911. She it was who built the "burh" as a fortified defence against the Danish invaders, one of several Midland sites chosen by King Edward the Elder for this purpose, Tamworth being of strategic importance because of its closeness to Watling Street.

'How did Brian Pickevance react to your plan to celebrate the twelve hundredth anniversary of Offa's death?' Tallyforth had then asked.

De Courcy had become somewhat animated.

'Initially, he wasn't interested,' he had replied. 'But when I explained that this would be a unique occasion and that no other school would be joining in the celebrations, he realised that it would be good publicity for the school. You may have realised by now, Chief Inspector, that Æthelfleda High School is not a high-achieving academic school, nor ever will be, given the nature of our catchment

71

area. So any chance to promote the school is one that the headteacher is keen on. I knew that. Plus I promised to oversee all the arrangements in my own time. I knew that would persuade him. Since then, of course, he's been milking it for all he can get - inviting television crews down to the school, talking to reporters from *The Times Educational Supplement,* giving interviews on Radio Four.'

'And what about those coins you mentioned?' Tallyforth had continued. 'Are they valuable?'

'Oh, yes, Chief Inspector! They are irreplaceable. They are part of our history. Some of the collections are valued at thousands of pounds.'

'Any kept locally?'

'None that are known of, no. There's a rumour that some local with a metal-detector has dug up some treasure trove recently and has it proudly adorning his mantelpiece.'

'Is there any truth in that?'

'Who knows? Of course, if they had, they would probably have sold it on to America by now. Of course I'm only speculating. There may be no such thing.'

Tallyforth was sitting in the bar of the Castle Hotel, with a pint of Burton ale in his right hand as he ran through the conversation he had had with Norman de Courcy. He had always been curious as to why the police force he belonged to had been given the name Mercian. His historical knowledge about the so-called Dark Ages, like most people's, was rather sketchy. De Courcy's eloquent and erudite explanations had given him a better understanding. It was all fascinating but it had little or no bearing on the case they were currently involved in, except to add to the picture of Pickevance slightly.

'Evening, sir.'

Tallyforth looked up to see George Elliott, still dressed in jeans and sweatshirt, standing above him. He could not help thinking what a good-looking woman she was.

'Sergeant, what's your poison? The Burton's rather fine. Alright for you?'

'Thanks, I'll have a pint,' she said, sitting down opposite Tallyforth's chair, which he had now vacated as he went to the bar to fetch her drink and to replenish his own half-empty glass.

'So?' he queried as he brought her beer to the table. 'La Bowen?'

She sipped deeply from her beer before answering.

'She admitted the affair straightaway,' replied George Elliott. 'There's very little side to that woman. Said it had been going on for the past year. Mostly they go to a cottage that they rent in Lichfield. Though occasionally he's stayed in her house in Church Lane in the town here. They were planning to set up home together in this place in Lichfield. After the inspection. And after his elder daughter had completed her A levels. So she says. And I'm sure she believed that was what was going to happen.'

'But you don't?' he asked, watching her carefully.

'Not entirely, no,' she said. 'At first sight, Pearl Bowen is hyper-confident, a modern woman, always demanding her equal rights, sure of herself. But underneath all that is a very insecure woman, who has been brought up like other little girls with romantic notions of the perfect love and is fighting a constant battle within herself between those romantic notions and the newer feminist ideals that she has embraced as she reached adulthood.'

'You sound as if you know this territory, Elliott,' Tallyforth mocked, smiling knowingly at her.

She pretended not to hear him, or at any rate not to hear his tone.

'What I'm saying, sir,' she said, stressing the 'sir', 'is that Pearl Bowen is in love with Pickevance. There's very little she wouldn't do for him.'

'Even commit murder?'

'I doubt that, sir, but I would want to reserve judgement. Love can be blind.'

'So, although Pickevance isn't your type, Sergeant, you now know whose type he is! Do you still think it was him?'

'Yes.'

'Time to bring him in, do you think?'

'Yes.'

'Let's just remind ourselves of all we know then. First, Stanton died of cyanide poisoning from drinking coffee that had been laced by person or persons unknown. Secondly, someone had apparently tampered with what Stanton had written on his computer in criticism of the school's management, presumably after Stanton was dead. Thirdly, Stanton had discovered that fifty grand had gone missing from the school's finances and would have revealed this in his report. Fourthly, the part of the building that Stanton and his inspection team were using was quite separate from the rest of the school and so it would have been possible for someone to enter and exit from there without being noticed by anyone, especially since Lashley the caretaker had been told to leave that part of the premises alone on the night in question. Fifthly, we now know for sure that Pickevance and his deputy, the Bowen woman, were having an affair, that many staff knew of this and that it was affecting the way the school was run. Have I missed anything, Elliott?'

'No, sir, not that I know of.'

'Wrong, Sergeant. There are one or two loose strands we have not untangled.

'If Pickevance was the killer, how did he get hold of the cyanide? And when and how did he get back into the school and into the room where Stanton was working in order to lace the coffee pot without being seen? And then there's Alfred Pugh.'

'Sir?'

'You heard of him? Bit of no good who was sacked last year. Had a letter in yesterday's *Tamworth Herald* accusing Pickevance of financial mismanagement.'

'So he knew of the missing money?' She looked earnestly at him.

'Well, his letter certainly hints at that. Now if he did, how would he know? Who else might have access to information about the school's finances?'

She shrugged her shoulders by way of answer. And then, her eyes suddenly lit up and she leaned forward towards Tallyforth excitedly.

'What about that finance woman, Mrs Hilton - she could have.... You think she told him?'

He looked across at her.

'Just before we bring Pickevance in, I think we could do with talking to Pugh and this Mrs Hilton. Agreed?'

She nodded. They drank up their beer and left the Castle Hotel.

'Brian? It's Pearl. Can you talk?'

'Yes. Just a minute. I'll take the phone upstairs to the study.' There was a pause.

'You alright? You sound anxious.'

'Brian, I've had the police here. That Sergeant Elliott. They know. About you and me. There was no point denying it.'

'Alright, calm down, calm down. What do you mean? How do they know? Who told them?'

'Apparently Stanton had found out. Don't ask me how but he did. And he had asked all of rest of them to check it out and it seems that half the staff know. And blabbed. What are we going to do?'

'Pearl, keep your voice down. Sarah's just downstairs. Now just keep calm. we haven't committed a crime.'

'But they'll suspect us of Stanton's murder!' she yelped from the other end of the phone.

'Don't be silly! Listen, we'd better not meet tonight. They may be watching for us and I don't want any suspicions being aroused. What about tomorrow afternoon?'

'Brian, I don't think I can manage this on my own. Can't you come round? Please?'

'Pearl, sweetheart, I can't. What would Sarah think if I went out at nine o'clock on a Saturday evening without any reason?'

'Can't you say you've had a call from the school? I'll meet you there if you like. Please, Brian, I really need you just now. Don't leave me on my own!'

There was another pause.

'Alright. I'll be at your place in twenty minutes. But I can't stay.'

Brian Pickevance pressed the disconnect button and moved back down the stairs of his house. As he reached the lounge, where his wife Sarah and their two younger children Becky and James were watching the end of *Casualty* on television, he called in:

'That was Gideon Lashley. He thinks there's been a break-

75

school. I'll have to go and check it out. Shan't be long, I hope. It's one thing after another just now.'

As he left the house, Sarah Pickevance looked down at the phone extension which she held in her hand. Her eyes began to water.

Although it was ten o'clock a night, it had been one of those early summer days and it was still warm enough that they didn't need jackets or coats. True, they were sitting in the front seats of George Elliott's blue Renault Clio, but they had been there for some time without any heating on in the stationary and silent car. They were parked in a nondescript street in the middle of the nondescript Belgrave modern housing estate, where acres of redbrick houses had sprung up in recent years on land that had once been countryside, as the town of Tamworth's population had exploded. A short distance down the street from where they were parked was Alicia Hilton's home, where the curtains were drawn and no lights showed. Tallyforth and George Elliott had rung the doorbell of the semi-detached house with its neatly-cut lawn and neat borders of primroses but, on getting no response, had determined to wait for a while to see if she re-appeared.

To while away the time, Tallyforth had been telling her about Offa and his rule in Mercia. She had listened politely but without great interest. The doings of the ancient Mercian king were of little relevance to her or, she believed, to the case they were engaged on. She was thinking much more of Pearl Bowen and the frankness with which the latter had spoken of her relationship with Pickevance, of the care he had shown for her when her father had died six months previously, of the risks he had taken to be with her at times when she was desperately lonely, of the affectionate gestures he was so capable of making. Was this really the same man whom they now suspected of being guilty of poisoning Hubert Stanton, the school's Registered Inspector? Surely, if he had loved her that much, he should have been able to face the ignominy and the shame of being revealed for what he had done! And what had he done anyway? As far as she could tell, his main crime had been falling in love with the woman who was his deputy at the school they both worked at. And as yet, they had no proof of anything other than that. Linking Pickevance to the missing money was pure supposition, based on his access to the school funds and to the assumption that Stanton had been murdered because he had discovered that Pickevance had been embezzling. But this was still mere supposition. The evidence was very, very thin. Surely they needed something more substantial to confront him with when they brought him in! Perhaps Alicia Hilton could help with that.

Just as she was thinking thus, a metallic-grey Vauxhall Calibra drew up outside Alicia Hilton's house and, shortly afterwards, Alicia herself emerged from the car and walked up to the front door to let herself in. The driver of the car, a short fat balding man, followed her in.

'Who's that?' demanded Tallyforth.

'Sorry, sir. Can't help,' she replied. 'Never seen him before. Her husband?'

Tallyforth turned towards her.

'Didn't I hear somewhere that she was divorced?'

'Possibly. I don't remember.'

He wound up his window.

'Come on, Elliott. We're going to talk to Mrs Hilton and her friend, whoever he is and if he wants to stay.'

They walked quickly from the car towards Alicia Hilton's house and up to the front door, where Tallyforth pressed the doorbell.

'Yes? Oh, Chief Inspector, it's you!' Alicia Hilton was genuinely shocked, as she peered round the edge of the door. 'I was just.... Is something wrong? I mean, what do you want at this time of night?'

Gradually she was regaining her composure.

'We'd like to ask you a few questions, Mrs Hilton,' explained George Elliott, leaning around Tallyforth's frame. 'Just routine enquiries. Sorry it's so late but we called earlier and you weren't in. And we really needed to talk to you tonight, if you wouldn't mind. Can we come in?'

Alicia Hilton looked at the two police officers hesitantly.

'I suppose so,' she said, pulling the door fully open. 'She gesticulated to the squat figure who was now standing behind her. This is Alfred Pugh, by the way. He's just given me a lift back from the Rugby Club. There was a social evening there.'

'I was just leaving as a matter of fact,' said Pugh. 'If you'll excuse me, Alicia.'

Tallyforth smiled.

'Not the Alf Pugh who writes to the *Tamworth Herald*? One-time teacher at Æthelfleda High School?' he queried.

Alf Pugh pulled up short as he was about to pass the two police officers.

'Yes, that's right,' he said. 'Why? Who wants to know?'

'A slice of luck for us here, sir,' smiled Tallyforth. 'We wanted to talk to you too after seeing that letter of yours in the *Herald*. Could kill two birds with one stone tonight. If you'll forgive a rather tired and inappropriate metaphor, sir. We're police officers, sir, investigating the death of one Hubert Stanton, the Registered Inspector who was leading the inspection of Æthelfleda High School. I believe you too might be able to help us in our enquiries, sir. We'd be much obliged if you could stay. We won't keep you long. Mind if we come in, Mrs Hilton?'

And Tallyforth and George Elliott crossed the threshold of Alicia Hilton's house and moved through the neatly-decorated hallway into the back room, preceded by Alf Pugh.

The room was furnished in the modern style with a settee and two armchairs. A teak-finished dropleaf table stood against one wall, with a vase of artificial lilies adorning its centre. The living flame gas fire was not switched on.

'Please sit down,' said Alicia Hilton, fussing round them. 'Shall I put the kettle on? Or would anyone like anything stronger?'

'Tea will be fine, Mrs Hilton,' said Tallyforth. 'We're on duty, remember.'

Alicia Hilton went out of the room into the kitchen.

'Mr Pugh, that was a very interesting letter of yours in yesterday's *Tamworth Herald*. Do you have any evidence to support your claim of financial mismanagement at Æthelfleda High School?' began Tallyforth, leaning back in the floral-covered armchair he had chosen.

Alf Pugh's mouth opened as if to speak, then closed again abruptly. This happened three times with never a word emerging.

He looked like a trout coming up for air. Finally, at the fourth attempt, he managed to speak.

'What I know is that Brian Pickevance got rid of four of his most experienced teachers last summer simply to balance the books,' he expostulated, his forehead beginning to ooze with sweat. 'Or so he said at the time. He used the financial shortfall as an excuse to get rid of people who disagreed with him. Egged on by that Bowen bitch, of course. I'm not sure now there was such a financial crisis as he made out.'

Tallyforth looked across at Alf Pugh, who sat forward on the settee opposite him, his legs crossed at the ankles and his knees akimbo, his forehead glistening with sweat.

'Go on, sir,' he said. 'You know something else?'

'Yes. I do now.'

'Well?'

But before Pugh could answer, Alicia Hilton re-appeared with the tea tray and offered it in turn to each of her three guests. She then carefully placed the tray on the dining table, took her own cup and sat down next to Alf Pugh.

'Strong enough for you, Chief Inspector?' she asked demurely.

'Thank you, yes,' Tallyforth replied. 'Mr Pugh here was just telling me about his suspicions concerning the financial affairs at Æthelfleda High School. You wouldn't have any knowledge of that, would you, Mrs Hilton?'

She blushed slightly.

'Well, I....' she began. 'I mean, I'm the school's finance director, so yes, I suppose I do know something about its financial affairs.'

'And the loss of five teachers last summer - you were aware of the financial situation which led to that loss?'

'Yes,' she replied. 'Or, at least I thought I was. I mean, I saw the figures that Bri...Mr Pickevance prepared before he went to the governors' meeting to say that he thought the school had to lose teachers.'

'And had Mr Pickevance prepared those figures himself?' asked George Elliott.

'Yes, as far as I'm aware.'

'So, now you're not so sure of what happened?' pressed Tallyforth.

Alicia Hilton glanced quickly at Alf Pugh sitting beside her, who gave her a reassuring nod.

'Tell them, Alicia,' he said quietly. 'Tell them what you told me.'

'Well, it was only two months ago, when I was preparing papers for the auditors that I came across some information which I didn't know about last year,' she began hesitantly, clasping her hands together tightly on her lap.

'Yes?'

'Well, the school didn't need to lose all of those teachers last year. You see, there was fifty thousand pounds more in the money that we were given last April than appeared in the budget that the governors approved in May. Somehow fifty thousand pounds disappeared between April and May of last year.'

'But didn't the auditors pick that up? Who were they anyway?' asked Tallyforth.

'It was Mr Ferris, one of the partners in Stevens, Stevens and Ferris Chartered Accountants. Mr Stevens is the Chairman of the Governors,' she replied.

Tallyforth sucked in his breath and glanced across at George Elliott, who was busy scribbling all this new information in her notebook.

'So you are suggesting that Pickevance and Stevens were working together to defraud the school of fifty grand? And that people lost their jobs because of this? Is that what you are suggesting, Mrs Hilton?' asked Tallyforth.

'I didn't... I don't know, Chief Inspector,' she answered, her eyes beginning to fill with tears. 'All I know is that I've been worried sick for the past two months, not knowing who I could tell about what I'd found. I couldn't tell Mr Pickevance because, well, just because. And when Mr Ferris said that everything was in order with the finances, I thought I must be going mad. So, after he'd gone, I checked again. And I knew I was right. There was fifty thousand unaccounted for from last April and the audit hadn't picked it up. What was I to do? That was when I told Alf here. I didn't mean to say anything but Alf has been very kind to me and the children and one evening, when we went to the Rugby Club for a drink, I was beside myself with worry and I just had to tell someone. I swore Alf to secrecy and he's been as good as his word.

We both thought the school inspectors would discover about the missing money but Alf felt that it was best to drop a hint. That's why he sent that letter to the *Tamworth Herald.*'

Tallyforth stood up.

'Mrs Hilton, I shall have to ask you to make a formal statement tomorrow morning. And you too, Mr Pugh.'

A bead of sweat on Alf Pugh's forehead began to run down towards his ear.

'But I don't know anything other than what Alicia told you,' protested Pugh. 'Surely you don't need me?'

'I'm afraid so, sir,' replied Tallyforth. 'I shall be opening an incident room at Tamworth police station tomorrow morning. I'd be very grateful if both of you could get there sometime before noon. And in the meantime, if any other detail comes to mind, please make a note of it and let us know tomorrow. Is that alright?'

Alicia Hilton and Alf Pugh looked at each other and then she nodded in Tallyforth's direction. Her face was drained while his forehead still glistened with sweat.

'We'll see ourselves out, Mrs Hilton,' said Tallyforth, as he headed for the front door, followed closely by George Elliott, to whom he added, 'I think it's time we brought Pickevance in. But he won't be going anywhere tonight. I'm dead beat - bed for me. Pickevance can wait till the morning. Agreed?'

'Yes, sir,' she replied. 'If you say so.'

'See you at headquarters in the morning then. Eight thirty. Be there.'

EIGHT

Tallyforth woke early. He had had a disturbed night's sleep, not because of the uncertainties about Stanton's murder but because of the message on his answerphone when he had arrived home shortly before midnight the previous evening. It had been from his daughter to say that she didn't want to go to the Van Morrison concert after all but would it be alright if she sold the two tickets and bought some clothes instead? He had suspected that his ex-wife had been behind that move. Although he could never prove it, nor did he ever take the time or trouble to ask about it, he was fairly sure that she frequently said things about him to his daughter when he wasn't there. And what was said, if he was right, was rarely complimentary to him. The bitterness of the marital break-up had never really disappeared from her, even though it was now ten years ago.

But why had his daughter agreed to come to the concert in the first place? When he had called on the Saturday morning, she had seemed genuinely pleased to see him, despite the lack of an obvious show of affection. He knew her well enough from looking at her eyes - they were always a give-away, even when the rest of her body was stiffened against him. And she had agreed to come to see this Van Morrison character in June despite the fact that she knew little about him and despite the fact that he was not one of the people whose music she was currently interested in.

So why the change of heart?

He had poured himself a good-sized glass of Jack Daniels, which he had taken to bed with him and sipped as he sat up in bed reflecting on this news. He had fallen asleep before finishing it and the last quarter of an inch of golden liquid sat in the small whisky glass beside his alarm clock on the bedside chest of drawers when he woke. He glanced at it as he sat up.

It was only six fifteen.

Tallyforth climbed out of bed and went to the bathroom.

What had she said? Could she sell the tickets and use the money to buy clothes? Part of him wanted to react furiously to this suggestion, as he had often done with his ex-wife when they were married and she had changed her mind about some event they had planned to go to and announced that she needed an evening in because she was exhausted and couldn't they just have a Chinese take-away and a bottle of wine instead. But another part of him refused to react thus, for he had realised that reacting in that way had been one of his failings and one of the causes of the marriage ending. And he was still feeling too guilty about all of that to refuse his children anything they asked for.

Tallyforth returned to his bedroom and pulled back the curtains. Despite the early hour, it was clear that it was going to be a fine day. The sky was cloudless and the April showers certainly did not seem intent on falling on this particular Sunday.

He selected a pale blue muslin shirt, grey slacks and casual brown slip-on shoes, then, just as he was about to leave the room and go to the kitchen to make coffee, he reached into his wardrobe to take out a thin maroon vee-necked sweater. However promising the weather looked, he reasoned, it was still only April. Summer's full heat was not yet here.

George Elliott too had risen early, though not as early as her boss. She had set her alarm for seven o'clock because she had wanted time to enjoy a bath before the day's work began.

The bath was now run and George Elliott threw her dressing gown on to the floor, climbed into the steaming water and lay back with her eyes shut, swirling the bubble bath's foam around her.

She was remembering the look on Pearl Bowen's face when she talked about Brian Pickevance, her lover. It was a look which mixed admiration with devotion. It was the look of love. It was the look that said "I don't care what happens. I'm in love with him and I can't help that. And nothing will ever change that. I'll go through hell for him."

When had she ever felt like that? she wondered. Indeed had she ever? Or was she incapable of such intensity of feeling?

She recalled the six years she had lived with Andy, the games teacher she had met in Coventry in her first posting after she had joined the force after leaving Swansea University. They had been good years, she recalled. It had not taken long after they had first met at a disco at his school, to which she had been summoned because of some minor fracas, before he had moved into her flat. They had got on famously. She enjoyed his crowd of friends and the parties they went to together. And they had become a good pair at badminton, supporting each other, cajoling each other, hugging each other with excitement when they won. And with the crowd of friends they had holidayed in Greece twice, Majorca twice and Italy once, each time renting out a large villa with its own swimming pool, so that they could get all-over tans. And then, after six years, Andy had applied for and got a job in another town and, although he came back every weekend, somehow it hadn't quite been the same. They had both recognised it and agreed a temporary separation, which became a permanent one quite quickly without either of them having to make a decision about it.

But had she really loved Andy? She guessed not. Otherwise they would have still been together, she supposed. But was that because she wasn't capable of giving any more emotionally? Neither of them had wanted children, so that wasn't the reason. No, they had shared good times together but that was all. Neither of them had really wanted to make it permanent. They were both ambitious in their jobs. They both agreed that marriage was an out-of-date concept. They had drifted apart quite naturally - no-one was hurt at the end of the day. They would have remained good friends, if they had stayed working in the same area, but they hadn't and that had been that.

She couldn't honestly say that she had felt for Andy anything comparable to what she had seen in Pearl Bowen's eyes when she spoke of Brian Pickevance.

And then there had been that passionate eighteen-month fling with Roger, whom she had met on her first training course to be a

84

detective. Roger Miles was as ambitious as she was, and harder than she was. His superiors had noted his hardness early on in his career - that steely gaze that he could hold unwavering for what seemed like hours, the refusal to concede any point in argument, the physical toughness which he was forever demonstrating. And yet she had known his softer side - the part of him he brought to her when they had been through a hard day's training together, watching a forensic scientist opening up the stomach of a murdered man perhaps or standing for hours in the freezing rain outside some suspect's place. The trouble was that Roger Miles was married and had two young children. And when he was spending time with George Elliott in her flat, his wife was having to cope with the demands of those two children on her own and in the belief that he was out on some night exercise.

Yes, she'd had her share of guilt over that but, such was the passion between them, that she couldn't give him up. Until one day he threatened her with a knife if she ever revealed the secrets of their affair to anyone. And that had been it. The passion she had felt for him for eighteen months evaporated instantaneously and was replaced first by fear and then, as he refused to leave her, by cold anger, which saw her shouting at him to go. And soon enough he went. Never to return. Though his marriage, as she found out subsequently, didn't last much longer. She hadn't been the first, nor was she the last. But his wife had found out about the next one and sent him packing. She did not know where he was now.

Surely that hadn't been love? And yet she recalled the tingling sensation she had felt when she had been waiting for him to visit and the yearning ache inside her when sometimes he had not appeared. But that was just physical lust, wasn't it?

There had been others, of course. One-night stands. Friendships. Sexual encounters. But nothing permanent, nothing that had reached the sort of intensity of feeling she had seen in Pearl Bowen. And she had been on her own, through choice, for the past three years.

So here she was, thirty-six years old, a career police officer. Single and apparently content.

But would she ever experience the kind of love that Pearl Bowen felt?

Tallyforth had barely sat down behind his desk when the door to his office was pushed fiercely open and the desk sergeant informed him that he had a visitor. Reluctantly, he got up from his chair and followed the desk sergeant through the building to the main foyer.

'In that interview room, sir,' said the desk sergeant, pointing across the corridor as he resumed his place behind the main desk. 'Lady called Mrs Pickevance. Says she needs to speak to you. About her husband. Says you know him. Says he's gone missing. Said she had to see you.'

Tallyforth's heart missed a beat. Pickevance gone missing? What could that mean? And they had intended bringing him in for questioning today. So, if he was the murderer, had they left him at large for too long? Should they have arrested him earlier? Then again, even if he was guilty, he was hardly a mass murderer. He didn't really constitute a threat to the public, did he? And where could he have gone? And when? And was that Bowen woman with him?

He pushed open the door of the interview room.

Sarah Pickevance - a tall, raven-haired woman whom Tallyforth put in her late thirties - sat behind a table in the bare interview room, sipping from a cup of tea. She wore a green cardigan over a creased white blouse and a nondescript grey skirt. She had obviously been crying.

'Mrs Pickevance?' he began. 'You wanted to see me?'

She looked up at him from her sad hangdog eyes.

'Chief Inspector Tallyforth?'

He nodded and pulled up a chair opposite her.

'My husband mentioned your name in connection with the death of that Registered Inspector at the school. I thought I should come and see you. I think I'm going out of my mind with worry. Brian's disappeared. I don't know when he's coming back. I just don't know what's going on. Help me, please.'

And her voice, which had gradually risen in timbre as she spoke, finally broke into a long uncontrolled bout of sobbing.

Tallyforth waited uncomfortably, knowing that she had been holding all her anguish and pain back until now, knowing too that that anguish and pain was not new-born but had been festering at the back of her mind for some time, maybe for years, but also recognising that he had to let it come out before he could press her for fuller information about her missing husband.

Eventually the sobbing subsided and Sarah Pickevance gained control of her emotions.

'I'm sorry, Chief Inspector,' she sighed, wiping her eyes with a paper tissue. 'I've been worried sick and I just couldn't tell the children anything. You're my only hope. Please find him. Please bring him home. I'm sure we can sort all of this out between us.'

'One thing at a time, Mrs Pickevance,' interjected Tallyforth, seeking to slow her down by reaching for his notebook. 'What do you mean your husband has disappeared? Since when?'

'Since last night.'

'You mean you haven't seen him since last night?'

'Yes. I mean, no, I haven't seen him since last night.'

Tallyforth winced. Should he reveal what he knew about the affair between Pickevance and the Bowen woman?

'Mrs Pickevance, there are any number of possibilities of where your husband might be. He may have gone to stay with friends. He may have.....He's been under a lot of stress this week. Maybe he just needed to get away. When did you last speak to him?'

'He went out at about nine o'clock last night. Just as *Casualty* was finishing. Said he had to go back to the school, because Gideon Lashley had phoned to say there had been a break-in. But I know that's not where he was going.'

Tallyforth looked up from his note taking.

'So where was he going, Mrs Pickevance?'

She scrunched up the paper tissue in her hand and stared down at the table for several long moments before she spoke in a quivering voice.

'He was going to see Pearl Bowen. I heard them on the phone just before he left. Brian was using the mobile extension. I had the main phone.'

So she knew.

87

'So you think that's where he's gone?'

'Yes,' she stared at the table again. She was having difficulty saying the words she had to say, as if keeping them back unsaid would make the act undone. 'They have been having an affair for the past twelve months. I've known about it for ages but I couldn't do anything - couldn't bring myself to say anything. I should have challenged him. Maybe if I had done, maybe if I'd stood up to him early enough, none of this would have happened.'

'So your husband isn't actually missing then, Mrs Pickevance,' said Tallyforth. 'Have you tried Ms Bowen to see if he's there?'

She looked crestfallen.

'I can't, Chief Inspector,' she sobbed. 'I just can't bring myself to speak to the woman. She's stolen my husband. She's stolen my children's father. I can't speak to her.'

'Mrs Pickevance, if you're right about your husband's whereabouts, and remember we don't know that for fact yet, and if he has left you, then at some point you are almost certainly going to have to talk to Ms Bowen.'

'Why? Can't you do it, Chief Inspector? Brian told me about Stanton's murder and about how you needed to keep in touch with him until the whole thing was cleared up. Aren't you just as anxious to trace him? Can't you phone her and speak to him? Please!' she begged him, kneading the paper tissue in her hands and gazing wistfully at him

'Did your husband take any of his belongings with him?' he asked. 'Clothes? Overnight bag? Anything like that?'

'I don't think so. When he went, he said he wouldn't be long. And, even though I knew where he was going, I assumed he would be back. He's never stayed away overnight before without telling me.'

'So it's possible that he may have gone somewhere else?' he pressed gently.

'But where, Chief Inspector? Where else would Brian go without telling me? Won't you please ring and find out? I've not slept all night. I have to know for sure.'

'What sort of car has he got?' Tallyforth asked.

'He took his car - it's a white BMW coupé,' she replied.

Tallyforth looked across the table at the disconsolate figure of Sarah Pickevance and recalled the final scene of his own marriage. If she was right, if Brian Pickevance had left her to live with Pearl Bowen, this was only the beginning, he knew, of a long and weary journey for all of them.

'If you'll just wait here, Mrs Pickevance, I'll go and do what you ask. Would you like more tea?'

She shook her head, tossing her hair back out of her eyes.

Tallyforth stood, turned from her and reached for the door handle.

George Elliott was in his office when he returned there. She looked agitated.

'Sir,' she began as soon as he entered the room. 'I've had Pearl Bowen on the phone just five minutes ago. There's been some development. She's had a letter from Pickevance.'

'A letter?' he asked, puzzled by this news. 'Why is he writing letters? Isn't he with her?'

It was her turn to look puzzled.

'Sir?'

Tallyforth sat down behind his desk and looked up at her.

'I've just spent the last half an hour with Pickevance's wife,' he explained. 'She says that Pickevance went out at nine o'clock last night, claiming that he had to go to the school because of some break-in, though she says she knows he was going to see this Bowen woman because she heard them talking on the phone. And apparently he never returned, so she believes he's stayed the night there, with Bowen. She knows about their affair and she assumes that he's left her. And now you're telling me that Pickevance has sent Bowen a letter! What's going on, Sergeant? What letter?'

'She rang me to say that, when she got up this morning, there was an unstamped letter from Pickevance lying in her hallway, saying that he was ending their affair and that he needed time to straighten himself out.'

'So he tells his mistress he's leaving her but he doesn't tell his wife that he's not coming home. What kind of a man is he?'

'Sir?'

'Did you find out whether he was there yesterday evening or not?' he queried, getting up from his desk and walking across the room to stare out of the window.

'She said that he had called to see her briefly yesterday evening, at about nine thirty, but that he hadn't stayed.'

'And there had been no hint of him doing a runner then?'

'Apparently not.'

'Elliott, there's something fishy going on here that I don't like. I want you to get over to this Bowen woman's place pronto and get hold of that letter. And, while you're there, see if you can get her to give you anything else he's written her. There may be some clue to his mental state somewhere. I'm going to take Mrs Pickevance home and see what I can find there. Meanwhile, we'd better put out an all-stations alert. He's driving a white BMW coupé. Maybe one of the motorway boys will see him. And if he really has gone missing, we'd better get a check arranged at all the airports. We don't want him skipping off abroad when we're looking for him, do we? I'll get that organised before I go. Keep in touch.'

George Elliott looked at him and saw the glow of expectation in his eyes.

Action at last.

NINE

George Elliott parked her car in the only space available in Church Lane and locked it. Behind her loomed the massive spire of St Editha's church, which was shrouded in scaffolding and plastic sheeting. A tarmaced footpath from the top of Church Lane led through trees and grey marble gravestones up to the church and a number of Sunday-dressed Tamworth citizens were making their way to the church entrance for the morning service.

She turned away from St Editha's and walked down the lane towards Pearl Bowen's end house. She rang the doorbell.

'Hello, Sergeant. Come in.'

Pearl Bowen looked haggard. The letter from Pickevance which she had discovered first thing in the morning had been a considerable shock to her, so much so that she had not yet bothered to apply her make-up. And she hadn't bothered much with her clothing either. She was dressed only in a red tee-shirt and black lycra leggings. For the first time since they had met, George Elliott reflected, Pearl Bowen looked her age, if not older.

'Here's the letter,' she said, as soon as they had gone through into the back room where they had had their previous conversation. 'Want some coffee? I must have drunk a gallon already this morning but what the hell! Shall I make a fresh brew? You happy with strong?'

'Yes, that'll be fine,' replied George Elliott, settling down in a chair to read Pickevance's letter.

Pearl Bowen went through into the adjoining kitchen area and refilled the coffee percolator noisily, as if by making a noise she could distract her overfull brain.

George Elliott carefully took Pickevance's letter out of its envelope and read:

Dearest Pearl,

I've started this letter five times already and scrapped it each time. This is one of the hardest letters I've ever had to write and please forgive me for not having the courage to tell you to your face.

I'm sitting here in "our" house in Lichfield. It's midnight and I'm on my own but the clock is ticking on the mantelpiece and I just have to write and tell you how I am feeling and what I have to do. It was lovely to see you again this evening, even though you were anxious, perhaps especially because you were so anxious, because when you are in that vulnerable state I really feel that you need me and that I need you. I wished I could have stayed like you wanted me to, but you knew that I couldn't because Sarah was expecting me back. But it was so hard to leave you and, after I got in the car, I decided to come here because I needed some space to think.

You see, I have been thinking for some time now that we ought to finish this affair. It's just not fair on Sarah or on Jim, and I don't really think I would ever have the courage to tell my children. And besides, as you said this evening, it's building up problems for both of us at school and we need to resolve that situation. So I'm writing to tell you that I want us to get back to the professional relationship we enjoyed when you first joined the school and nothing more. I know it will be difficult but I believe we can manage it. I have decided to take a few days off next week - I shall get Sarah to ring in on Monday morning to say that I am sick, so you will have to look after things for a few days while I'm away. When I get back, we can talk things out properly.

I want you to know, though, that I wouldn't have done without this last year. Thank you for everything you have given me - for sharing your life with me, for letting me share your life. You have made me happier than I have ever been in my whole life. Every new day of this past year has been like a journey of discovery into my soul. And every new discovery has made me surer that what we have shared has been more than enough to last me for ever. No-one can take away from me what you have given me. I truly believe that what has happened to us only happens once in a lifetime and only to a few lucky people, so because it's so precious we must make sure we remember it.

But, my darling, I have got doubts - not about you but about me. I don't think I have the strength to give everything up, to leave my children, my home, everything I have worked for all these years. And I doubt if you will still want me in a few years time when I'm old and even greyer than I am now. And I have doubts about the school. If what that police sergeant told you is true, then there would be big trouble in the school if I were to leave Sarah to live with you. Remember that my Becky's in Year 8 - how would she handle all of that? I just can't put her and the others through that kind of suffering.

It's late now and I'm tired. Part of me is just so happy because you've loved me and I've loved you, but another part of me is just so sad that it has to end now. Please understand, darling, I love you more than I ever thought it was possible to love someone. And I want you so much right now, want your body next to mine, your legs entwined with mine, your fingers clasping mine. You're the most wonderful person I have ever known. But I have to face reality and I know this has to end. Forgive me, Pearl, I'm just not strong enough.

I'm going to drive back to Tamworth now to put this letter through your letter-box. I'll be back at school later in the week. Forgive me.

Brian
XXX

She folded the letter and put it back in its envelope.

'Thank you,' she said, as Pearl Bowen passed her a steaming beaker of freshly-made coffee. 'And thank you for letting me see this letter. It looks like, when he wrote it, he was intending to go home.'

'What am I going to do?' Pearl Bowen asked, distraught, and not really taking in George Elliott's words. 'He can't just walk out on me like that! And then tell me that he's not coming into school at the start of the week, when Hubert Stanton's murder hasn't been resolved, when nobody knows what's going to happen about the inspection and when, if what you're telling me is right, half of the staff think I'm responsible for taking Brian away from his wife and children! Help me!'

George Elliott looked across at Pearl Bowen, who was pacing mindlessly around the room, clutching her mug of coffee to her chest and staring blankly ahead of her.

'Pearl,' she began. 'There's something else you should know. Brian Pickevance didn't go home last night. His wife has been at the station this morning to tell us that he's gone missing. She suspected he was with you.'

Pearl Bowen stopped her distracted perambulation and stared at George Elliott, her mouth falling open in surprise.

'Didn't go home!' she said. 'Didn't go home! So where is he?'

George Elliott stood up.

'Exactly what we want to know, Pearl. Is there a telephone at this place in Lichfield?'

'No! That was one of its attractions. When my friend left it, she arranged for the phone to be cut off, until such time as someone bought it.'

'So there's no way of finding out if he's there or not.'

'No, not without going to see. I'll show you where it is, if you' ll let me come with you. I want to speak to him. Please let me come, Sergeant.'

George Elliott looked doubtfully at the distraught, pleading figure of Pearl Bowen. Why not? she thought. Pickevance probably wasn't there anyway. And if he was, what harm could be done by letting him face Pearl Bowen? And maybe something would be said in her presence, some slip of the tongue, some seemingly incongruous detail, that might give a clue to Stanton's murder.

'Alright, Pearl. You can come with me but I have to get a message to my chief first. And you'll have to stay in the car when we get to Lichfield. I want to speak to Brian Pickevance first. If, that is, he's there at all! Agreed?'

Pearl Bowen's face showed relief and consternation simultaneously, as she struggled with conflicting feelings.

'OK,' she said at last.

'One other thing,' said George Elliott. 'Do you have any other letters that he sent you that might give us a clue to his mental state?'

'What for?' returned the distraught Pearl Bowen, a sharp look of concern suddenly appearing in her eyes.

George Elliott did not reply immediately.

'I don't want to have to get a search warrant, Pearl,' she eventually said, her voice lowered.

'You think he murdered Stanton, don't you? You think that's why he's gone missing, don't you?' Pearl Bowen's voice quivered in a mixture of anger and fear. 'You're wrong, Sergeant, wrong. Whatever Brian has done, he's not a murderer, believe me.'

'Are there any letters?'

'Bugger you! You can take a look at what you want. All my correspondence is in that drawer over there.'

She pointed at a dark oak bureau standing against one wall, then stalked out of the room to change into something more suitable for their journey.

George Elliott moved across to the bureau, opened the drawer indicated and flicked through its contents. Two envelopes in Pickevance's distinctively feminine handwriting stood out in the mass of other correspondence. Carefully she took these two letters and pocketed them.

Tallyforth hadn't taken Sarah Pickevance home as he had intended, because just before he was about to leave his office Superintendent 'Nobby' Clarke had walked in, waving a piece of paper.

'New evidence, Tallyforth,' he said, holding the paper in front of Tallyforth's face. 'Message from the front line. Looks significant.'

Tallyforth looked up at his superior officer and noted the gleeful look on his face. Superintendent Clarke had never lost the thrill of the chase, even though he had been promoted away from it. Even more he loved the thrill of causing his maverick chief inspector to review the lines of his current enquiry by bringing new information to his attention.

'What is it, sir?' queried Tallyforth. 'And can it wait? I was just on the point of taking the headmaster's wife back to her home. There's been a significant development in the Stanton murder, sir. The headmaster, Pickevance, has done a runner. He was our prime suspect. We were about to wheel him in for questioning.'

'Tallyforth, I know what case you are involved in and this fax I am holding is also significant and related to that case. It is possibly more significant than you realise. Her Majesty's Chief Inspector of Schools has only just been told about Stanton's death and has forwarded this to us,' replied Clarke. 'You need to read it. Get someone else to take Mrs Pickevance home. '

And he dropped the paper, which Tallyforth could see was a lengthy fax, on to the desk between them, then spun on his heel and marched out of the office.

Tallyforth lifted the paper up and saw that it was from OFSTED and bore the stamp of HMCI - it was from the Chief Inspector himself and addressed to Hubert Stanton, Registered Inspector. The date of the fax was Wednesday 24th April 1996 and it was timed at 14.00 hours. It had been sent to the Granada Lodge Motel where Stanton and his fellow-inspectors had been staying. Presumably Stanton would not have seen the fax until he arrived back at the Motel in the evening of that day. The message on the front cover of the fax said: 'Please note the enclosed'.

He lifted his phone and issued instructions for Sarah Pickevance to be told that her husband had not yet been traced and then for her to be taken home, ensuring that the driver waited after delivering her, in case there had been some message from her missing husband.

Tallyforth then picked up the fax again, turned over the front page and read:

Dear Sir,

We are writing as concerned parents to tell you about some of the things that are going on at Æthelfleda High School where our children are pupils. All we want is a good education for our children but we think that the Headmaster is not setting a very good example.

First of all, we think it is very wrong that four experienced teachers were made redundant last summer. We have had children at this school since 1988 and two of us were pupils at the school ourselves and those experienced teachers were the best teachers in the school, because the children respected them and knew that if they stepped out of line they would be punished severely. One of those teachers, Mr Pugh, has been at this school for the past twenty-five years and everyone round here knows him because he stands no nonsense. He is tough but fair and he had very good discipline. Since him and the others have gone, standards have gone down and Mr Pickevance does not support the teachers against the children, especially some of the tougher ones who now rule the roost and do what they want in the school.

Secondly, we were told last year that the money that was going to be saved by making those experienced teachers redundant was going to be used to improve the resources in the school but all we know about is that all the teachers have got their own computers. Where's the fairness in that? Why haven't our children got more computers? If Mr Pickevance wants the teachers to have computers, he should get them to buy their own. Our children should have the money spent on them that the council gives the school to spend.

Thirdly, Mr Pickevance and his deputy Miss Bowen do not set a good example to the children. Everyone round here knows that they are having an affair. They're always leaving the school together and people have seen them holding hands in restaurants and somebody saw them walking together in Lichfield one weekend with their arms around each other. He is a married man and his own daughter is in the school, so what does he think he is doing? How can he set a proper example to our children?

Fourthly, we have been told that a lot of money has gone missing from the school fund and people say that it has been used by Mr Pickevance to buy some old coins that were dug up in this area recently. We think this is disgusting and just shows why he should not be headmaster of this school any longer.

We hope you will take these things seriously and ask your inspectors to investigate carefully and to take the proper steps to ensure our children get a good education.

Yours sincerely,
Several concerned Tamworth parents

P.S. We also think that Mr Stevens the Chairman of Governors is in league with Mr Pickevance.

Tallyforth pursed his lips and quietly whistled. This was getting to be dynamite. If this letter were genuine - and he had to reserve judgement a little because of its anonymity - then it wasn't just Alf Pugh that was gunning for Pickevance. If the parents of the school, or some of them at least, had begun to express doubts, then who else knew what Pickevance had been up to? And what was all this about him buying old coins? Could they be the pennies and *sceattas* from King Offa's time that Norman de Courcy had told him about? Had there really been some treasure trove discovered locally? And if so, what did Pickevance want with it?

But then Tallyforth stilled his racing brain. There was something very fishy going on here. Why had these anonymous parents written to HMCI in London and not to Hubert Stanton himself? Why had the Chief Inspector faxed the letter on to Stanton without letting him know in advance? Or had he been warned in advance to expect it? And, if so, had he told any of his colleagues, William Reynolds for example, about it? And did the Chief Inspector expect him to take it seriously? And had the rest of the inspection team been told about its contents? Had Pickevance been told? And where did these "concerned parents" get their information? OK, some of what was said could be gossip but some of it sounded suspiciously like inside information, particularly the bit about the missing money and about the involvement of the chairman of governors. So who had told these parents about all that?

Or was the letter from parents at all? Was it perhaps another strand in Alf Pugh's vendetta against Pickevance?

Tallyforth decided that he needed to question Pugh more fully before looking any further for the writers of this letter. He remembered that he had asked Pugh and Alicia Hilton to call at the Tamworth police station before noon and here he was sitting in his office at headquarters in Birmingham. He glanced at his watch and saw that it was still only nine thirty in the morning.

Time to get going.

'Sir? I'm with Pearl Bowen. She hasn't seen Pickevance since last night. Seems he went to this place in Lichfield and wrote her a letter, delivered it, then disappeared. It's possible he's gone back there, so we're going to take a look.'

Tallyforth heard George Elliott's distanced voice over the police radio in his Range Rover as he drove down the almost-deserted Sunday morning M42.

'Elliott, keep a....' He paused, realising that Pearl Bowen could hear all he was saying into the microphone of the police radio. 'Keep me posted. There's been another development at this end. I'm on my way to Tamworth. I need to talk to this Pugh character. I hope I get there before he arrives.'

There was a momentary silence on the police radio.

'Sir?'

'What is it, Elliott?'

'What if he's there?'

'Where, Elliott? Where are you talking about?'

'This house in Lichfield, sir. The one that Pearl and him have been using. The one where he went last night to write this letter.'

'If he's there, then bring him in, of course. We need to talk to him. Bring him straight to Tamworth. I'll be there. I've rung ahead and asked them to clear a room for us.'

'What if he's dead, sir? Taken his own life?'

Tallyforth heard a strangled cry down the airwaves. He guessed that it was Pearl Bowen, realising this possibility for the first time. Or at least admitting it to herself for the first time.

'Elliott, don't presume. One death is enough in this case. I don't want any suicides cluttering things up. Just get there quick. And let me know as soon as you arrive. Clear?'

'Yes, sir. Roger, wilco, and out, sir.'

Cheeky young prat, he thought. And drove on through the early morning sun.

TEN

Built on the site of the former Marmion School which has long since disappeared, Tamworth Police Station is a nondescript, modern, four-storey building in Spinning School Lane, close to the centre of the town but because of its modernity not a part of it. The room that had been vacated for Tallyforth to use as an incident room bore all the signs of recent occupation - a mass of old notices on the walls, filing cabinets with spider plants to decorate them, an ash-tray that had been emptied but not cleaned, a waste bin full of torn paper, cigarette butts and a pizza box.

As he entered the room, Tallyforth recoiled slightly at the putrid aroma, then settled himself on a chair and reached for the telephone.

'Yes, Alfred Pugh. Has anyone of that name been in this morning?' he said into the mouthpiece. 'You sure? Well, when he appears, let me know. I asked him to come and make a statement. About the Stanton murder. Yes, that's right, I want to see him when he gets here. Clear? Good! Oh, and if a Mrs Hilton is with him, ask her to come up as well. And can you get someone to come and empty the bin in here? It stinks! Thanks.'

He put the phone down.

Local bobbies, he thought. Same everywhere. Not very bright. Which is why they stayed local bobbies. And that reminded him - there was something else local he needed to check up on.

He picked up the phone again and dialled.

'Is that Norman de Courcy?' he said and, when he received confirmation, continued, 'this is Chief Inspector Tallyforth of the Mercian C.I.D. We met yesterday, if you remember, and you were telling me about those coins from Offa's time.'

100

He paused to hear the other man concur before continuing.

'When you mentioned the rumour about some treasure-trove being discovered lately in this area, you didn't mention where you'd heard this rumour. Can you remember?'

He listened.

'So you're saying that you heard it at school, in the staffroom. Can you remember exactly who mentioned it to you?'

He listened again.

'You think it was Jon Mitchell, the music teacher, and that he heard it from someone in his band? You mean his own band, sir, or one of his school bands?'

A further pause, longer this time.

'Let me just get this right, sir. You're saying that Jon Mitchell came into school one Monday morning and buttonholed you in the staffroom before lessons began to tell you that the father of one of the pupils in one of his bands had been out with his metal-detector around Borrowpit Lake the previous weekend and had found some unidentifiable old coins. And that he had cleaned them up during the week and taken one of them to his local pub and showed it to a mate of his who was the curator at the Tamworth Castle Museum. And that he had said that the coin looked exactly like one they had in the museum which dated from Offa's time. How did Mitchell know all this, sir?'

He listened to the reply.

'He'd been where the previous evening? The Edge night-club? In Tamworth? And one of his bands had been playing there and this pupil from the band, had told him all this? But you thought it was all nonsense. Why was that, sir?'

Tallyforth nodded as he heard de Courcy's explanation for not giving credence to the story.

'You've always been sceptical of Jon Mitchell's stories because he's a romantic. So it never crossed your mind that there was any truth to the story. Would it surprise you to know, sir, that there is a strong possibility there was such a find? And that we have received an anonymous tip-off that your headmaster, Brian Pickevance, has paid a large sum of money for those coins?'

There was no reply. De Courcy was stunned by the news.

'Mr de Courcy, I would be grateful if you could keep this to yourself. There may be nothing in it, as you originally surmised, but we have to keep an open mind on these matters. Particularly in the current circumstances. If you could find out the name of the man who is alleged to have found these coins, without arousing any suspicions, it would be helpful. I'm based at Tamworth police station now and you can leave a message at any time. Meanwhile, thank you very much for your assistance.'

Tallyforth put the phone down, pushed his chair back and stretched his legs out. Maybe there was some substance to the accusation in that anonymous 'smoking' fax! But he needed even more now to talk to Pugh.

There was no sign of Brian Pickevance at the house in Lichfield - another end-of-terrace Victorian property which had been renovated attractively. George Elliott had gone in first, as they had agreed and as Pearl Bowen had come to realise was best, just in case there was something she didn't want to see. Using Pearl Bowen's key, she had unlocked the door and made a fleeting visit to each room to see if anyone was there. But there wasn't and the two of them had conducted a fuller search then to see if he had left any indication of where he might have gone but again there was nothing. Pickevance had apparently disappeared into thin air.

'Did he seem to you to be under particular pressure, Pearl? After all, you know him as well as anybody,' George Elliott asked when their search had proved fruitless. They were standing in the kitchen and Pearl Bowen was putting water into the kettle.

'No more than usual,' came the reply. 'The last twelve months have been a real strain for both of us, as you can imagine. In fact, we've split up twice. Only for a few days each time admittedly. But the strain of things caused us to row over silly little things.'

'Such as?'

'Oh, you know, why he couldn't arrange to stay the night when I was alone. Me being completely unreasonable, I know. But I just got so lonely at times and I needed him there. So, even though we'd agreed that nothing would happen until his elder daughter had finished her A levels and the OFSTED inspection was over, I was just impatient. And we rowed. And I told him it was all over.

102

And he left with that look of a wounded bloodhound that he can't help.'

'And then what happened?'

'Oh, we'd spend a couple of days trying to avoid each other at school or looking into the distance when we had to talk to each other. Once he locked himself in his study for a whole day and refused to answer the telephone. I had to deal with everything and make up some story for Alicia Hilton and the other clerical staff about him working on some important document and needing to be free of disturbance.'

'What happened?' George Elliott queried, as they stood in the kitchen of the house, waiting for the kettle to boil.

'He came out eventually. At about three o'clock. I pushed him back in, shut the door behind me and....'

'Yes?'

There was a pause before Pearl Bowen replied.

'You can imagine, sergeant,' she said eventually, her eyes sparkling at the memory and a smile playing across her face. 'Sex in forbidden places is very special, you know?'

'No, I wouldn't know,' answered George Elliott dryly, trying hard not to think of the two of them making love on the floor of the head's study. Or was it on his desk? She covered her momentary embarrassment with a cough. 'Did he ever talk about any particular place that he was fond of? Anywhere he used to go on holiday, for instance? Here or abroad?'

Pearl Bowen unplugged the kettle, which had now boiled, poured a splash into the Wedgwood-style china teapot, emptied it, dropped in two teabags then filled it.

'No, not that I can remember. They used to have a caravan and go to Padstow in Cornwall a lot, I remember him saying that. When the children were much smaller. But the last few years they'd been on package holidays to Greece and Spain. Nothing exceptional. He worked too hard and didn't have the time or energy any longer to organise anything more adventurous. And Sarah just wanted to lie in the sun, so he said.'

She poured tea into matching Wedgwood-blue cups.

'Thanks. Nowhere local?' persisted George Elliott. 'Nowhere he used to walk locally, for instance?'

Pearl Bowen sipped her tea and thought.

'He used to walk in the Kettlebrook Park in the evenings. I remember him telling me that. When he wasn't with me, that is. He used to find it relaxing. And he lives over that way. But there's nowhere there he could have slept. Sorry. I can't help. Where the hell is he, Sergeant? Why has he cleared off like this?'

'I wish I knew, Pearl,' said George Elliott quietly. 'I wish I knew. But I think you'd better come back to Tamworth with me. My chief will be waiting for news. He may know something himself. Are you fit?'

Pearl Bowen drained her cup of tea and nodded.

'I'll just wash these cups,' she said.

It was almost noon when Alf Pugh eventually turned up at the police station. He was wearing a light green anorak over an open-necked yellow shirt and green corduroy trousers. A few wispy hairs blew gently around the tweed cap that covered his bald head and his walrus moustache drooped over his mouth. He was accompanied by Alicia Hilton, dressed in a prim navy woollen twin-set and with make-up artfully applied to enhance her high cheekbones and hide the age-lines. The duty desk sergeant took them straight up to Tallyforth's office.

'Good morning, Chief Inspector,' began Pugh, doffing his cap. 'Here we are, as you asked. We've come to make statements, as you asked. Alright if we do this together? Only Mrs Hilton's a bit nervous about all this. Never had any dealings with the police before, you know. Told her not to worry but she asked me to stay with her. If it's alright with you, like, Chief Inspector.'

Tallyforth motioned to them to sit down, then picked up the phone.

'Bring us some coffee, will you, Sergeant? Thanks.'

He looked across at his two new companions. They both looked more composed than they had the previous evening. Probably planned together what they were going to say. Though they didn't know what he was going to ask, did they? he thought to himself.

'Morning, Mrs Hilton. Morning, Mr Pugh. Good of you to spare the time,' Tallyforth began. 'Yes, it will be perfectly in order for you both to stay. But before you make your statements, I'd be grateful if you could answer one or two more questions. You see, there's been some further developments since last night.'

Alf Pugh and Alicia Hilton looked at each other.

'What's happened, Chief Inspector?' she asked nervously.

'We're not altogether sure yet, Mrs Hilton,' Tallyforth replied, 'but it seems that your headmaster, Brian Pickevance, has gone missing.'

He watched their reactions carefully. Alf Pugh looked almost smug, as if Pickevance's disappearance was an outcome he cheerfully welcomed. Alicia Hilton, on the other hand, became very agitated. She crossed and uncrossed her legs, leaned forward as if to say something then sat back without doing so, looked anxiously at Pugh as if for guidance, then clasped her hands tightly together on her lap.

'You seem concerned, Mrs Hilton,' said Tallyforth at last. 'Have you any idea where he might be?'

'N..no,' she stammered. 'It's just that.....'

'Now then, Alicia, calm down. The chief inspector's only doing his job,' said Alf Pugh, leaning across towards her and patting her hand patronisingly.

'Yes?' queried Tallyforth. 'What were you about to say, Mrs Hilton?'

She looked appealingly at him.

Just at that moment the desk sergeant pushed the door open with a tray containing three mugs of coffee, which he deposited on the table in front of Tallyforth before leaving the room without saying anything.

'It's just that....he threatened to do that once before,' she blurted out as the door closed, casting her eyes down at the floor.

'Alicia!' interjected Pugh.

'Go on, Mrs Hilton,' said Tallyforth.

'There was an incident three years ago. Bri...Mr Pickevance got very upset about it and talked about quitting. You see, although he's very strong on the surface, he gets very hurt underneath and finds it difficult to cope at times.'

Tallyforth watched her face as it struggled to contain the mixture of emotions that were coursing through her mind. There was more to this confession than was currently apparent, he could swear it.

'What was the incident, Mrs Hilton? Do you remember?'

She looked quickly up at him.

'Oh, it was nothing really. Just something that he'd got blown out of all proportion.'

'Even so, it might help if we knew what it was.'

She bit her lip.

'I'd made an error in copying out something he'd written. And he hadn't checked it, like he normally does. And it had gone out to all the staff and several of them complained. It was nothing really. Storm in a teacup,' she answered.

'And he threatened to quit over a trivial thing like that?' asked Tallyforth, incredulous.

'Y...yes.'

'Surely there was something more than that, Mrs Hilton?'

She bit her lip again and stared down at her clasped hands.

'Chief Inspector, when my husband left me, Mr Pickevance was very kind to me. He and his wife used to invite me over to their house on Sundays. Their eldest are the same ages as my two children. If it hadn't been for their kindness in that first year when the divorce was going through, I don't know what I'd have done. All our friends were my husband's friends and they all deserted me. I expect he told them some story about how it was all my fault, how I'd not been sexually adequate or something along those lines. That's the sort of thing he used to accuse me of. Anyway it took me over a year to get back on my feet. And Brian and Sarah, that's Mr and Mrs Pickevance, were marvellous to me. So you see, I know him quite well, Chief Inspector.'

'And how is all this connected to his threat to quit?'

He watched her, like an angler watching a fish that has just bitten at the bait and knows its end is now certain but still feels the need to resist. He was certain that there was something significant, something deeply significant, that lay just below the surface of what Alicia Hilton was telling him. He couldn't quite put his finger on what precisely this mystery was but his instincts told him it mattered. And it mattered like hell.

So he watched and waited.

'It wasn't just that,' she continued, her bottom lip quivering. 'You see, Chief Inspector, because I'd become a sort of friend of the family he had confided in me and told me certain things that perhaps he should not have told me.'

'Go on, Mrs Hilton. I'm listening,' said Tallyforth. 'Please, do have a drink. Sorry, I forgot. That sergeant certainly knows how to pick his moment.'

She reached across and took one of the mugs of coffee, stirring sugar into it before raising it to her lips. Alf Pugh also took a mug.

'He told me that he and Sarah, that's Mrs Pickevance, well, they were having problems,' she whispered.

'You mean marital problems?'

She nodded.

'What sort of problems? Arguments? Fights? That sort of thing?'

She shook her head.

'What then? Was there someone else?'

Again she shook her head, though he noticed her glance up at him quickly and then her gaze fell back on to her hands.

'Mrs Hilton?'

Again she flashed him a look. Then she spoke.

'In bed,' she whispered.

'You mean sexual problems?' said Tallyforth, relieved to have finally got there.

She nodded.

'So he was threatening to run away from her then. Is that what you mean? He wasn't threatening to run away from the school, he was threatening to run away from everything! Is that it?'

She nodded agreement once again.

'And the mistake you made was just the trigger that sent him over the edge. Is that it?' asked Tallyforth, standing up now and moving across the room in thought. 'So what happened?'

'Nothing,' she said, regaining her composure. 'I talked him out of it. I suggested that he and Sarah might get counselling but he wouldn't have any of that. He was convinced there was nothing wrong and that it would sort itself out in time. He just put it down to the stress of the job.'

Tallyforth wheeled round to face her.

'And that was it? Nothing more? No further incidents?'

Alf Pugh, who had remained conspicuously silent throughout

107

this conversation, suddenly intervened.

'Nothing since that Bowen woman arrived,' he said. 'Alicia confided all this to me last year, when she told me about the missing money. She told me about Pickevance and the Bowen woman. She caught them at it in his study one day. Or near as good as. The man should be shot.'

Tallyforth sat down again.

'So what you're saying is that Brian Pickevance calmed down once his sex life improved, in other words when he and Pearl Bowen began their affair,' he said.

Alicia Hilton blushed and stifled a sob.

'Sorry, Mrs Hilton, but I have to get this absolutely right,' apologised Tallyforth.

'I wish the bugger had gone off,' said Alf Pugh angrily. 'If it hadn't been for that Bowen woman, I'd have still had my job! And the school wouldn't be in the mess it is now.'

'Mr Pugh, you wouldn't know anything about a fax sent to OFSTED, would you?' queried Tallyforth suddenly.

Alf Pugh's bald forehead began to sweat and his eyes flitted from side to side.

'Don't know what you mean, Chief Inspector,' he said.

'I think you do, Mr Pugh,' continued Tallyforth. 'A fax from some "concerned parents" which made certain accusations against Brian Pickevance - accusations which I am fairly sure could only have been made by someone who knew a lot about the school, someone who was employed there, I should say. You told him about the missing money, Mrs Hilton. You told us that last night. Did you also tell our friend here about collusion with the chairman of the governors? And what collusion are you taking about? And what's all this about Pickevance buying old coins with the school's money?'

She began to sob deeply.

'Chief Inspector, you have no right!' began Alf Pugh, standing up and moving over to Alicia Hilton's side where he put his hand on her shoulder. 'We came in here quite voluntarily to make statements and you start accusing us of things we know nothing about.'

Tallyforth opened his mouth to speak then decided against it.

Instead he smiled grimly. And waited.

Gradually her sobbing died away and she wiped her eyes with a paper tissue rescued from her handbag.

'Yes, Chief Inspector, you're right,' she said quietly but firmly. 'I sent the fax. I told you last night that I had been worried sick about the missing money after I discovered it. And when Mr Ferris, who audited all the school finances, said there was nothing wrong, I just guessed that Mr Stevens was colluding with Mr Pickevance. I didn't know what for. Perhaps you ought to talk to him. But I knew there was something wrong and I knew I was the only one who knew about it. Apart from Mr Stevens and Mr Pickevance that is. And I had to make it known.'

'So the anonymous fax to OFSTED as well as Mr Pugh's letter to the *Tamworth Herald*? Just to make sure?' asked Tallyforth.

She nodded. Alf Pugh stood beside her squeezing her shoulder and looking uncomfortable. He had wanted to brazen it out.

'And what about the coins?'

'That was just a rumour,' answered Alf Pugh. 'Jon Mitchell, the music teacher, told me that the father of some kid in one of his bands had found some old coins worth a lot of money. Come across them with his metal detector. He said they were supposedly from Offa's time. Jon said that they'd been sold privately for fifty thousand quid and nobody knew who the buyer was. I just put two and two together. It didn't really matter, did it? If Stanton and his mob asked questions and found there was no truth to it, so what? The point was they would have been alerted to the missing money. And to Pickevance's shady dealings. That was all we wanted.'

'Mr Pugh, you are making serious allegations against Brian Pickevance, which unfortunately he is not here to defend himself against. I'm not condoning the way you behaved. You should have come to the police in the first place,' said Tallyforth, placing himself in front of them. 'And you, Mrs Hilton. If, as you say, you had evidence of some criminal action, you should have told the police. That's what we're here for.'

'But you'd never have taken it seriously, would you?' sneered Alf Pugh. 'You're only here now because there's been a murder, not because of a few quid gone missing and people lost their jobs through it.'

Tallyforth stared at Alf Pugh coldly. And he held the stare until the other man looked down.

Then he turned his back on them, moved to the telephone and lifted it to his mouth.

'Sergeant, come and take statements from Mrs Hilton and Mr Pugh, will you? I have work to do.'

ELEVEN

By mid-afternoon that Sunday Tallyforth felt a need to clear his brain a little, so he left the Tamworth Police Station and walked through the town past the imposing black marble statue of Sir Robert Peel outside the Old Town Hall towards the Castle Pleasure Gardens and the riverside. He had left instructions for George Elliott to join him as soon as she returned from taking Pearl Bowen home. By Peel's statue, he paused to read the inscription on the plinth below it.

It was an odd coincidence to be here in Tamworth where the founder of the modern police force had lived, Tallyforth reflected. What would the town's most famous son make of the current case?

He passed through he deserted market-place and followed the path that wound through the Pleasure Gardens, noticing the Norman castle that stood proudly but uselessly now on its mound. Was that where Offa's castle had been as well? he mused. Must ask de Courcy. Out of curiosity. He supposed it was likely, given its position, but maybe the Mercians hadn't built castles to defend themselves against their enemies! Maybe they were just domestic centres - semi-permanent shelters against the ravages of the weather. He really did feel very ignorant about the history of the Dark Ages. What pictures he did have, he realised, came largely from the television adaptation of *Hereward the Wake* he remembered watching when he was much younger.

He continued on his way through the terraced gardens with their flower beds of purple, pink, yellow and red tulips, of sweet-smelling white and maroon hyacinths, of variegated pansies, and passed a plaque set into the wall on the way to the riverside which read:

111

> **ST. RUFFIN'S WELL**
> **ACCORDING TO TRADITION THIS WELL WAS**
> **DEDICATED TO ST. RUFFIN THE MARTYRED SON OF**
> **WULFHERE WHO WAS KING OF MERCIA IN THE**
> **SEVENTH CENTURY. THE RESTORATION WORK WAS**
> **CARRIED OUT TO COMMEMORATE THE**
> **1200TH·ANNIVERSARY OF THE ACCESSION TO THE**
> **MERCIAN THRONE IN 757 A.D. OF KING OFFA, WHOSE**
> **ROYAL PALACE STOOD IN THE NORTHERN PART OF**
> **THESE GROUNDS WHEN TAMWORTH WAS THE**
> **CAPITAL OF THAT KINGDOM**

He had never heard of this well or of St.Ruffin. He moved closer to look for the well but could see no sign of water. Obviously, it had been dammed up or diverted, he thought. But thoughts of King Offa began to surface again in his mind.

Tallyforth looked to his right and across the River Anker he could see the green and cream Snow Dome building, which proudly boasted that it housed the country's first indoor real snow ski slope. What would Offa have made of that? he wondered.

Tallyforth sighed.

When he reached the riverside, he found a bench and sat down, stretching his legs out in front of him and his arms along the back of the bench. A group of mute swans swam gently in his direction, no doubt hoping for breadcrumbs or something similar. When they realised that there was nothing forthcoming, they sailed serenely off down the river, their necks arched and their orange black-tipped bills pointed forwards.

Threads, he mused, threads. In any murder case there were threads that had to be followed, some that led nowhere and some that led in the direction of the solution. He knew that only too well. But there were usually other threads that occupied his mind in any murder investigation - threads that came from he knew not where. And he had become used to the fact that it wasn't just because any human being in any situation had their own preoccupations coursing through their minds as well as the particular business they were supposed to be engaged on. No, he was aware of such preoccupations and that subterranean layer of thought that never ceased. No, there were other threads that seemed to pull at him in whichever murder investigation he was involved. It was almost as if the air itself was filled with hidden threads looking for something or someone to cling to. He had never understood this but he had learned to pay attention to the phenomenon.

So now he sat on the park bench and let his mind meander through the happenings of the last few days.

First of all, there was the obligatory mental filing of all that was so far known about Stanton's death. He rehearsed the details slowly in his mind.

Stanton had last been seen by his deputy William Reynolds in the boardroom at Æthelfleda High School just after eight o'clock on Thursday 25th April. The evening before he had received a fax from HMCI, which they now knew originated from Pugh and Alicia Hilton, accusing Pickevance of having an affair with his deputy, Pearl Bowen, and of financial irregularities. On the morning of that fateful Thursday Stanton had asked his inspection team to find out if the staff of the school had confidence in the headmaster and at their evening meeting he had learned that the staff were against the headmaster, because of Pearl Bowen and her influence over him. Some time after all his fellow-inspectors left the premises, some for the Granada Lodge Motel and others for home, Stanton who had stayed in the school to work on his draft report had drunk the fatal cup of coffee which had been laced with cyanide. He would have died quickly.

The following morning, the Friday, Stanton's body had been discovered by Gideon Lashley, the school's caretaker, or premises manager as they were determined to call him, whose suspicions about the light being left on the night before had not been aroused because he had been told that the inspectors might need to work late and Stanton had his own key to the building they were working in. He had phoned Pickevance who then phoned the police.

Since then, all the evidence, admittedly circumstantial but nevertheless seemingly of great significance, pointed overwhelmingly towards the guilt of Brian Pickevance - the changes in the report on Stanton's laptop computer which would have made it less critical of the school's management, the revelation from Alicia Hilton of the fifty thousand pounds apparently missing from the school accounts, the admission by Pearl Bowen of their year-long affair and their plans to set up home together. And now, to cap it all, Pickevance had gone missing. As if admitting his guilt.

It was all very neat. Too neat, thought Tallyforth not for the first time, as another family of swans sailed inshore in his direction. Too neat. He knew from experience that life and death were rarely as straightforward as all that. He also sensed from the invisible threads that hovered in the air around him that there were things being ignored, things that mattered, things that might lead to a different resolution.

He leaned his head back and stared up into the sun, as if he might make those threads visible.

Offa and all his works - that was one thread that kept recurring. The king of the Mercians who had built his royal palace at Tamworth, whose name was now celebrated only on a stretch of the new ring road. The celebrations planned by Norman de Courcy and the Mercian Society of the twelve hundredth anniversary of Offa's death - celebrations that involved Æthelfleda High School considerably. The treasure-trove of coinage from the time of Offa which had allegedly been found by the parent of one of the pupils in the school and, again allegedly, purchased by Pickevance for fifty thousand pounds. Why? What could he want with these coins? If, that is, there were any truth in the allegations. And just now, St.Ruffin's Well - another link to Offa.

Then there was Alf Pugh, the sacked teacher who seemed to be conducting a one-man vendetta against Pickevance. The letter to the *Tamworth Herald,* carefully timed for maximum effect. The fax to OFSTED sent by him and Alicia Hilton. Was there anything more to him than just this personal hatred of the man who had once been his boss? Was there any other motive to his actions?

And then again there was Alicia Hilton. The school's finance director who had apparently been befriended by Pickevance when her marriage had broken down and had thus become party to his confessions about the failings of his own marriage. It was she who had discovered the fraud and told Pugh about it. Was there anything other than a desire for integrity and an anxiety about

114

dishonesty in her motives? Was there perhaps some jealousy at the influence of Pearl Bowen on Pickevance? A feeling, maybe, that she had been displaced as a confidante?

And Sarah Pickevance, the scorned wife. How long had she known about the affair with Pearl Bowen? How desperately unhappy had she been through this period? And if, as Alicia Hilton had said, the Pickevances' sex life had been problematic for a long time, how had she coped with this? How desperate might she have become? They hadn't really talked to her at length, as if she were almost an appendage to the main investigation. Maybe she was more important than they had so far allowed.

What else was there?

Well, there was this music teacher, Jon Mitchell, who had been on the school premises till quite late on the night of Stanton's death and who was now, apparently, the source of this story about the discovery of the treasure trove. What did they know about him? Nothing much, apart from the fact that he ran four rock bands in the school and also fronted his own band. They certainly needed to talk to him about this treasure trove story at least and maybe about his movements on the night of the murder.

Perry Stevens, the senior partner in Stevens, Stevens and Ferris and chairman of the governing body at Æthelfleda High School, who had now been implicated by Alicia Hilton in the alleged fraud, also needed to be seen and spoken to. Fleetingly the thought crossed Tallyforth's mind that he might need to be careful there. The man was also a Conservative politician, who would doubtless have connections. He might even be a mason! Tallyforth had his own suspicions of the brotherhood's influence within the Mercian Force.

Anyone else? Gideon Lashley? Pearl Bowen? The thin-voiced William Reynolds? Any of the other inspectors? Any of the other teachers?

Making a mental note that they might have to go back to these people if their present line of enquiries didn't produce a solution soon, he dismissed all these possibilities for the moment. Nothing they had found so far suggested the involvement or implication of any of these people.

Tallyforth opened his eyes which had closed themselves in this reverie. The sun was still shining. A few families were strolling along the riverside.

He remembered his own family and more specifically his daughter. He still hadn't spoken to her about the Van Morrison concert and her decision not to go with him. Maybe he could still persuade her to go. Maybe he could give her some money and use the tickets himself. Maybe George Elliott would like the tickets. He must ask her for more about this Van Morrison character.

Just as he mused thus, George Elliott herself appeared, bearing two ice cream cones, and sat down beside him. She passed him one of the cones.

'Thanks,' he said as he took the cone and licked round its edge where the ice cream had started to melt. 'Sergeant, were you aware that Sir Robert Peel, the founder of the modern police force and of the modern Conservative Party, hailed from Tamworth?'

She glanced at him over her ice cream, whose edges she too was licking clean, her face turned sideways in order to achieve this and her left hand held cupped underneath the cone to prevent the ice cream droplets from falling on to her long blue denim dress.

'I was, actually,' she replied, once her tongue was free from its work. 'We did something at police college about all that. Peel was Home Secretary at the time and managed to persuade all the rest of the members of parliament to vote for his bill to create a Metropolitan Police Force to patrol the streets of London and make them safe from highwaymen like Jonathan Wild, otherwise known as the Thief-taker General. Peel was also Prime Minister ten years later when the Birmingham Police Act was passed. And that led indirectly to the creation of today's Mercian Police Force.'

She licked her ice cream again.

'I hate smart-arsed, college-trained cops like you, Elliott,' Tallyforth said, but without venom - it was part of the banter he had established with and for her. 'Go on. Tell me all. I'm desperate to hear.'

She smiled. She enjoyed having some superiority over him and accepted the put-downs with which it was inevitably accompanied.

'The Metropolitan Police Act of 1829 which created the Metropolitan Police divided the Met. district into seventeen police divisions, each with one hundred and sixty five men, including one superintendent, four inspectors and sixteen sergeants. Their uniform was a blue-tailed coat, blue trousers and glazed black top hat with thick leather crown, and they carried a rattle and short truncheon beneath tails of their coat. Policemen had to be under thirty five, of good physique, at least five foot seven, literate, and of good character. Ranks up to superintendent were to be drawn from within the force. A wage of one guinea a week was paid in order to deter the officer class. The first superintendent of A Division was an ex-sergeant major who interviewed the first applicants. The police force, from the beginning, was to be in tune with the people, understanding the people, belonging to the people, and drawing its strength from the people,' she recited from memory.

He looked at her, holding his almost-eaten cone away from him.

'Have you been rehearsing that?' he asked in amazement. 'You planning to go on *Brain of Britain* or something?'

She grinned.

'That's not all,' she continued. 'One thing they didn't teach us at police college but that I know from university is the part played by the novelist Henry Fielding in the development of law enforcement in London.'

'Who's he? Never heard of him.'

'Never heard of *Joseph Andrews*? *Tom Jones*?'

'You mean the Welsh singer?'

She refused to rise to his bait.

'Fielding was Chief Magistrate at Bow Street in the middle of the eighteenth century. He started the Bow Street Runners. And they were the forerunners of Peel's Metropolitan Police,' she finished triumphantly.

He took a handkerchief from his pocket and wiped his hands, now empty of the ice cream cone.

'Very interesting, Elliott,' he said dryly. 'And talking of runners, any news of our friend Pickevance?'

'Only that his car has been spotted in three different parts of the country in the past twelve hours,' she replied.

'Go on.'

'Well, the police in Lincolnshire have reported a white BMW

coupé seen driving into Grantham, though they lost it.'

'That would be ironic, eh, Elliott? Pickevance visiting the spiritual home of the inventor of privatisation?'

'Sir?' she queried.

'Don't you know anything except what they teach you at police college or university? I suppose you're too young. That's where Thatcher's father had his grocer's shop, where she apparently learned that there's no such thing as society.'

'Oh,' she said. She had remembered but she liked to see him getting angry. It was only on political matters like this that he could be really aroused. Professionally he was ice-cool. 'I don't understand the relevance.'

'Pickevance and his Grant Maintained school - that's the result of Thatcher's privatisation schemes!' he cried. When he saw that she still wasn't interested, he continued:

'Where else?'

'There's been a report from motorway police in Leicestershire of a sighting on the M1 and another supposed sighting just outside Inverness.'

'That's unlikely,' he said gruffly. 'Even in a BMW he wouldn't have got that far. Unless he'd driven all night. And why Inverness? Why Scotland? My guess is that either or both of the other two are possible. I think he's just driving around. I think he knows that everything is pointing at him and he doesn't know how to get out of the fix he's in. If he is the murderer, then of course he'll go down for life. If he isn't the murderer, then it seems likely that he'll get done for fraud at the very least, assuming that the allegations are true. And if they're not substantiated, then his marriage is probably finished and I wouldn't give too much chance of his job surviving either. And do you think this Bowen woman will want him then?'

George Elliott licked the remains of her ice-cream and considered. A couple of teenage girls passed them, giggling.

'You're probably right,' she said at last.

He stood up suddenly.

'Come on, Sergeant. Enough philosophising for one day. We've got work to do.'

She looked up at him, saw the determined grimace on his face and realised that he had a plan.

'Where are we going?'

'We're going to see our artist in residence,' he said, smiling in advance of his witticism. 'And I don't mean your Tom Jones, I mean Jon "Rock n' Roll" Mitchell.'

TWELVE

They drove in Tallyforth's Range Rover, with him driving, to the picturesque village of Abbot's Bromley where Jon Mitchell and his partner Margi Benetti lived. Their house was an old black and white cottage on the main thoroughfare that took travellers through the village. Its frontage was directly on to the pavement outside the house but it had a lengthy rear garden, which stretched out to the fields beyond.

'Yes?' asked Margi Benetti as she opened the door to the two police officers. She was dressed in denim jeans and a navy blue sweatshirt that bore the message 'Legalise Pot'. Her olive skin colour and dark hair spoke of her Italian origins.

'Is this where Jon Mitchell lives?' asked George Elliott. 'We're police officers, investigating the murder of a Hubert Stanton on the premises of Æthelfleda High School last Thursday evening. We believe your husband may be able to help us in our enquiries.'

'We're not married,' Margi Benetti flashed back at her. 'Jon is my partner. Come in. He's in the garden.'

They were led through the low-ceilinged cottage with its dark exposed beams and stripped wood doors, past the deep inglenook fireplace with its quarry-tiled hearth, past the decoratively hand-painted kitchen furniture and into the rear garden via a stable door. There was a pungent aroma that filled the house, which they both recognised.

Jon Mitchell, his blond hair swept back into a ponytail as usual, his earring glistening in the sunlight, sat on a deckchair facing the garden which had largely been left to its own devices but which at this moment was flooded with a carpet of wild bluebells. He was smoking a thin, hand-rolled cigarette whose smell was identical to that within the house. On a table at his side were a four-pack of Guinness, a half-drained pint glass of the same dark liquid, an old tobacco tin, a Zippo cigarette lighter, a portable C.D. player and an opened C.D. case. The C.D. player was playing an up-beat rhythm and blues number with a driving drum and organ sound punctuated regularly by a sharp brass section. Jon Mitchell's' head, fingers and feet moved in time with music.

'Jon, it's the fuzz,' said Margi, sitting down on the deckchair next to him. 'They want to talk to you.'

Jon Mitchell looked up.

'Yeah?' he said, grinding his cigarette butt into the concrete beneath his feet hastily. 'What d'you want?'

George Elliott glanced at Tallyforth, who shook his head once. They were not here to investigate the smoking of marijuana. That could wait. If they even were to bother.

'Sergeant Elliott and Chief Inspector Tallyforth of the Mercian Police Force. We're investigating the murder of Hubert Stanton, who was leading the inspection of the school you work at, Mr Mitchell,' began George Elliott, having to raise her voice above the music which he made no effort to turn down, as Tallyforth looked around them. 'We would appreciate it if you would answer a few questions. It might help us in our enquiries.'

'Sure,' Jon Mitchell replied. 'Please. Sit down. Don't know how I can help. But....'

He shrugged his shoulders and reached over to turn down the C.D. player, which was now playing a slower number which featured a moaning harmonica.

As he sat down on the wooden bench to which they had been directed, Tallyforth picked up the C.D. case and looked at its contents.

'You like this Van Morrison character?' he asked casually, holding up the case of the Irish singer's *Enlightenment*. George Elliott looked sharply at him. What was the point of this? she wondered.

'The greatest,' replied Jon Mitchell. 'I've been a fan since I was a kid. My old man took me to see the Man in concert when I was seven years old. I've been hooked ever since. Got all his albums, including the bootlegs. Go to see him in concert every year when he does his tour of the U.K.'

121

'Strange choice for a music teacher,' mused Tallyforth, staring at the unusual design on the C.D. cover, which looked like a carnation bursting out of a crater on the moon's surface.

'Not really,' replied Jon Mitchell. 'My dad was a hippy in the sixties and I was brought up rather unconventionally but one thing he taught me was how to play the guitar. And he made me have piano lessons, because he'd never learned to play and always wished he had. So I had this kind of unusual musical education, listening to all the music of the sixties while I was growing up and going through all that classical piano tuition at the same time. It was only when I got to music college that I found I wasn't the only one who'd had that range of influences.'

'But teaching?' repeated Tallyforth.

'Yeah, that was a bit of a surprise really,' said Jon Mitchell, rather more apprehensively and glancing at Margi Benetti who sat silently watching him. 'My first wife. Got pregnant and we were broke. Made me go into teaching to support the little one. And I've now got four of them to support, two from each wife! I don't seem to have ever escaped.'

'But you still want to?' persisted Tallyforth.

'I guess so,' came the hesitant reply. 'Though I think it's more likely through one of the school bands now than through my own work.'

'Tell me about these bands of yours,' said Tallyforth, tapping the C.D. case against his hand in time with the music which was much gentler now and featured a tinkling piano above a bass and snare drum accompaniment to a spoken voice.

> *In the days before rock 'n' roll*
> *In the days before rock 'n' roll*

Tallyforth could remember them.

But Jon Mitchell was speaking again.

'I run four bands at the school. There's a rap band called the LieQs, a rock band called Spirit, a heavy metal band known as the Warlords, and another rock band called Gutter Press. They're all talented and they could all make it. But there's a lot of luck. They've got to be in the right place at the right time. But they've got the hunger - and that's important. They're all from working class backgrounds. Or non-working class, I should say. That's why they're hungry. It was maybe my problem. I didn't have that hunger.'

'But you have a band of your own?' queried Tallyforth.

'Mm, the Falling Leaves. Margi's our vocalist,' he nodded in her direction and a fleeting smile passed across her face. 'We do alright but it's just local gigs really. Apart from Margi, we've all got other jobs and we can't travel far. But I need to play music. And I like the buzz of an audience. Even the drunks at a Working Men's Club or a Rugby Club!'

Jon Mitchell smiled thinly to himself.

'Odd name for a band,' said Tallyforth.

'It's from one of my favourite Irish songs - one that Van the Man sang with the Chieftains. *Raglan Road*. On the *Irish Heartbeat* album. Margi sweetheart, could you get it?'

Margi Benetti stood and moved back into the cottage, then reappeared at the stable door.

'Would you two like a drink?' she asked.

'Tea would be nice,' said Tallyforth without looking up. 'Alright with you, Elliott?'

George Elliott nodded.

'I'll come and help you,' she said and followed Margi Benetti into the kitchen.

The music had changed again.

> *Memories*
> *All I have is memories*
> *All I have is memories*
> *Memories of you.*

Tallyforth's heart lurched. Memories of the children raced across his mind. Memories of their births. Memories of them starting to walk and talk. Memories of them starting school. Memories of you, indeed. His heart wept, though his face maintained its outward calm.

'Is that a mandolin?' he asked.

'No, electronic keyboards. I used to think that. But it's definitely keyboards. I can get the effect myself. Mind if I have a slurp?'

Jon Mitchell lifted his glass of Guinness to his mouth.

'You were in the school on the Thursday evening when Stanton died, weren't you?' asked Tallyforth. 'Band rehearsal, wasn't it? One of the bands you just mentioned?'

Jon Mitchell put his glass down quickly and wiped the froth from his lips with the back of his hand..

'Yes, that's right,' he began. 'Gutter Press. They've got a gig coming up in a club in Swadlincote soon. I was leading them through their set.'

'And what time did you leave the school?'

'Must have been about seven,' replied Jon Mitchell. 'Can't remember precisely. Ask Margi. We went to the cinema that evening, I know that. Went to Derby to see that Ken Loach film *Land and Freedom* - brilliant. You seen it?'

'No,' said Tallyforth. 'Who else was on the premises when you left? Do you remember?'

'I don't think there was anyone,' said Jon Mitchell, taking another ruminative sup from his beer. 'Except the inspectors. But we'd been told that they'd be working late. God knows what they do. The music bloke was alright, though, I have to say. Got on OK with him.'

'So there was no-one else that you saw?' asked Tallyforth again.

'No.'

'The headmaster? The deputy?'

'They left before us, definitely. They came in to see the band and said goodnight. I remember that. About half an hour before we went.'

Tallyforth put down the C.D. cover that he had been holding, as Margi Benetti and George Elliott came out from the kitchen with three cups of tea.

'Not for you, lover. Yeah?' quizzed Margi Benetti, cocking an eye at Jon Mitchell.

'Right, sweetheart,' he replied, raising his glass of Guinness in acknowledgement.

'So you went straight home from the school?' repeated Tallyforth.

'Not quite,' said Jon Mitchell. 'I knew we didn't have much time so I called in at the Indian take-away for some food.'

'Which one?' asked Tallyforth.

'There's only a few in Tamworth, worse luck,' butted in Margi

124

Benetti. 'No Indian restaurants at all and only a few take-aways. We have to go to Derby or Birmingham for a decent Indian meal.'

'Just a minute,' said George Elliott. 'Did you say there wasn't an Indian restaurant in Tamworth, only take-aways? What's the name of the one you used?'

'The India Palace. In Church Street,' Jon Mitchell said.

George Elliott looked meaningfully at Tallyforth. He saw the look but did not respond.

'D'you want to hear this *Irish Heartbeat* album?' asked Jon Mitchell, when he noticed that Margi had brought it with the tea and placed it on the table by the C.D. player. 'It's the one with The Chieftains. The one with *Raglan Road* on it. Yeah?'

'OK,' said Tallyforth. 'And while we're listening, could you tell us about the treasure trove that was found around Tamworth?'

Jon Mitchell paused as he was taking the C.D. from its case. He cast an anxious glance at Margi Benetti, who shrugged and smiled supportively.

'Sorry,' he said. 'What would that be?'

'I think you know exactly what I mean,' said Tallyforth, a menacing tone creeping into his voice for the first time since they had arrived. 'Coins supposedly found by the father of one of the kids in one of your bands. With a metal-detector. Around by Borrowpit Lake. Believed to be *sceattas* from Offa's time. Remember now?'

Jon Mitchell pressed the button to begin the C.D. player.

'Oh, that,' he said. 'That was Jimmy Page's dad. Bit of a nutter. Spends all his time hunting for treasure with his metal-detector, since the pit was closed down he used to work in. Did you know that Jimmy Page - that's the original Jimmy Page, who's a better guitarist than Clapton, though he's never been recognised for it - played guitar behind Van's vocals on *Baby Please Don't Go,* which was one of the hits that Them made? His Dublin band. In the sixties.'

'And how did you find out? About the coins being found, I mean?' pressed Tallyforth, ignoring the musical history lesson.

'Jimmy told me one night. He's in the Gutter Press and they'd had a gig at The Edge. It's a club in Tamworth. I manage their affairs, so I was with them. He was telling the rest of the band and

125

I heard it. I thought it was probably just a story, so I didn't ask any more.'

'And the fact that they'd been sold privately for fifty thousand pounds. Was that just a story too, as far as you knew?' asked Tallyforth.

'Yes.'

'Nevertheless you thought it was worth repeating to your colleague Norman de Courcy and to your ex-colleague Alf Pugh. Why?'

Jon Mitchell laughed.

'Norman's obsessed with this Offa character,' he explained. 'I just like feeding his obsession. It was just a laugh really. I don't think he really believed me. Even though I told him to check with Jimmy Page.'

'And Pugh?' continued Tallyforth.

'Pugwash they call him,' interjected Margi. 'He's stupid. He thinks that the headmaster sacked him because he didn't like him. Everybody knows that Pugwash was having an affair with Alicia Hilton and that she'd been thrown over by Pickevance when Pearl Bowen appeared on the scene. And that he was trying to get revenge on Pickevance for Alicia.'

George Elliott took in a deep breath. Tallyforth looked at Margi Benetti, then turned his gaze slowly on to Jon Mitchell.

'So you told this Pugh character about the supposed discovery of the coins and about their supposed sale for fifty thousand pounds?' he asked. 'Why?'

'I knew he was convinced that Pickevance was nicking money from the school accounts. Everybody knew about this place in Lichfield that he and Bowen used to go to. It had to be paid for somehow. Pugwash reckoned Pickevance was laundering money from the school accounts to pay for it. But he couldn't prove anything,' replied Jon Mitchell.

'So what would he want with these coins?' asked George Elliott.

'Search me,' said Jon Mitchell, a look of genuine ignorance on his face. 'That's just Pugwash's fantasy. Better ask him. Better still ask Pickevance.'

Tallyforth looked at George Elliott, whose face betrayed the excitement she was feeling as this new evidence about an affair between Pickevance and Alicia Hilton came to light.

'Listen,' said Jon Mitchell suddenly, holding his finger to his lips and urging them to silence. 'This is *Raglan Road*.'

They listened as the Uileann pipes of Paddy Moloney ushered in the rich voice of Van Morrison:

On Raglan Road on an Autumn day
I saw her first and knew
That her dark hair would weave a snare
That I might one day rue.
I saw the danger, yet I walked
Along the enchanted way
And I said let grief be a falling leaf
At the dawning of the day.

On Grafton Street in November
We tripped lightly along the ledge
Of a deep ravine where can be seen
The worst of passions pledged.
The Queen of Hearts still baking tarts
And I not making hay.
But I loved too much. By such and such
Is happiness thrown away.

I gave her the gifts of the mind.
I gave her the secret sign
That's known to all the artists who have
Known true gods of sound and time.
With word and tint I never did stint.
I gave her reams of poems to say
With her own name there and her shiny black hair
Like the clouds over fields of May.

On a quiet street where old ghosts meet
I see her walking now
Away from me so hurriedly
My reason must allow.
For I have wooed not as I should
A creature made of clay.
When the angel woos the clay, he'll lose
His wings at the dawn of the day.

'See?' said Jon Mitchell in the moment's silence that followed, as he switched the C.D. player off.

'I see,' said Tallyforth quietly.

'I don't,' said George Elliott. 'Sorry, I just don't get the significance.'

'Never been in love with a bastard?' asked Margi, scanning the varnish on her fingernails. 'If you had, you'd understand.'

George Elliott blushed. Roger was the closest she had come to a bastard, she thought. And yes, she had cared for him more than she had admitted. But she had closed down on those feelings after he went, had concentrated her energies on her career, had convinced herself that love had passed her by.

There was a long silence, as each contemplated the haunting words of the old Irish melody.

A cuckoo's distant call cut into the silence.

'I understand,' said Tallyforth. 'I see why you call yourselves the Falling Leaves. I guess you've known grief, even at your age.'

'Age doesn't come into it,' said Jon Mitchell. 'Grief can strike you any time.'

Tallyforth looked at him with a new respect.

'You don't have anything about this Van Morrison character, do you? I'm supposed to be taking my daughter to see him in Birmingham in June. It would help if I knew a bit more. It was my sergeant here who recommended him,' he said.

'Sure, there's an article from *The Observer* from just before last Christmas. Remember when Bill Clinton went to Belfast to try and breathe new life into the peace process? Van was there too. Story is the President wanted to jam with him but his security people wouldn't hear of it. So Van performed *Days Like This* outside City Hall for sixty thousand people.'

'Really? I don't remember reading about that,' said Tallyforth.

'Hang on, I'll get you the article. I know exactly where it is.'

And Jon Mitchell unstretched himself from his deckchair and strode into the cottage, whence he emerged a few minutes later bearing the newspaper article he had promised.

'Thanks. I'll return it to you when I've copied it,' said Tallyforth, folding the newspaper page carefully and putting it in his pocket.

'No rush,' said Jon Mitchell.

Tallyforth stood and George Elliott followed his example.

'Mr Mitchell, we're very grateful for your help,' said Tallyforth. 'And you too, Ms Benetti. And now you'll forgive us if we leave. But we have a lot to do. We have to catch Stanton's killer.'

THIRTEEN

'Sarah, it's Brian.'

Sarah Pickevance felt her heart skip a beat. It was Sunday evening and they were watching television when the telephone rang. She had hardly slept the night before when her husband had failed to return and she was now dog tired. So, in order to hasten her sleep, she had opened a bottle of Liebfraumilch and was on her second glass, which she was sipping as she sat on the settee with her legs curled up underneath her. Her daughter Pam had taken time off revising for her A levels in order to sit with her mother and she too had a glass of wine in her hand. She had been sworn to secrecy about the disappearance of her father and the two younger children, Becky and James, knew only that he was staying with friends for a couple of days. There had been no need to cause them unnecessary upset, Sarah Pickevance had decided. Likewise, she hadn't said anything to Nick when he had made his weekly phone call from university that afternoon. It was too soon to alert them all to her husband's disappearance but she had needed to get Pam's support. Pam and she were more like sisters than mother and daughter. They were both the same height at five foot four, both were size twelve, and both wore size five shoes. They also shared a common dress sense, so that each would raid the other's wardrobe frequently, though it was more commonly daughter borrowing from mother. But Pam had also been her mother's confidante and friend for a long time.

During the course of that Sunday, as the hours and minutes ticked by and no news was heard, Sarah Pickevance had begun to prepare herself for the non-return of her husband. She could not explain precisely what was making her do this - partly, she supposed, it was because she had been half-expecting him to leave for some time, ever since she had first suspected about his affair with Pearl Bowen, but partly also because there was something else that was telling her to think about a future without him.

So when the phone rang shortly after nine o'clock, the last person she had expected to hear from was her husband.

'Brian, where are you? What's happened?' she cried, all her doubts and uncertainties temporarily forgotten as the relief of knowing that he was still alive surged through her heart.

She had not realised it until then but there had been a half-formed thought at the back of her mind that her husband might have committed suicide because he couldn't face up to what he had done.

'I'm alright, Sarah, but I need to talk to you,' he said.

'Wait a minute, Brian,' she interjected, as she realised that the two younger children were in the same room and had already heard too much.

She motioned to her daughter Pam that she was going to take the call on the other phone upstairs and then got up from the settee and went to their bedroom.

'Brian, where are you?' she began again, as soon as she heard the click as her daughter returned the downstairs phone to its cradle.

'I can't tell you, Sarah,' he replied. 'But don't worry. I'm alright. I just needed to get away for a little while to think things over. I've had a lot on my mind just recently.'

'You've had a lot on your mind!' she cried. 'What d'you think you're doing to the children? What d'you think you're doing to me? Brian, what is going on? Where are you?'

There was a moment's silence at the other end of the line and she wondered if he was going to ring off.

'Sarah, I'm sorry, truly sorry,' he said at last. 'I've made a complete mess of everything. I've realised over the last twenty-four hours that I need you, Sarah, and I need my children and that I've let you all down. And I'm just dreadfully sorry, sorry, sorry. I don't know what I can do.'

His voice had broken down into uncontrolled sobbing. Sarah

Pickevance controlled her own quivering heart. All her old instincts returned for taking over unstable family situations, developed with each of her children over the years as her husband had become more and more embroiled in his career and then during the past three years with him as both of his parents had died and he had been unable to control his grief at their loss.

'Brian, just tell me where you are and I'll come and get you,' she said firmly now. 'Whatever's wrong we can sort it out between us. As a family. Just tell me where you are.'

There was another pause, longer this time, before he replied. She could hear distant sniffing as he sought to control his tears.

'I can't,' he said. 'Not just yet, Sarah. I need some more time. But I'm alright. Please ring the school in the morning and tell Alicia that I'm ill and won't be in until the middle of the week. Please, Sarah. I need some space.'

'Brian, it's too late for that,' she replied impatiently. 'The police are looking for you.'

'Police! Why?' His voice took on a sharper, more anxious tone.

'Because I told them you were missing,' she said. 'I was worried about you. This Stanton business at the school. I thought....'

'You don't think I did it?'

'No, no!' she said, more confidently than she felt, for why had he run away if he was completely innocent?

'I knew that Tallyforth had it in for me,' said Brian Pickevance. 'I could tell from the way he was asking me questions last Friday. But it was nothing to do with me, Sarah. Please believe me!'

'Then why don't you come back and tell them,' she insisted. 'If you've done nothing, there's no need to stay away.'

'So what else did you tell the police?' he asked.

She bit her lip. Much as she wanted him back to complete the family, much as she wanted him back because, despite everything, she still loved him, much as she wanted him back, because she wanted to prove to the world that she was, in his eyes at least, far better than that Bowen woman, she was hesitant about how much she should tell him now. But then, she reasoned, he would find out soon enough after he returned, because the police would tell him. And, if he really was not going to return just yet because he needed time to think about things, then it was probably, no, almost certainly best to get everything out into the open.

'Brian, I know about you and Pearl Bowen,' she began. 'I heard you on the phone to her last night just before you went out. I knew you weren't going back to the school. I knew you were going to see her. I thought that's where you were last night. I thought you'd left me to go to her.'

The pause this time was even longer. She could almost hear his heart beating faster.

'Sarah,' he began. 'I don't know where to begin. I don't know what to say. I don't know what to do.'

'Just come home, Brian,' she instructed, more sure of herself now, more in control. 'Just come home and we can sort it out. One way or the other. But let's get it sorted. Now.'

'I can't,' he wailed. 'I can't. Don't you see? If the police think I killed Stanton, they'll arrest me as soon as they find me and all they'll want to do is interrogate me about that. They won't give a damn about us, Sarah. I can't come back yet. Give me space. Please. I need more time. I'll ring you tomorrow.'

'Brian, don't hang up,' she called, her control faltering and disappearing as quickly as it had appeared.

But it was too late. The line was dead. She dialled one-four-seven-one, forlornly, but the source of the call was not acknowledged. Brian Pickevance's whereabouts remained a mystery.

Tallyforth was sitting in the incident room at Tamworth police station. He had sent George Elliott to run further checks on the police computer on Alicia Hilton, Alf Pugh, Brian Pickevance, Jon Mitchell, Margi Benetti and Perry Stevens. Meanwhile he was absorbed in reading the article about Van Morrison that Mitchell had given him. As he read, the haunting melody of *Raglan Road* kept running through his mind, although the only words he could remember were:

> *I saw the danger, yet I walked*
> *Along the enchanted way*
> *And I said let grief be a falling leaf*
> *At the dawning of the day.*

As he read about the Irish blues singer, renowned for his truculence and refusal to be interviewed about anything other than his music, indeed preferring not to be interviewed at all, Tallyforth began to feel an odd affinity with him. Like Van Morrison, Tallyforth had believed for a long time that people's professional work defined them, not their private lives. He read with interest of the singer's upbringing in a Protestant working-class Belfast home, the son of a shipyard worker who collected blues, gospel and jazz music and a religiously devout mother who mixed being a Jehovah's Witness with being a jazz singer. He followed his progress from the early Belfast showband The Monarchs, where he sang and played the saxophone, into the formation of Them in 1963 as Northern Ireland's answer to the Rolling Stones. He read of Van Morrison's disillusion with Them and his relaunching of himself on a successful solo career in America, where he produced what has been described as one of the greatest rock albums of all time *Astral Weeks* in 1969 and where he married Janet Planet, one of his backing singers, who subsequently gave birth to his only child Shana, who had recently duetted with him on *You Don't Know Me*. The marriage had not lasted long. And then the details of the subsequent musical career, spanning over a quarter of a century, uninterrupted except for a brief spell in 1974 when Van the Man announced his retirement. Apart from the public acknowledgement of the singer's debt to the great blues singers like Leadbelly, Muddy Waters and John Lee Hooker, Tallyforth was surprised to read about the wide-ranging literary references in his music - John Donne, Jack Kerouac, Tennessee Williams, Blake, Byron, Rimbaud, Beckett being some of the names mentioned. This, he thought, was more up George Elliott's street than his - he must check out that she knew all this. Finally he read of the singer's relationship with Michelle Rocca, the former Miss Ireland and Eurovision Song Contest presenter, who had appeared on the album cover of the 1995 album *Days Like This*. The suggestion of the article was that the curmudgeonly singer had at last mellowed because of this relationship.

He put the newspaper cutting down on the table when he had finished reading. He still hadn't decided finally what to do about the concert tickets. Should he try his daughter again? Or should he ask George Elliott if she wanted them? Or should he maybe ask her if she would go to the concert with him? He had become personally intrigued to see this Van the Man.

'Pearl, it's Brian.'

Pearl Bowen nearly dropped the phone when she heard his voice. It was after ten o'clock on the Sunday evening and she had had a dreadful day, which had begun with the discovery of Brian Pickevance's farewell letter on her doormat that morning and then been rapidly followed by the news from George Elliott that her erstwhile lover had disappeared completely, and then the momentary hope and simultaneous fear that he might be in the house in Lichfield. The fact that he had not been at the latter venue made his actual whereabouts even more troubling and Pearl Bowen had spent the afternoon and early evening attempting to fill her mind with other thoughts. She had tried to keep busy by phoning Jim in London, who was back from his weekend conference in Brussels, by speaking to her mother at length about events back in South Wales where she originated, by speaking to her former headteacher about the OFSTED inspection and the strain it had been on all of them. She had been for a long walk along the river bank, feeding the mute swans on her way; she had ironed all her clothes; she had dusted throughout the house; she had prepared all her week's lessons. But nothing could drive away that nagging worm of worry that ate away at the back of her brain.

'Brian? What's happening?' she managed to blurt out, her voice seemingly controlled by something other than her brain.

'Pearl, I'm alright,' he continued. 'I've just spoken to Sarah. She told me. About everything. About the police and everything. And she knows about us. Did you get my letter?'

'Ye...es,' she almost whispered.

'I'm sorry, Pearl,' she heard him say. 'I've got to put a stop to all of this. And I've got to do it now. I can't live with myself any longer.'

She took a deep breath. Was he going to do something foolish? She had to talk to him now.

'Brian, can't you come and see me tonight? Can't we talk about this face to face? Where are you?' she asked.

'No, that's not possible,' he replied. 'I can't tell you where I am. I just want you to know I'm alright. And that I'm sorry. Sorry for everything. But I'm not going to do anything silly, so you don't have to worry about me. I've asked Sarah to ring Alicia in the morning to explain I'm ill and I won't be in school for a few days. I intend to return mid-week when I've got everything sorted out. But it's over, Pearl. You and me. I'm staying with Sarah, if she'll have me. And the kids. I can't face being without them. Please understand. I've thought long and hard about this. And I'm determined. Please don't try and change my mind. Maybe you should stay away for the back end of the week. Maybe if we didn't see each other at school for a week we could manage things better. And it will soon be half term.'

'Aren't you forgetting one thing?' she said, recovering her composure as she listened to his outburst.

'What?'

'Hubert Stanton was murdered at the school last Thursday evening,' she responded. 'Or had you forgotten? And the police have not arrested anyone yet. In fact, I don't think their enquiries are leading them anywhere conclusive. But I'll tell you one thing, Brian, and that's that you and I are high on their list of suspects. And your disappearance has probably put you right at the top of that list. Can't you see, Brian, that the longer you stay away the more suspect you seem?'

'I didn't do it, Pearl,' he said earnestly. 'You've got to believe me. It was nothing to do with me.'

She sighed in exasperation.

'But you've got to come back to clear your name,' she said.

'I'm sorry, Pearl. I need some space. I need some time. Please try to understand. Take care of yourself.'

And for the second time that evening, Brian Pickevance put down the phone to end his conversation.

Pearl Bowen stared in disbelief at the buzzing phone in her hand. Should she ring the police now? Tell that Sergeant Elliott? Or should she wait till the morning?

She put the phone back in its cradle and glanced at her watch.

It was ten twenty.

Forty-five minutes earlier George Elliott, feeling tired from the long day that they had spent on the case, re-entered the incident room where Tallyforth still sat reading.

'Have you found anything?' he asked, barely deigning to look up.

'Not a lot,' she started, glancing down at her notebook. 'Just that Pickevance's speeding offence was in Grantham, so it's possible he's got some connection with the place. I haven't tried his wife about that yet. Only just found it and it's a bit late. What d'you think?'

He looked up at her.

'Yes, you're right,' he said. 'The morning will do. Anything else?'

'Pugh,' she said, almost sneeringly, for she had taken an instant dislike to his squashed nose and leering manner. 'Done for assault a couple of times when he was younger. Nothing serious. Once when he was a student in Wales and one other occasion. Both times he was drunk. Both times connected to rugby matches. Nothing significant really, I suppose.'

Tallyforth grunted non-committally.

'Yeah?'

'Absolutely nothing on the computer about the others,' she said. 'Jon Mitchell and Margi Benetti never convicted for smoking dope, though we could change that, I suppose. Alicia Hilton and Perry Stevens not known.'

'Is that all?' he said testily. 'What have you been doing all this time? I think I know the Van Morrison story inside out and upside down now!'

She snorted and then looked doubtfully at him. She knew how he would react to the piece of information she was about to give him, not because of its substance but because of its source.

'I spoke to Steve,' she began. 'About Stevens.'

'Can't we ever get through a case without that little creep from the Home Office sticking his nose in?' he asked contemptuously. 'What is it this time?'

'Sir, I've told you before, the Home Office has access to information we don't have,' she explained, not for the first time. 'And you know what Steve tells us is worthwhile. And he's going over the limit for us. You know that. Be grateful!'

He looked at her and the hard look in his eyes softened, as he realised that she was telling him off and he was taking it. He wasn't reacting angrily or sullenly as he always seemed to in such a situation. Did this mean anything?

'Go on then,' he mumbled, with half a smile playing on his lips. 'What have you got?'

'Perry Stevens, the chair of governors,' she began. 'We know his firm was responsible for auditing the school's finances and we know he's the leader of the Conservative group on the Borough Council. But Steve says he's also a freemason. Grand Master of one of the main lodges in the West Midlands. And it's believed that several senior officers from the Mercian Force are in the same lodge. Including Superintendent Clarke. We'd better watch our backs, sir, if that's right.'

'What are you saying, Sergeant?' Tallyforth stood up, as he spoke. 'Are you saying that there might be some corruption in the Mercian Police Force? Be careful! But we need to speak to this Stevens character anyway about this alleged embezzlement. He can wait till tomorrow though. And maybe Pickevance will have turned up by then as well, hopefully with a signed confession to Stanton's murder.'

He strode across the room and reached down for the door handle.

'Come on, I'll buy you a pint. I want to know what you know about Van Morrison and Jack Kerouac. OK?'

She smiled and preceded him out of the door.

FOURTEEN

It had rained overnight and the clouds were still heavy as Tallyforth drove towards Tamworth on the Monday morning.

They had arranged, at George Elliott's suggestion, to meet in the Rock Island Diner in the Services complex at Junction 10 of the M42. Tallyforth carefully parked his Range Rover and walked up to the Diner which looked little more than a portakabin on stilts with a Stars and Stripes flag fluttering outside. As he entered, he noted the young waitresses in their uniforms with Stars and Stripes insignia pinned to the breasts of their white or red blouses. He also noted how they were all singing along to the loud music coming from the jukebox, which was or at least looked very much like a genuine nineteen-fifties model. The record playing as he entered was the Everly Brothers' *Wake Up Little Susie*.

George Elliott had beaten him to it. She was sitting at a table just inside the door with a cup of coffee in front of her.

'Morning, sir,' she said smiling up at him. 'Breakfast?'

He grimaced.

'I don't think my stomach could cope with greasy burgers at this time of day,' he replied. 'What time d'you make it anyway?'

She glanced at her watch.

'I make it nine,' she said. 'Sleep well?'

He grimaced again.

'No, not really,' he answered, taking a seat opposite her. 'Kept waking up in the night.'

'Bad dreams, sir?'

'No, nothing like that,' he began. 'Coffee for me, please. How about you, Elliott? Another? Anything to eat?'

The latter was addressed to the pony-tailed waitress who hovered at the side of their table to take their order.

'Yes, I'll have another,' replied George Elliott, looking up and smiling at the waitress. 'Cappuccino please. And a chocolate muffin.'

'Same for me,' repeated Tallyforth. 'Though I shouldn't really. I've had my muesli already. And that's all I'm supposed to have in the morning. Cholesterol management, my doctor calls it. Still, what the hell!'

Tallyforth sat back. George Elliott watched him bemused.

'I've been waking up in the night confused,' he began again, as Freddie Cannon's *Tallahassie Lassie* replaced the Everly Brothers. 'There's something wriggling away at the back of my subconscious trying to tell me something. But every time it tries to get out, something drives it back into hiding again.'

'How d'you work that out?' she asked, curious about this explanation he was now giving for the intuitive gift for detection he always claimed to have.

'I know that the last time I woke in the night, which was exactly four-thirty because I looked at my alarm, I was absolutely certain the moment before I woke that I had the answer. But then, when I sat up in bed to turn the light on, whatever it was that a second earlier had been on the point of revelation had disappeared.'

She looked across at him, giving him a quizzical stare.

'That's just like any dream,' she said. 'I wake up sometimes just as a dream is on the point of something huge. Isn't that just normal?'

Tallyforth sipped from the coffee which had by now been placed in front of him and began to tear the wrapping from the muffin. As he did so, he glanced across at his sergeant. She was wearing a cream turtle-neck sweater under a brown suede jacket. He could smell her Chanel perfume.

'Elliott, you wouldn't like to come and see this Van Morrison character with me in June, would you? My daughter's not keen. I tried her again last night. So I'm stuck with two tickets. And I've got quite intrigued from what I was reading last night. How about it?' he asked suddenly.

George Elliott smiled slightly to herself.

'Second best, is that it?' she queried with a jocular laugh, which did not quite cover up the gravity of her tone.

140

'For Christ's sake, no! Nothing like that,' he replied. 'I just thought, you know, since you like the bloke as well... You do, don't you? Like him, I mean?'

'Yes,' she answered. 'I think he's brilliant. OK, you're on. But you have to let me pay for my own ticket. How much?'

Tallyforth's face lightened.

'You can't afford it on sergeant's wages,' he said, smiling at her and holding her gaze momentarily. 'My treat this time. Maybe you another time. OK?'

'OK.'

She glanced away, raised her muffin to her mouth and took a bite. Buddy Holly's *Heartbeat* pounded through the Rock Island Diner.

'We've got to talk to Stevens but we're going to have to be very careful with him,' began Tallyforth again, changing tack and getting back to their enquiry. 'If what you hear is correct about him being a mason, then he will have friends in high places. And I'm not ruling out 'Nobby' Clarke. I suggest we call at Stevens's office on the way into Tamworth and ask him to accompany us to the police station, before he can contact anyone else. We'll just say it's routine enquiries about the school. Agreed?'

George Elliott nodded, her mouth full of chocolate muffin.

'And leave the questioning to me,' he insisted. 'We have to be very cautious.'

She looked up at him. The moment had gone when they had behaved like two equals. It was back to master and servant.

They finished their coffees, paid and walked out into the still cloudy morning. The temperature had dropped appreciably since the previous week. She pulled her jacket around her.

'Follow me in,' he said. 'We'll leave your car at the station and go for Stevens in mine.'

'Mr Stevens, we're very grateful to you for giving up your valuable time to help us with our enquiries,' began Tallyforth, shepherding Perry Stevens, who was dressed in dark pin-striped suit and shining black shoes, to a seat on the opposite side of the table from where George Elliott was already sitting. 'You know, of course, about the murder of Registered Inspector Hubert Stanton at Æthelfleda High School last Thursday evening and you will know that so far we have not been able to trace the killer?'

'Of course, Chief Inspector,' replied the suavely-spoken Stevens, crossing his legs carefully and ensuring that the creases on his trousers stayed intact. 'How can I help?'

George Elliott opened her notebook.

'Would you mind telling us, sir, when you became Chairman of the Governors at Æthelfleda High School?' asked Tallyforth.

'That would have been in nineteen eighty-seven, Chief Inspector. I'd been on the governing body for some time but my colleagues elected me Chairman in nineteen eighty-seven.'

'And were you then also on the Borough Council?'

'Most certainly,' came the reply. 'I was in fact Leader of the Council at the time. Political control of the Borough Council swung back and forth in the nineteen eighties but at that time my party was in overall control.'

'So you were carrying a lot of responsibility at the time, sir?' quizzed Tallyforth.

'Chief Inspector, ever since I entered local politics I have made it my duty to work for my community. I felt it was a privilege to be invited to stand for election as Chairman of the school's Governing Body.'

'So it was nothing to do with the move to Grant Maintained status?'

Perry Stevens uncrossed his legs, straightened the creases once again, coughed lightly and resumed.

'Chief Inspector, I am a loyal member of the Conservative Party. I believe that what Margaret Thatcher achieved for this country was remarkable. When the Education Bill was going through parliament in nineteen eighty-seven with its proposals for Grant Maintained schools, I believed that this would be a further plank in the Conservative revolution to free our schools up from local government red tape. You may be aware, Chief Inspector, that the schools of Tamworth are administered by the county, whose Labour administration is solely interested in the schools of the northern part of the county around the Potteries. I wanted to get control of our schools back into local hands, where it ought to be. The opportunity to show through the example of Æthelfleda High School how much better local control could be was one that I relished. So, yes, of course I saw the opportunity opened up by the Education Act as an attraction to me as Chairman of the Governing Body. But I must make it clear that I would have continued serving the school whatever the outcome of the parental vote.'

George Elliott was busy scribbling down the detail of Stevens's lengthy reply.

'So you were Chairman when Brian Pickevance was appointed?' asked Tallyforth.

'Most certainly,' came the reply. 'An outstanding candidate. Clearly the best. We have been very fortunate in Brian.'

'And when the matter of Grant Maintained status was first brought to the governors in nineteen eighty-eight, they rejected the idea, is that right?

'That's correct, Chief Inspector. They felt it was too big a leap of faith at the time, though Brian was very keen.'

'And you, sir?'

Perry Stevens coughed again and knitted his thin hands on his knee.

'I have to say that I was as keen,' replied Stevens. 'Although, as Chairman, I had to try to contain my enthusiasm somewhat.'

'But, when the matter was raised again the following year, the governors had changed their minds. Why was that, sir?'

'We were fortunate that a number of new governors were in place by then and, when the Borough Council became Labour-controlled in December of that year, we all felt that we had to make the move immediately before political pressure forced us to rethink.'

'Were these new governors Conservative supporters then, sir?'

'No, I wouldn't say that, Chief Inspector. Political affiliation wasn't the most important factor. What we wanted and what we were able to get were people with business experience. Æthelfleda High School serves a deprived area, Chief Inspector. Large numbers of children come from one-parent families and many of them don't know who their real fathers are. Their mothers are very inadequate, living off social security and spending the money on drugs and alcohol. There's a lot of prostitution. Lots of the children don't get any breakfast before they come to school in the mornings. We wanted people on the governing body who would join Brian Pickevance and his team in changing the ethos of this school and that's why we wanted people from business, people who had benefited from the freedoms opened up under Margaret Thatcher, people who knew that change is painful but necessary.'

Perry Stevens had sat forward during this peroration, his eyes moist with excitement as he recalled the early days of his stewardship of the school.

'And the loss of four experienced teachers last year, sir,' continued Tallyforth. 'How did that come about?'

'Chief Inspector, what Brian Pickevance has done for this school has been exemplary,' Stevens began again. 'But we were faced with a situation which even he could not prevent. Although Æthelfleda High School is funded directly from central government, its funding is based on that which it would have received from its Local Education Authority and I have to say that our county is very profligate. It spends far too much on central administration. Consequently, when the government determined the Standard Spending Assessment for the county, it set this at a low figure in order to teach the Labour politicians in the north a lesson. Unfortunately, there has been a knock-on effect from this on to our own budget. The result was that we had to make five teachers redundant, including four very experienced ones.'

'And was it difficult identifying those teachers?'

Perry Stevens looked down at his hands, which still clasped his knee. George Elliott looked up from her notes. Tallyforth sat back in his chair.

'No, not really. We went through all the appropriate procedures but at the end of the day it was clear to the governors that only five people fitted the requirements. Two of those were known to me, I have to say, because I am a past president of Tamworth Rugby Club where they were members - John Clayton, who was one of the deputies, and Alfred Pugh, who was a year head.'

'Did they try to pressurise you?'

'Pugh did, yes. He telephoned me one day but I had to tell him it was not just me, it was the whole Governing Body and I couldn't discuss the matter in public. John Clayton accepted it. He's moved down south now. To Bournemouth, I understand.'

Tallyforth stood up and moved across to the window, making a gap for himself in the vertical blinds.

'Your colleague Mr Ferris acts as auditor for the school. Is that right?' he asked, his back turned on Stevens.

'Yes, that's right.'

'Rather unusual, isn't it, sir? I mean, with you being the Chairman of the Governing Body?'

'No, it's quite straightforward, Chief Inspector,' replied Perry Stevens, his face revealing not the slightest sense of discomfort. 'Matthew Ferris is a partner in the company but he is an independent auditor of a body's finances. It's all within the Association's laws.'

'And he has not uncovered any financial irregularity in the past year?'

'Certainly not, Chief Inspector.' Stevens bristled slightly. 'What are you implying?'

Tallyforth turned from the window and looked down at Perry Stevens.

'There has been an allegation that fifty thousand pounds of the school's money has gone missing,' he snapped. 'And that the loss was not shown up in the financial audit of the school done by your colleague Mr Ferris.'

'Who on earth told you that?' blustered Perry Stevens, sitting back in a well-rehearsed gesture. 'It's absolute piffle whoever it was.'

'Oh, it is a very good source, sir, I assure you,' said Tallyforth, moving back to the table and leaning on to it to stare at Stevens.

Perry Stevens focused on George Elliott, who had looked up temporarily from her scribbling. Then he gazed blankly at Tallyforth. Then he crossed and uncrossed his legs again. Then he sat up straight in his seat, unclasping his hands and pointing the index finger of his right one at Tallyforth..

'Chief Inspector, are you suggesting that my firm is responsible for some financial irregularity? Are you implying perhaps that I am linked to this alleged financial irregularity because of my position as Chairman of the Governing Body of the school in question? Is that what you are saying?' His voice was angry now. 'Because if so, I will have to warn you that my lawyers will be informed of this and your superior officers will also be told. How dare you treat me like this? I came in here quite voluntarily to help you in your enquiries and now I find that you are accusing me of complicity in something I know nothing about. You will excuse me, Chief Inspector. I am a busy man.'

And, so saying, the elegantly-suited Perry Stevens stood to his full height, put his head in the air and marched out of the room.

George Elliott looked at Tallyforth, who was still standing with his hands splayed on to the table. He was smiling gently to himself.

'Cat among the pigeons, Elliott,' he said at last. 'Hold on to your safety belt - things will get hotter now.'

She grinned feebly back. Was this the wisest choice of action? she wondered. After all, it was less than two hours previously that he had been warning her of the need to take care.

At eleven o'clock that Monday morning, Norman de Courcy walked into the Tamworth Police Station and asked to see Chief Inspector Tallyforth. The desk sergeant, who knew de Courcy slightly from a time when there had been a rather noisy political rally in the middle of the nineteen eighty-seven General Election, led him up to the incident room and showed him in.

When they saw de Courcy's short balding figure stood in the doorway, Tallyforth and George Elliott looked up from the notes they were reading.

'Good morning, Chief Inspector,' de Courcy began. He was wearing his customary bow tie and a leather-elbowed brown sports jacket. 'I had a free period at school so I arranged with Ms. Bowen to come and see you. Mr Pickevance isn't at school today. It seems he's not well. I have some information for you, information I believe you may find of value in your quest.'

'Please, sit down,' said Tallyforth, motioning to the empty chair. 'I don't think you've met Sergeant Elliott, have you?'

George Elliott smiled a greeting in de Courcy's direction. De Courcy returned the greeting and proceeded to sit down, fetching a notebook out of his briefcase as he did so.

146

'Chief Inspector,' he began in a hushed and almost conspiratorial voice. 'I have conducted some enquiries as you suggested. Into the alleged find of treasure trove.'

George Elliott looked at her chief quizzically. He had not told her about de Courcy being involved thus.

'According to one of the most respected members of the Mercian Society, who is also on the trustees of the Tamworth Castle Trust, the person who found the coins with his metal-detector was a certain James Page, an ex-miner from Tamworth. His son is a pupil at our school. Quite a talented guitarist, I understand.'

He looked across at them.

'Go on,' said George Elliott. 'Where did he find the coins? How many were there? Are they really Mercian coins?'

'One moment, please, Sergeant,' pleaded Norman de Courcy. 'The coins were apparently found in the field surrounding Borrowpit Lake. It's all been dug up there in the last few years as part of the development that's been taking place. As far as I can make out from my source, there were twenty silver coins found. It is believed, though remember no-one who knows about these things has actually seen these coins yet, that they are all of the wolf-whorl type, which are alleged to have been made at the royal mint in Tamworth during Offa's time. If that is so, and I am stressing if, they are extremely rare. There has never been a find like this in the Tamworth area. We know there was a royal mint here, though we believed that it was operating from the tenth century onwards and therefore not in Offa's time. However, we do know that Offa struck coins of this type. We know he had his royal palace here. We know that *sceattas* with this wolf design have been discovered elsewhere in England. But never as close to what we believe was the heart of Offa's kingdom. It is possible, therefore, that these coins could have been minted here. If true, it would be a remarkable discovery. It would rank alongside the discovery of the watermill uncovered in nineteen seventy-one and provide us with invaluable new information about Mercian rule.'

'So how do you know these coins are genuine?' asked George Elliott.

'We don't,' replied de Courcy, resting his notebook on his knees. 'Not yet. The only person who will admit to having seen one is the

147

person who works in Tamworth Castle to whom James Page showed one of the coins. He claims that it was remarkably similar to one that is on display in the Castle Museum but he is far from being an expert. I've got some pictures here of the sort of coins we are talking about. You can have these.'

Norman de Courcy opened his briefcase and extracted a sheaf of papers on which photographs of Mercian coins had been photocopied.

'What about Page, sir?' interjected Tallyforth. 'Have you visited him?'

'He's denying the whole thing,' said de Courcy despondently. 'Though I have to say, his denial was not very convincing.'

'Why d'you say that?'

'Chief Inspector, I used to teach the man,' came the reply. 'He was a pupil of mine twenty years ago, when the school was a secondary modern. And I have to say he was a rogue then. Always in trouble. Always in detention for some minor misdemeanour or other. And in my experience the child is father to the man. I didn't believe his denials when he was a young boy. And I still don't. I'd swear that he knows more than he is willing to tell me. And, from the smirk on his face when I left him, I'd say that, if you get him to tell you the truth about those coins, you'll be close to resolving the murder of that Stanton fellow. But now, if you'll excuse me, I have to go. I have my examination class this afternoon and there's only a few weeks left till the exam. Thank you for listening, Chief Inspector, Sergeant. I wish you luck.'

'Before you go, Mr de Courcy,' said Tallyforth, 'can I just check something else? You are on the Tamworth Borough Council, aren't you?'

Norman de Courcy looked surprised.

'Yes.'

'And you obviously know Mr Perry Stevens?'

'Yes.' Norman de Courcy's face became agitated. 'I have spent a large part of my political life fighting the sort of things that Stevens supports. It's one of the reasons why I didn't retire from the school earlier, when it first became grant-maintained. I'm completely against the whole idea on principle, as you can imagine, but I wanted to keep a watch on what Stevens was up to. That's why I'm one of the teachers on the Governing Body.'

George Elliott and Tallyforth exchanged meaningful glances.

'And have you had a need to keep watch on him, sir?' asked Tallyforth.

'Chief Inspector, the condition of liberty is eternal vigilance, as someone once said,' replied de Courcy. 'You may be interested to know that the same Perry Stevens is currently negotiating to sell off part of the school's playing fields to McDonald's as a burger joint. Of course, he will deny it if you ask him. But I have it on good authority from someone in the Conservative Party that this is true. I'm just waiting for it to appear on the Governing Body's agenda. But I really must go. Please excuse me.'

And Norman de Courcy put his notebook back in his briefcase, stood and left the room.

'Elliott,' ordered Tallyforth curtly, 'I think this Mr Page deserves a visit, don't you?'

'What about Stevens?' asked George Elliott. 'Don't we need to find out about this sale of the playing fields?'

'I think he can wait,' said Tallyforth, getting up from his seat. 'Remember he threatened us with his lawyers. He won't be going anywhere and it will be useful to be one up on him. Besides, I don't really think that has anything to do with Stanton's murder. Come on.'

She followed him out of the room.

FIFTEEN

The Page family lived in a nineteen-fifties council house on the estate that surrounded Æthelfleda High School. It was typical of its era and had not been significantly improved since it had been built, nor had it been maintained other than superficially over the ensuing years. The wooden gate into the front drive was hanging on by one hinge and the grass was overgrown. The paint on the windows was cracked and peeling.

George Elliott knocked on the front door, while Tallyforth stood behind her, looking up and down the dismal street.

'Hey up, me duck! What can I do for you then?' asked the burly, unshaven figure, wearing only a grimy white vest and track suit bottoms, who opened the door to them.

'We're police officers. Mercian Police Force,' said George Elliott, showing her identity card. 'Are you James Page?'

He looked surprised but not taken aback.

'I am that, me duck,' he replied. 'What can I do you for?'

'Can we come in, Mr Page?' asked Tallyforth over her shoulder. 'We have some questions we'd like to ask you.'

'Of course you can, me duck,' came the cheery reply and James Page stood back to allow his visitors into the house.

They stood in the cramped hall for a moment until Page ushered them into the front room of his house, which they were surprised to find was well furnished with a mocha three-piece suite and a red, deep-pile carpet.

'D'you like a cuppa summat?' Page asked. 'The missus can easily put the kettle on, y' know."

'Not for me,' replied George Elliott. 'But thanks anyway.'

She chose an armchair and sat down.

'I wouldn't mind,' said Tallyforth. 'Tea, please. Not too strong. Thanks.'

James Page leaned out of the doorway into the hall and called out in the direction of the back of the house:

'Phyllis! Mek us two cups of tea, will you, love? We've got visitors. From the police!'

He came back into the room and sat down opposite George Elliott, his legs apart and his elbows resting on his thighs.

'Now then, me duck,' he began cheerily. 'What can I do you for?'

George Elliott opened her mouth to speak but, before she could do so, Tallyforth had butted in.

'Mr Page, do you own a metal-detector?' he asked, still standing up.

'I do that. Nowt criminal in that, is there?'

'And have you used that metal-detector in the vicinity of Borrowpit Lake in the last few weeks?'

James Page looked up at him with a twinkle in his eye.

'I have that,' he replied. 'Yes, that's true. The ground around Borrowpit Lake's had a good churning over the last few years, what with all the new roads they've been building around here.'

George Elliott waited for Tallyforth to continue but there was a moment's silence.

'Is this your son?' asked Tallyforth, holding out a photograph in a gilt-edged display case which he had taken from the mantelpiece above the gas fire.

'It is that!' replied the ex-miner proudly. 'Him with his electric guitar. Bought it for him when he was nine. And now his group's on the way to fame and fortune! We hope.'

He stood up and took the photograph from Tallyforth, holding it fondly in his large hands.

'It's the only way out for his generation,' he began. 'Sport or music. That's all. There's no proper work around here now the pit's gone. And there never will be. Just serving in supermarkets or stacking in warehouses. That's all there is in Tamworth now.'

George Elliott was puzzled. James Page was not conforming to the picture she had had of him from what de Courcy had said about him. She had expected someone quite different.

'You've got high hopes for him then? Your boy?' continued Tallyforth.

The two men were standing facing each other now, almost oblivious of George Elliott who was still seated.

'The second Jimmy Page,' came the reply. 'This kid's got the makings. He could make it real big. If he gets the breaks, of course. Lot of luck in the music business. Gotta be in the right place at the right time. That Mitchell bloke at the school, though, he'll see them right. Should've been teachers like him when I was a kid.'

'You resentful of your education then, are you?' asked Tallyforth.

James Page squinted fiercely at him.

'You joking?' he asked. 'Call what I had an education! Ten years and they still couldn't teach me to read! I got out as soon as I could. Went down the pit like me dad had. Waste of time, school were!'

'Mr de Courcy was one of your teachers, wasn't he?' continued Tallyforth.

A look of realisation suddenly dawned on Page and his voice filled with anger.

'Is that what you're here about?' he said. 'Has he been saying something to you about me? Bastard! I never liked him when I was at the school, him and his bow ties and his lah-di-dah ways. Always keeping me in detention for nothing. What's he been saying then?'

George Elliott butted in.

'He came to talk to you about some coins you'd found,' she said. 'Around Borrowpit Lake.'

'That's right,' replied Page suspiciously. 'So?'

'So you did find some coins there?' she queried.

'Maybe's I did and maybe's I didn't,' he answered. 'Why d'you want to know?'

'But you told Mr de Courcy that you hadn't found anything?' she asked again.

'It were none of his business,' said Page bristling with anger now. 'What I find with my metal-detector is my business. And before you say anything, I know the rules about handing in anything valuable.'

'Mr Page,' said Tallyforth quietly, 'did you discover twenty old coins, believed to date from the time of Offa the king of the Mercians, in the fields around Borrowpit Lake? Yes or no. Tell the truth, man. It's for your own good.'

James Page suddenly sat down and began to laugh. His laughter grew in intensity and loudness and didn't cease for several minutes. Tallyforth and George Elliott looked at each other in bewilderment.

Eventually Page managed to control his laughter. He wiped his eyes with the back of his hand.

'Believed to date from the time of Offal?' he said. 'Who the hell's he when he's at home? Yes, I did find some coins. And yes, there were twenty. And yes, they are old. But not that old!'

And he started laughing again.

'They're from the eighteen hundreds,' he explained. 'I knows a bit about coins now, since I've been using the metal-detector. And I had them checked out by a mate of mine who works at the Castle.'

'So they're of no great value?' asked George Elliott.

'Few quid maybe,' replied Page. 'Nowt much though, worse luck! Who told you they were from that Offal bloke you mentioned?'

'Your son apparently told his music teacher, Jon Mitchell, that you'd found some treasure-trove,' answered Tallyforth. 'It was Mitchell who told de Courcy.'

Page laughed again.

'Look, I'll show you them,' he said, standing up again and reaching down behind the chair that George Elliott was sitting on. He brought out an old shoe box and took the lid off. He reached in and took out a piece of cloth, which he carefully unwrapped to reveal the twenty coins he had found. They were Victorian sixpenny bits.

'That's your Offal coins, me duck!' he said, his eyes twinkling. 'Good old Victorian tanners!'

Tallyforth took one, held it up to the light, grimaced slightly, then replaced it in the cloth that James Page was holding.

'Mr Page, I'm sorry we've wasted your and our time,' he said briskly. 'Come on, Sergeant. We've seen all we need to see.'

'Don't you want your tea, me duck?' said Page plaintively, as Tallyforth brushed past his wife as she came into the room.

There was no answer.

....

153

Tallyforth was driving the Range Rover at speed, his teeth clenched, his eyes staring straight ahead. She could tell by looking at him that he was angry. And she knew why. The connection with Offa, the king of the Mercians, which he and he alone had been pursuing in his mind, had suddenly collapsed with Page's revelations about the coins. He had not confided in her that he suspected some link, other than the obvious one about the coins, but she had sensed over the past couple of days, particularly because of his reluctance to call Pickevance in for questioning at the earliest opportunity when everything pointed suspiciously in his direction, that her chief was following one of his hunches again.

And now, as she watched his body tensed over the Range Rover's steering wheel, she realised fully the hunch he had been following. He had picked up on the Offa connection and convinced himself that it was linked to Stanton's death. Somewhere inside the great detective's head there had grown a fancy which linked the exploits of the Mercian king to the events currently engaging them. Quite how such a link had been made she did not know and now she was unlikely to find out. Even if, she surmised, he knew himself. He probably could not make it explicit, because it was something snatched from the darkness of his unconscious, something intangible, something impossible to quantify or qualify. It was Tallyforth's normal way of working, which, allied to her methodical and logical methods, made them the Mercian Force's leading murder investigators.

The coins had seemed to provide a physical representation of that intuitive connection but, now that Page had shown them the Victorian sixpences and given proof positive that de Courcy's story and Pugh's suspicions were unfounded, Tallyforth was having to reject that intuitive guess. His anger, she could tell, was focused as much on himself for giving too much credence to this intuition.

For several minutes they drove in silence, seemingly at random.

'Where are we heading, sir?' she asked, glancing studiously at him and not wishing to upset him further by some untoward choice of phrase or tone.

In response Tallyforth suddenly braked hard and swung the car round in a one hundred and eighty degree turn.

'I want to speak to that Bowen woman again,' he said through gritted teeth. 'And Lashley, the caretaker. There's something being kept from us that's crucial. I'm going to the school.'

She looked across at him. The tension evident on his face only a few seconds previously had vanished and been replaced by a look of grim determination.

Very soon they were driving through the gates of Æthelfleda High School, past the netball court where Denise Hadlington was coaching two teams of over-enthusiastic girls, and into the main car park.

'I want you to talk to Lashley,' Tallyforth explained, as he pulled the handbrake on and switched the engine off. 'Get him to go over again who was in the school on the evening of Stanton's murder, what time they left, and anything else that occurred on that evening. And find out who had keys to that bit of the building the inspectors were using. And who had access to the poisons in the science area. I'm going to talk to Ms. Bowen about Pickevance. Meet me back here in an hour. Okay?'

She nodded and climbed out of the car.

'Come in, Alicia. Sit down. The chief inspector wants to talk to us both together,' said Pearl Bowen with a grim smile. She was sitting in Pickevance's office, behind his desk, with the photograph of his family facing her. She was heavily made up and wore a dark blue suit with a red silk scarf tied carefully around the top of her crisp white cotton blouse.

Alicia Hilton had been summoned, at Tallyforth's request, from her own office. She was dressed as demurely as ever in a lightweight summer dress of a faded yellow colour which swished around her legs as she entered the headteacher's office.

She sat down on one of the armless chairs against the wall and waited.

Tallyforth had changed his mind. He had decided that he wanted to talk to both of them together. To do so, he had had to promise Pearl Bowen that he would not mention the affair between her and Pickevance, not just to save her embarrassment but also because he was more concerned to discover their feelings about his mood leading up to and during the OFSTED inspection. What he didn't tell Pearl Bowen, of course, was that he also wanted to see how the two of them reacted to each other under public scrutiny. For these two women, next to his wife Sarah, probably knew Brian Pickevance better than anyone else. And in fact they probably saw more of him than his wife did, given the demands of running a school in the nineteen-nineties. But he also knew that Alicia Hilton had been close to Pickevance - how close he wasn't clear about, though Margi Benetti had suggested that they had been very close before Pearl Bowen's arrival. So he wanted to see them together under some pressure.

'Now, you two have a lot to do with Brian Pickevance in the normal run of things,' he began, pacing up and down the room between the two of them. 'How would you say he was in the weeks leading up to the inspection? Was he worried? Unduly stressed? Overanxious? Were there any signs of unusual behaviour - you know, excessive coffee drinking, bouts of quick temper, sudden lurches in decision-making, anything like that?'

Alicia Hilton looked up at him.

'He always kept himself under perfect control,' she answered. 'Mr Pickevance is a gentleman. He would not adopt inappropriate behaviour in front of one of his staff. I certainly didn't see anything unusual in his behaviour. But Ms. Bowen saw more of him than I did.'

Tallyforth noticed the quick flash from Pearl Bowen's eyes in Alicia Hilton's direction.

'Only because there was a lot of planning and managing to do, Alicia,' she said, smiling fiercely across the room at Tallyforth. 'Chief Inspector, it won't surprise you to learn that not all the teachers at Æthelfleda High School are brilliant. Some of them have their weaknesses, I'm afraid, and we had to support them as best we could. I expect it's the same in the police force - not everyone's perfect. But one of the tenets of good management is that any enterprise is only as good as its weakest members, so we have to find ways of supporting those and helping them to be better.'

Tallyforth watched Alicia Hilton as Pearl Bowen spoke. He noticed that she was fiddling with the cord that went round the waist on her dress. There was a nervousness about the way she did this that Tallyforth was curious about. Was she anxious that something was going to be touched on that she didn't want touched on? Or was she perhaps disputing Pearl Bowen's strictures on management?

'Were the non-teaching staff as anxious about the OFSTED inspection?' he asked her, pausing in his stride in front of her and cocking his head on one side as if to look for the answer forming itself in her larynx before emerging through her mouth.

Alicia Hilton looked up.

'Naturally, Chief Inspector,' she replied. 'Even though Mr Pickevance took us through the whole process and explained that we were not likely to be seen very much. But it's a big thing, an inspection. And we saw all the teachers panicking and I guess some of that rubbed off on us.'

'In what ways?' he probed.

'We're only human, Chief Inspector,' Alicia Hilton replied. 'We were being asked to produce paperwork at a much faster rate than normal. Some of the requests seemed a little excessive.'

Tallyforth almost felt the sharply-tipped dart that flew with these words across the room to the seat where Pearl Bowen sat contemplating the paint on her long finger nails.

'So you were put under a deal of pressure in the run-up to the inspection,' Tallyforth summarised. 'And did that lead to any significant difficulties in your relationships with the school's management?'

Alicia Hilton's eyes opened wide as she looked up at him.

'Why, no, Chief Inspector!' she said, feigning surprise that he should have the nerve to ask such a question. 'We gained the Investors in People Award here last year because of the school's commitment to meeting the professional needs of all its staff. We all accepted that, because of the OFSTED inspection, we had to work harder. After all, the success of the school is due to the hard work of everyone involved in it.'

Tallyforth grimaced. He could see that he wasn't getting anywhere with this line of questioning. Time to change tack, he thought.

'Was Brian Pickevance worried that the school might fail the inspection?' he asked Pearl Bowen. 'They do fail schools, don't they?'

Pearl Bowen's face paled.

'That's correct,' she said quietly. 'But Æthelfleda High wouldn't have come into that category. True, neither our attendance rate nor our examination rate are that good but, considering the quality of our intake, we believe that we are adding significant value to children's attainment levels. Did you know, Chief Inspector, that over half of our intake have reading ages at least two years below their chronological age? When you're battling against that, I think we do remarkably well. Brian has a lot to be proud of. We were certainly not afraid of OFSTED. We regarded it positively.'

Tallyforth had positioned himself against the door, watching her face as she spoke. She certainly had her answers off pat, he thought. But something wasn't quite right. He had noticed the paleness of her look and the quietness of her voice at the start of her reply.

'So there's no reason to suppose that Pickevance's disappearance is anything to do with the stress of the inspection?'

'No, I'm sure that's not the reason,' answered Pearl Bowen.

'What do you mean disappearance?' asked Alicia Hilton suddenly. 'I thought he was ill!'

Tallyforth's gaze switched between the faces of the two women in the room.

'And nothing to do with the missing money?' he tried again.

This time it was Pearl Bowen's face that fell in astonishment.

'What missing money?' she asked, genuinely bewildered.

Tallyforth watched them both again. Clearly each was learning of something they had known nothing of before. Each had a secret that the other was desperate for. But how could Pearl Bowen reveal her knowledge of Pickevance's disappearance without publicly admitting to her affair with him? And how could Alicia Hilton reveal her knowledge about the missing fifty thousand pounds without implicating herself and Alf Pugh in their attempt to inform Hubert Stanton of the embezzlement?

They met back in the car park as arranged.

'Anything?' he asked.

'Nothing new,' she answered. 'Lashley's story matches the one he told you originally. The girl's P.E. teacher and her netball team, de Courcy, Mitchell and one of his bands, Pickevance and Bowen. But all well gone by the time the inspectors left the school. And apparently Stanton left there on his own.'

Tallyforth pulled a face.

'What about the poisons?' he tried again.

'Kept under lock and key in the prep. room in the middle of the science labs. It's got no windows and is impossible to break into. The only people who have keys are Lashley, the head of science Mrs Field and, of course, Pickevance, who by the way teaches some chemistry. Lashley volunteered that bit of information.'

'So, not only did he have the keys to the poisons, he also knew what cyanide could do! Why the hell didn't we arrest him two days ago?'

It was George Elliott's turn to pull a face.

'Search me!' she said, but the implication was clear. She blamed Tallyforth and his predilection for hunting for exotic irrelevancies. 'Did you get anywhere with Pearl Bowen?'

'Yes and no,' he answered teasingly. 'I talked to her and Alicia Hilton together. Very interesting. The dynamics that is. They clearly despise each other. And, of course, the Hilton woman knew nothing about Pickevance's disappearance, while your friend Pearl knew nothing about the missing money. What you might call a steep learning curve for both of them.'

Tallyforth smiled to himself. For, although the interview with the two women had failed to produce evidence of any value, it had shown up the animosity between the two of them clearly. And maybe that animosity was based on jealousy, he surmised. Maybe, just maybe, there had been something more between Pickevance and Alicia Hilton than they knew.

Just then George Elliott's mobile phone chirruped.

'Yes?' she spoke into the mouthpiece, then listened carefully.

After a moment she held the phone out to him.

'It's for you. William Reynolds. Tamworth police gave him this number. Needs to talk to you. Says it's urgent.'

Tallyforth took the phone from her.

'Mr Reynolds, how are you?' he asked. 'How can I help?'

He listened to the reply, nodding gravely to himself.

'You've been told by Her Majesty's Chief Inspector that

159

Æthelfleda High School has to be deemed as failing because of what happened to Hubert Stanton? Surely that can't be a reason for failing a school, sir! After all, that's got nothing to do with the quality of education offered there, has it?'

He listened again to Reynolds's thin voice, which sounded even more shrewish through the airwaves.

'Her Majesty's Chief Inspector is adamant you say,' he repeated. 'What's wrong with him? Is he off his trolley? I'm conducting a murder investigation here. And the chief suspect, Brian Pickevance, the headteacher of this school, has disappeared. We're trying to locate him quietly so as not to frighten him into doing something stupid. The last thing I need is his school being pilloried in the popular press. Can't you stop it?'

The reply was clearly negative.

'Then I'm going to have to go above your head, sir,' bellowed Tallyforth. 'Thank you for the information. No doubt you will hear more in the near future. Goodbye!'

He pressed the red button to terminate the call and handed the phone back to his sergeant.

'That's all we need,' he sighed.

But that wasn't all they got.

When they arrived back at Tamworth police station, there was a lengthy message from Superintendent 'Nobby' Clarke telling them that Peregrine Stevens's solicitor had complained about their harassment of his client, who was an upstanding member of the local community, respected by all and sundry for his good works in the town for over a quarter of a century. His client's reputation had been sullied by the implications of the line of questioning adopted by Detective Chief Inspector Tallyforth and Detective Sergeant Elliott and he demanded that they be suspended from duty pending a full inquiry.

'So what does our great leader do?' asked Tallyforth rhetorically. 'What does he do to protect his officers? Does he tell this solicitor to go hang himself? Does he tear the affidavit into a thousand little pieces and flush them down the toilet? Does he hell! What he does is give you and me forty-eight hours to sort out this murder or we'll be suspended. How's that for you, Elliott?'

She smiled bleakly. It didn't surprise her.

'The brotherhood, sir,' she said. 'Remember the curse?'

'Bugger that, Elliott,' he fumed. 'Come on, let's get back to Birmingham and have some decent food. Balti suit you?'

'Brilliant,' she answered.

SIXTEEN

They went to Adil's on Stony Lane in Balsall Heath, where almost every other building is a Balti house and where the Balti experience really began in England. Unlike some of the more recently-opened Balti restaurants in Birmingham and elsewhere in the West Midlands which had sought to go upmarket in their decor and ambience, Adil's retains its authentic original style with its long tables and glass tabletops, underneath which were the menus.

Tallyforth broke the top two poppadums on the pile that had been casually set in front of them by the swarthy, moustachioed waiter. He took a large piece and dipped it in the mint yoghurt sauce in the small silver bowl beside him on the table.

'So, Elliott,' he began, munching ruminatively on his poppadum. 'Proverbial chickens coming home to roost, I think. Stevens threatening us with harassment, Bowen and Hilton about to scratch each other's eyes out, Pickevance's school about to be declared a failing school with him still tooling round the country somewhere. If that lot doesn't produce a solution to Stanton's murder, I don't know what will.'

She was looking at the menu while nibbling on her piece of poppadum.

'Mm,' she replied.

A crowd of male students, all in black jeans and tee-shirts, entered Adil's noisily and sat down at a table near them, where they continued with their loud, joky conversation.

'Know what you're having? Starter?' Tallyforth asked.

'Think I'll have chicken tikka,' she said, glancing over the table at him. 'Then the vegetable balti.'

'I'm having a couple of samosas, then, I think, the special balti.'

They gave their order to the waiter, who scribbled it down on his notepad but made no attempt to engage them in any form of conversation. The fawning behaviour of waiters in posh restaurants is not on the menu at Adil's.

'And a naan,' added Tallyforth. 'For two.'

'What about Pugh?' she asked, *á propos* of nothing in particular. 'And de Courcy? Maybe Lashley even. Or Jon Mitchell. They were all there on the night in question. Are you including them in your list of suspects?'

He looked up at her. Was she teasing him? Or was she just being her usual methodical self? They were both aware that the endgame was near.

'Where the hell did you get that lot from?' he barked. 'You know we've not been looking at any of them. They're not in the frame at all.'

She smiled at his momentary bad temper. She was used to it, sometimes deliberately provoked it.

'Okay, so let's just talk about them. You've taught me never to discount any possibility until it's been thoroughly looked at. Well, we haven't looked at any of those people.'

'Because they have no motive,' he butted in.

'As far as we know,' she responded. 'But that doesn't mean we can automatically eliminate them. I mean, take de Courcy. We know he didn't like the way Pickevance had led the school into becoming Grant-maintained and we know he had huge political differences with Stevens. We also know that he has an obsession with this whole Offa business and experience tells us that obsessives can often be so blinkered that they only see what they want to see.'

Tallyforth smiled across at her. This was his meticulous sergeant doing what she did best, that is being meticulous.

'Not the type,' he said. 'You've seen him, haven't you? Definitely not the type.'

'Looks can be deceptive,' she replied. 'You taught me that. And those lives of quiet desperation you've often reminded me of are lived by people like de Courcy. Didn't he spend years caring for his first wife before she died? And then years as the only Liberal on the Borough Council? And all that time he's spent trying to preserve the memory of Offa! Don't you think he might have cause to be bitter?'

'Yes, bitterness I can see,' sighed Tallyforth, breaking off another slice of poppadum and dipping it into the sauce. 'But bitterness at life's injustices is not the same as a desire to kill. Where's the motive, George? Where's his motive?'

She blushed slightly. He rarely referred to her by her first name, normally preferring the formality of either title or last name. But she chose to ignore this lapse.

'I don't know that,' she answered, regaining her composure quickly and keeping the conversation along its proper lines. 'But remember it was de Courcy who sent us on that wild goose chase about the Mercian coins!'

'But only because of what Mitchell had told him,' he answered. 'And we know that Mitchell did it to wind him up. Thanks.'

The last comment was addressed to the waiter who placed his samosas and her chicken tikka on the table in front of them.

'You want a Stella?'

When she nodded, he poured them a glass each from one of the cans they had bought from the off licence just up Stony Lane. The group of students at the nearby table continued to be loud, which kept their own conversation appropriately inaudible.

'What about Mitchell then?' she asked between a mouthful of spicy chicken tikka. 'He was on the premises till quite late on the night. In fact, he was the last to leave, according to Lashley. He could have hidden himself somewhere in the school after his band had left, waited for the rest of the inspectors to leave, slipped into their room on some pretext and offered to make fresh coffee. If Stanton was preoccupied with writing his report, he might not have noticed anything untoward.'

'Stop right there,' said Tallyforth, holding up a hand to echo his words. 'You're probably right about the last bit. Whoever put the cyanide in the coffee probably came into the room in the way you've just described and was therefore certainly known to Stanton. And trusted by him. But what could Mitchell's motive have been? He wasn't threatened by the inspection. He had nothing to gain from Stanton's death. It's the same as de Courcy.'

'Maybe someone had found out about his pot-smoking? Maybe

questions had been asked about the fact that he was managing these four bands? Maybe he was making money out of them?'

'You're guessing, aren't you?' Tallyforth smiled. 'You know that Mitchell's a rogue but he's not a murderer. Besides, how would he have got access to the cyanide? You're forgetting that part of the equation.'

There was a pause. George Elliott speared a piece of tomato, dipped it in the yoghurt sauce, then raised it towards her lips.

'Okay then,' she began again. 'You're assuming that the cyanide came from the science labs. And we haven't checked out yet whether any is missing. But, if you're right, then what about Lashley the caretaker? He has keys to the whole building. And, remember, it was him that found the body. And it was him who said that he had ignored the light left on in the inspectors' room all night.'

'Motive again, George,' said Tallyforth, picking up the last crumbs of his samosas with his fingers. 'Yes, Lashley had the opportunity but what could he possibly hope to gain from killing Stanton?'

She chewed the last piece of chicken tikka thoughtfully and took a slurp of her beer. He had used her first name again. Was this some new stage in their relationship? She wondered again about his reasons for asking her to go with him to the Van Morrison concert in June. But she had to admit he was right. The three people they had just considered had to be discounted.

'Now Pugh is a different matter,' Tallyforth said, reaching for his beer. 'Alfred Pugh is a kettle of very different fish. We know that he has it in for Pickevance and he admits it. He believes he was unfairly sacked last year.'

'Made redundant,' George Elliott corrected.

'Same difference,' he continued. 'Oh, right, thanks.'

The waiter arrived with a large golden naan bread on the table between them, then quickly returned with their main dishes, served in the traditional black balti pans.

Tallyforth leaned forward and sniffed the strong aroma from his dish.

'Wonderful,' he said. 'Really looking forward to this. Haven't had a balti for ages. Must be at least a week!'

She laughingly tore off a hunk of naan and dipped it into her vegetable balti.

'So why would Pugh want Stanton dead?' she quizzed.

'Just consider,' he said. 'Pugh was sacked by Pickevance last summer. Pugh wants revenge. He finds out from Alicia Hilton about the missing money. He thinks he can bring that to the attention of the OFSTED inspection team, hence the fax to OFSTED in London and the letter to the *Tamworth Herald*.'

'So,' she interjected, 'why do anything else? Surely, if Stanton had found out that money was missing, that would have been enough to finish Pickevance, wouldn't it? Why would Pugh want Stanton dead? Surely he'd be better off alive!'

'Just possibly,' replied Tallyforth. 'But remember, desperate men do desperate things. Maybe he wasn't sure that Stanton had got the messages. Maybe he wanted....'

'Too many maybes,' she said. 'Why would Pugh murder Stanton?'

'To implicate Pickevance of course!' he crowed. 'Pugh knew about the missing money. He knew about the school's academic record and its attendance record. He knew that most of the staff were brassed off with the Bowen woman and her influence on Pickevance. He knew the two of them were having an affair. And he hoped that it would all burst out as a result of the inspection. What better way to ensure that Pickevance got nailed than by ensuring he got framed for murder?'

She paused from her eating to enjoy another drink.

'A bit far-fetched, isn't it?' she said at last. 'Why go to those lengths when the guy was going to be nailed anyway?'

'But Pugh didn't know that, did he?'

Tallyforth scraped a piece of naan along the side of his bowl to collect as much of the delicious mixture as he could.

'So who's your money on?' he queried.

'Pickevance,' she answered without hesitating.

'Not the women?' he asked.

'Pearl Bowen is loud and flash,' she began. 'But she's also open. That's her big problem really. Subtlety is not her middle name. And that's why she's antagonised so many of the staff at the school. That's probably why Pugh had it in for Pickevance. She no doubt was involved in the decision to make Pugh redundant. She may even have been the messenger that gave him the news. So he probably blames her. His vendetta against Pickevance owes its origins to Pearl Bowen. But she's hardly a murderer. I can see her blasting someone to metaphorical smithereens with her ferocity but nothing more than that. Besides, what possible motive could she have, to use your argument?'

Tallyforth laughed.

'She could be in cahoots with Pickevance,' he offered.

'I still don't think so. I think it's down to him on his own,' she said firmly. 'Anyway what about Alicia Hilton?'

'No! She's definitely involved with Pugh over the fax and the letter to the newspaper and she clearly resents the influence that the Bowen woman has on Pickevance, though we don't know what her relationship with him was beforehand. All we know is what she's told us about Pickevance's support for her after her husband left. But no-one's got her on or near the premises at the time in question. And she didn't have keys to the school from what Lashley says. If she is involved, it's only as an accessory because of what she's told Pugh. I still think he's hiding something.'

She glanced at him as he mopped the last of his chicken balti with the naan bread.

'But surely we've got to get hold of Pickevance to question him first,' she said. 'After all, he has done a runner in the middle of a murder investigation. That does look a trifle suspicious, doesn't it?'

The last bit was said with heavy sarcasm.

'True,' he replied. 'I wonder where the bugger is right now.'

Monday 29th April 1996. 8.05 p.m.

'Sarah? It's Brian. Look, I need to talk to you.'

'Where are you?'

'Never mind that. I'm not far away. Are the police still looking for me?'

'Yes, as far as I'm aware. But where are you?'

'I told you, I'm not far away. Are the police outside the house? Are they waiting for me there? I really do need to talk to you before I speak to them.'

'I don't think they're out there. I haven't seen anyone. Unless they're in an unmarked car.'

'Sarah, I've made a mess of a lot of things and I want to talk to you before I talk to that Chief Inspector Tallyforth. But not like this, not over the phone. If you're sure it's safe, I'll be with you in an hour.'

'Please take care, Brian. They think you murdered that Mr Stanton, you know, I'm sure they do.'

'Sarah, believe me, I didn't do it. I may have done a lot of stupid things but I did not kill Stanton. Why should I? What would I have to gain?'

'I just don't know anything any longer, Brian. Please take care.'

'See you in an hour.'

Monday 29th April 1996. 8.15 p.m.

'Pearl, it's Brian.'

'What the hell are you doing? Where are you?'

'Calm down, I'm all right. How are you?'

'Just about sane. No thanks to you, you bastard!'

'Is everything all right at school?'

'Jesus wept! Is that all you've got to think about? I've had Tallyforth in interrogating me and Alicia today, telling me that there's money missing from the school finances. I've had just about every newspaper in the land phoning up for information about the death of Stanton. I've had Norman de Courcy pestering me for extra money for his bloody Offa celebrations. And all the time I'm having to cover up for you, pretending that you're at home ill. What the hell is going on with you, Brian?'

'I just needed some time and space. To think things over. I meant what I said in that letter, Pearl. I haven't changed my mind on that. I'm staying with Sarah. I'm going to see her tonight.'

'Well, bully for you, Brian Pickevance! Back to your cosy little fireside, eh? Back to the woman you told me you'd never loved. Back to her whimpering, whining ways. Back to a screw every Friday night and never any other time. Back to the missionary position and no other. Sounds wonderful!'

'Pearl, don't.'

'Pearl, don't! You bastard, what's going to happen to me now. I can't carry on working here with you. So where do I go?'

168

'We need to talk about that.'

'Don't patronise me, you bastard! If you meant half of the things you said to me, you wouldn't try and treat me like middle management. What am I going to do, Brian?'

'I told you. I intend being back in school on Wednesday. I suggest you take the rest of the week off. We can meet up again next Monday to discuss everything. That will give everything time to settle down.'

'And what about the police? What about Stanton's murder? What about this missing money? How the hell are you going to let all that "settle down"?'

'I shall see Chief Inspector Tallyforth tomorrow and explain everything. Pearl, I have to go now. Please don't think too badly of me.'

Monday 29th April 1996. 8.30 p.m.

'Alicia? This is Brian. Brian Pickevance. How are you?'

'I'm very well, thank you.'

'Alicia, what's all this about money missing from the school finances?'

'I don't know anything about that, Mr Pickevance.'

'Alicia, why are you being formal with me? It's me. Brian. Remember?'

'I think it best if we maintain a professional relationship, Mr Pickevance.'

'Alicia, what is going on? After all we've been through together! I know you're still bitter about Pearl but that's over a year ago now. I thought we'd got through all that. Can't we behave like civilised human beings? Can't we be adult about these matters? Can't we still be friends?'

'It's easy for you, isn't it? You and your smooth talking. You think you can talk anyone round to your way of thinking, don't you? Well, it won't work with me any more.'

'Alicia, I'm sorry, I really am. I'm truly sorry that you got hurt. That wasn't what I intended. You knew that things weren't right between us. They hadn't been right for ages and you know that. There was no way we could have continued the way we were. And

169

you knew I couldn't leave Sarah.'

'But you were prepared to leave her for Pearl Bowen, weren't you? That's why you've run away, isn't it? Because you can't face reality, can you? You live in a fantasy world, you do. A world where everything and everyone bows down to your wishes. The hero headmaster with his nice little wife and his nice little mistress. Well, let me tell you, such a world doesn't exist. Too many people, including Sarah and myself, have given in to you and let you live in that silly little fantasy world but it's falling apart now, isn't it? And you don't know how to cope, do you?'

'Alicia, what is all this?'

'You know what I'm saying. You know it's true. You just don't want to face up to it.'

'Alicia, what about this missing money?'

'I don't know anything about that. Mr Pickevance.'

'Alicia!'

'I'm sorry. I have to go now. Goodbye.'

'Alicia!'

Monday April 1996. 9.00 p.m.

They were getting into Tallyforth's Range Rover when the police radio came crackling through with a message for Tallyforth.

Three phone calls from Pickevance had been intercepted.

SEVENTEEN

The Tuesday morning broke fair and sunny. George Elliott, dressed in a short denim skirt and a cream tee-shirt, sat on the desk in the office they had been given. She had risen early to get to the Tamworth police station in order to hear the tapes of the tapped phone calls. For once she had beaten Tallyforth.

She was replaying the third phone call, the one to Alicia Hilton, for the fourth time. She did not hear Tallyforth's entry to the room because of the headphones she was wearing to listen to the tapes.

He tapped her on the shoulder to get her attention and she whipped the headphones off.

'Sir, you need to listen to these. They're dynamite,' she said, indicating the tapes and the tape recorder.

Tallyforth looked down at the equipment and nodded.

'Do we know where the calls were made from?' he asked.

'Yes, apparently they were from three different phone boxes, adjacent to each other, outside Burton-on-Trent railway station. That's why it was difficult to trace him quickly enough. Just as a car was on the way to pick him up, he was making his second call and the driver was told to wait. By the time the second trace had been made and the driver alerted, Pickevance was phoning Alicia Hilton. And again there was a delay. It took some dimwit several minutes to realise that the three phone calls were made from adjacent phone boxes and by that time the bird had flown,' she explained.

Tallyforth picked up the transcripts of the tapes and took them to his desk, where he sat down and began to browse.

'Seems like he was heading for home,' he said, looking up from his reading, 'going to see his wife. Didn't anyone try there?'

171

She pulled a chair up opposite him.

'Must have changed his mind,' she said. 'He never made it.'

'Any reason?' he queried. 'Anybody spoken to Sarah Pickevance yet?'

'No. Everyone's waiting for you. I thought you'd want to speak to Alicia Hilton.'

'Why?'

'You really need to listen to their conversation. You need to hear the tone in her voice, not just read the words on the page. You'll hear the bitterness for yourself. And her denial of knowing anything about the missing money. She's obviously playing some kind of game.'

Tallyforth looked across at her.

'Okay, give me the tape and the machine.'

George Elliott reached behind her for the equipment and passed it to him. Tallyforth donned the headphones and pressed the play button.

As he was listening, the phone suddenly rang. Tallyforth motioned to George Elliott to answer it. She did so.

'Yes, this is Detective Sergeant Elliott. No, Detective Chief Inspector Tallyforth is busy at present. Can I help?' she said into the mouthpiece.

There was a pause as she listened. Her eyes initially opened wide, as she took in what she was being told, then narrowed.

'Where is she now?' she asked.

The answer was brief this time.

'And is she all right? Is there any news yet?'

Tallyforth had realised from the look on George Elliott's face that there was something wrong. He took the headphones off and questioned her with his eyes. She waved him away.

'Okay, we're on our way,' she said into the phone. 'Keep us posted about her condition. I'll get someone from here to the hospital as quickly as possible.'

She put the phone down and sighed.

'It's Pearl Bowen,' she began by way of explanation. 'She's been found collapsed in the head's office at the school. Been taken to the General Hospital. And there was a pot of fresh coffee in her office.'

172

'Still alive?' Tallyforth asked, rising from his seat.

'Apparently. Seems she'd come in early and was working in Pickevance's office. Was found by guess who? Alicia Hilton. Claims she had called in for some papers she needed. Bit dodgy, don't you think?'

'Go on.'

'Well, it's obvious, isn't it? What better way of covering up for yourself than being the one responsible for the discovery?'

'What are you saying, Elliott?' Tallyforth asked in exasperation.

'I bet that wasn't the first time that she'd been into the office. I bet she'd had an opportunity to get into the office beforehand, that she offered to make the coffee, and that she laced it with something. Probably cyanide again.'

'You're jumping to conclusions, aren't you?' he said.

'Have you heard that tape?' she riposted.

'Yes, but....'

'Then I think we know our murderer.'

'What about Pickevance? You had him in the frame last night. Listen, I hear what you're saying. And I accept there's something wrong about that woman. But I'm not yet convinced. There's too many other loose threads. We really need to speak to Pickevance. Why the hell did those telephone buggers cock it up?'

'Sir, I've said we'll be at the school. Shall we go? And we need to get a bobby to the hospital.'

'Yeah, okay. You go. I need to sort out things with Stevens's solicitor and try to get this failing school business stopped. We need to get Superintendent Clarke working for us for once rather than dumping problems on us. I'm going back to Birmingham to see him. Talk to the Hilton woman but be careful. Remember we don't have any evidence yet. You're speculating that Pearl Bowen has been poisoned and that the poison was cyanide. We need to know about that before we press any harder. If I hear anything here, I'll let you know. Keep your mobile on. And while you're there, see if you can get the poisons in the science labs. checked. See if there's anything missing. Especially cyanide. If we can trace that, at least we can begin to feel a bit more confident.'

'Okay, see you shortly. Good luck with 'Nobby' Clarke.'

Unlike just about every office that Tallyforth had ever worked from or in, Superintendent Albert 'Nobby' Clarke's office was immaculately tidy. His desk was empty apart from a telephone. In front of that desk the small coffee table, which he kept together with the two leather armchairs for more informal discussions, was similarly uncluttered apart from a small potted busy lizzie. The only decoration in the austerely-furbished room was a reproduction of a Paul Klee cubist painting, whose stark lines seemed to echo the mood of the rest of the office. The painting was on the wall behind the desk at which Clarke was sitting, his close-cropped silver hair and his sharply-creased white shirt complementing the room's coldness.

'Sit down, Tallyforth,' ordered Clarke, as his chief inspector appeared at the door. 'I've been reading your notes on this school murder case. Odd business.'

This was typical of Clarke, whom no-one could ever accuse of having been educated at a charm school and who appeared never to have learned the social niceties of small talk.

'Yes,' replied Tallyforth, selecting one of the leather armchairs and sitting down. He was used to the power-games that Clarke enjoyed playing, had learned to cope with them and at times to play them to his own advantage. So he refused to be cowed by the inferior physical position he had been deliberately placed in, with Clarke above him behind his spartan desk.

'Are you close to a result?' pressed Clarke. 'That headteacher's gone missing, hasn't he? Any sign yet?'

'Not yet, sir, no,' replied Tallyforth. 'We were close to him last night. Phone intercepts. But one of the local peelers fouled up. But we'll get him soon, sir. Trust me.'

'And is he the solution, Tallyforth?' queried Clarke, swivelling lightly in his chair and tapping lightly on his desk.

'We're not convinced, sir,' said Tallyforth, watching Clarke's face carefully for some clue as to his state of mind. 'There are others who could be in the frame. But we need to talk to Pickevance first. He's certainly a key player.'

'And what about Perry Stevens?' Clarke's voice became slightly more steely in a way that would have been imperceptible to anyone who didn't know him well but which was immediately picked up by Tallyforth, who crossed his legs and coughed lightly.

'Sir?' he said, playing for a little time, although he had known this was coming, had considered his various options and had decided which to take. But caution had long taught him to make one final mental check before committing himself in speech.

'This business about you supposedly harassing him over money missing from the school's accounts. What did you say to him, Tallyforth? You're tangling with someone who is not without political influence, you know.'

Tallyforth watched his chief's face with an unperturbed expression.

'Leader of the depleted Conservative group on Tamworth Borough Council, sir! Not really a big fish, is he?' he pushed back at Clarke.

'Tallyforth,' Clarke began again quietly, the steely tone re-entering, 'Perry Stevens was a courtier of Margaret Thatcher, I understand. It is a mistake to believe that the only people she dealt with were parliamentary members. She knew that her appeal was as much to the knights of Middle England as to the sycophants in parliament who subsequently brought about her downfall. Perry Stevens is in touch with grass-roots opinion in the country and was one of those knights she spoke to regularly to gather opinion. It's a little-known feature of her reign.'

'May I ask how you know so much about him, sir?' queried Tallyforth, feigning insouciance.

Was there just the tiniest shattering of ice? Was that tiny red discoloration on Clarke's left cheek an indication of blushing embarrassment?

'Tallyforth, it is part of my role as Chief Superintendent to be politically alert. Although I no longer work at the operational level, police work does not only include murder investigations, you know. There are other elements of public life we have to concern ourselves with,' came the reply. And the red spot had disappeared before Clarke had finished speaking. 'Now, did you harass Stevens?'

'No, sir,' explained Tallyforth. 'We merely asked him if he was aware of a large discrepancy in the school accounts which had been audited by one of his partners and passed as okay. He immediately became very defensive and threatened us with his lawyers. We still haven't got a full answer from him.'

'Tallyforth, I have in the top drawer of my desk a sworn affidavit from Perry Stevens to state that he knows nothing about any alleged missing money from the school accounts and that his partner Richard Ferris audited the school's accounts in a complete and proper way and found no evidence of any malpractice. Stevens's lawyer also tells me that his client is taking advice as to whether he has grounds for suing the police force over wrongful accusations. I am instructed that I will hear further. What have you got to say to that, Tallyforth?'

Tallyforth leaned forward slightly and smiled.

'I think you might ask him about his involvement in seeking to sell part of the Æthelfleda High School's playing field to McDonald's for a drive-in restaurant before he issues any writ against us,' he countered. 'And, while we're on the subject of harassment, is there any chance of you using your influence to get the Chief Inspector of Schools to delay his decision to announce that Æthelfleda High is a failing school. We need to find Pickevance and we don't want him finding that out or he'll run even further away!'

Clarke blanched slightly, but this time the change in his expression and his manner was evident.

'I'm not with you, Tallyforth,' he said, sitting forward and clasping his hands together. 'Where did you get this business about selling playing fields off? And what's all this about the Chief Inspector of Schools?'

Tallyforth told him about de Courcy's accusation and about the news from William Reynolds about HMCI's decision to pronounce Æthelfleda High School a failing school.

'I'll see what I can do about the latter,' said Clarke. 'I don't see why the announcement could not be delayed a few days. Certainly until after you've found this Pickevance character. It seems an odd reason to fail a school anyway, doesn't it? But I'll ask the Chief Constable to intervene.'

'Thank you, sir, that would be very helpful, replied Tallyforth, beginning to get up from his seat. 'And Stevens? Sleaze is not a stranger to the Conservatives, you know, sir!'

Clarke looked at him through narrowed eyes.

'I think you'd better leave that with me as well, Tallyforth,' he said bleakly. 'But get it sorted, man. Find this Pickevance and get him put away, if it was him. And if it wasn't, then whoever. But a result, Tallyforth. A result.'

'Yes, sir,' came the reply, thrown over Tallyforth's shoulder as he headed towards the door.

By the time Tallyforth reached Æthelfleda High School later that morning and caught up with George Elliott, news had already been received from the General Hospital that Pearl Bowen was all right. She had had her stomach pumped and was being kept in overnight for observation, but there was no expectation of any complication. The coffee pot and its contents had been sent off to Jake Clifford at the forensic laboratory but there had been no result as yet.

'What's the mood like?' asked Tallyforth.

They were sitting in the boardroom where a few days previously Hubert Stanton's body had been discovered. Each was munching an apple which Tallyforth had collected from the school's dining room as he arrived.

'Grim,' George Elliott replied. 'None of them liked the woman but there's a sense of foreboding about the place. Nobody knows quite what to do. There isn't another deputy head any longer after last summer's cuts so Norman de Courcy, as the senior member of staff, is looking after things until they know what's what.'

'Governors? Stevens?' Tallyforth queried.

'De Courcy's spoken to him, I gather.'

'The Hilton woman?'

'I've taken a statement from her about how she found Pearl Bowen and what she did. She claims she only saw her first thing this morning as she arrived and hadn't been near the head's office since. Till she went in with some papers and found her slumped over the desk. Just like Stanton.'

'D'you believe her?'

'It's hard to tell,' she sighed. 'You know I've felt all along that it was Pickevance who poisoned Stanton. Until I heard that telephone intercept this morning. That changed my view of Alicia Hilton. And I'm not sure now. She plays this prim and proper act to perfection so it's difficult to pick up on any emotion underlying that appearance. If she is guilty, she's bloody good at concealing it.'

Tallyforth stood up and walked across the room.

'Did you get anywhere with the science labs? Any missing poisons?'

'Yes,' she replied. 'Small bottle of cyanide missing, as suspected.'

'No news of when, I suppose?' he asked.

'No, afraid not. The head of science Pat Field hadn't checked since last week. No reason to, she said. Which is fair enough. We should have done that last week.'

'Okay, so we know where the cyanide came from, which means that we were right about it being an inside job. Anything about locks being tampered with or broken?'

'No. Whoever took the cyanide had a key.'

'And we know that the only people with keys were Pickevance, Lashley and the Field woman, yes?'

'That's right, sir.'

'Elliott, I think we need to talk to Lashley again. I have a feeling there's something he's not telling us. Or maybe something we're not asking him. Yet.'

'Shall I fetch him?' she asked.

'Just ring through. He won't be far away.'

Gideon Lashley's curly ginger hair kept nodding in time with his face as he listened to what Tallyforth was saying.

'Oh ah, Inspector, That's roight what I towld the sergeant 'ere the uther day. The ownly wuns what 'as master kays am the 'eadtaicher Mr Pickevance, the deputy 'ead Mrs Bowen, an' me,' he began.

'You never mentioned Ms. Bowen to me,' interrupted George Elliott sharply. 'You only told me about Pickevance and yourself having master keys.'

Gideon Lashley jangled his bunch of keys a little nervously. He was never comfortable with powerful women.

'Day oi? Well, oi meant to,' he said, stroking the left arm of his creased boiler suit. 'Sorry abaht that, Inspector.'

Tallyforth caught George Elliott's eye. He had picked up Lashley's awkwardness at her questioning.

'Now what about keys to other parts of the building,' he asked in a gentler tone, seeking to encourage Lashley's co-operation. 'Who would have had keys for particular buildings?'

Lashley's hand moved off his boiler suit and rested on his knee.

'Well, Mrs Field 'as kays for all the science block, loik oi've towld yow,' he began again, mollified now to be talking to another male. 'An' Mrs 'Adlington 'as kays fer the changing rooms an' the sports 'all.'

'Isn't that next to the science area?' asked Tallyforth.

'Oh ah,' replied Gideon Lashley. 'But they 'ay cunnected in enny way. Just boy a corridor.'

Just then there was a commotion in the corridor outside the boardroom. Someone was rushing along the corridor, calling out something indistinguishable but the sound of panic was obvious.

The door burst open and Norman de Courcy, breathless from having run across from the main block, stood there, leaning against the side of the door and holding on to its handle.

'Chief Inspector, you'd better come quickly,' he wheezed, gasping for breath. 'Something terrible's happened.'

'Tallyforth and George Elliott were already on their feet and moving towards him. Gideon Lashley too rose and stared in bewilderment at the small, bow-tied, bald-headed figure of the head of history whose chest heaved as he struggled for breath.

'What is it, Mr de Courcy,' asked Tallyforth. 'What's happened?'

De Courcy gulped for fresh air.

'It's Alicia,' he exhaled. 'Mrs Hilton. She's collapsed. I think she's been poisoned too!'

EIGHTEEN

By the time they had got across to the main school building and reached the finance director's office, Alicia Hilton had revived somewhat and, though she wasn't able to make coherent sense, she was able to sit up and her eyes were flickering.

Denise Hadlington, the girls' physical education teacher who was a qualified first-aider, was standing beside her holding a small bottle of smelling salts which she had obviously used to revive Alicia Hilton. Her white blouse had been unbottoned at the neck and her linen jacket was draped over a chair.

Tallyforth, George Elliott and Norman de Courcy stood in the doorway, breathing heavily from running between buildings as they looked at the scene before them.

Tallyforth's eyes scanned the room. Nothing unusual. A desk, dominated by a computer monitor, filing cabinets, telephone, charts pinned to the walls. But no coffee-making device.

'Has she said anything?' he asked aloud.

Denise Hadlington looked round at him.

'Nothing that makes any sense,' she replied. 'Just moaning and groaning. I've phoned for an ambulance. She needs a proper examination and treatment.'

'Do we know if she was on any medication?' enquired George Elliott. 'Or if she'd drunk anything in the last hour or so? Coffee? Tea?'

'Don't know anything about medication,' replied Denise Hadlington. 'You could try her handbag, I suppose.'

She nodded at the floor beside her.

George Elliott took two steps towards the desk, lifted the handbag from the floor, looked inside and shook her head.

180

'She had a cup of tea with me after lunch,' interjected Norman de Courcy. 'There was some paperwork she needed to go through with me.'

'And you're okay, sir?' asked Tallyforth.

'Apart from being rather breathless, yes,' de Courcy answered. 'Why?'

'It's just that Hubert Stanton died after drinking coffee that had been laced with cyanide, Pearl Bowen had been drinking coffee before she collapsed, and now Alicia Hilton. And there's a small bottle of cyanide apparently gone missing from the science labs,' explained Tallyforth, guiding Norman de Courcy out of the finance office. 'Mind if I use your phone, sir? I need to contact the forensic laboratory.'

'Of course, Chief Inspector, of course,' de Courcy said, ushering Tallyforth in the direction of the headteacher's office. 'But what about Mrs Hilton?'

'When the paramedics arrive, tell them to get her to the General Hospital quickly and tell them about Pearl Bowen. At least that will give the doctors somewhere to start. Even though it was tea and even though you drank it too.'

Tallyforth marched briskly into the headteacher's office where a few days previously he had first interviewed the missing Brian Pickevance. Norman de Courcy returned to the stricken Alicia Hilton.

He was swivelling in Pickevance's black executive chair, his brow knitted in concentration, when George Elliott found him.

She closed the door behind her.

'Any news of Pearl Bowen?' she asked.

'Yes, it was cyanide in the coffee. Clifford's confirmed it. Fortunately, it was only a small dose and they got her to the hospital quickly enough for the medics to clear her stomach,' he answered. 'She was lucky.'

George Elliott looked at him.

'Sir, I don't get all of this. Who is doing all this poisoning?'

'You mean you don't suspect Alicia Hilton any more?' he queried with a slight touch of irony, for he felt she had fallen rather quickly for that solution.

'How could it be? She's a victim herself, isn't he?'

'Possibly,' he said. 'Though her collapse may not be connected. Remember that de Courcy shared a pot of tea with her and he's okay. You'd better search that office of hers after she's gone. See if there's any evidence of anything she might have taken.'

'You mean like a small bottle of cyanide?'

'It's just possible she has taken some herself to divert suspicion.'

George Elliott gave him a quizzical look.

'Bit far-fetched, isn't it, sir? How would she know she'd be found in time?'

Tallyforth looked up at her exasperatedly and pointed at the reproduction of Kipling's 'If' that Pickevance had framed on his office wall.

'Remember the unforgiving minute, Elliott. Just organise the search. We've got to stop all this. And at once. It's getting out of hand.'

'Yessir.'

She almost felt like saluting. She hated it when he got in one of his bossy moods. It meant he really was as confused as she was.

'I demand to see Chief Inspector Tallyforth.'

Perry Stevens's smooth voice had been transformed by events. He was now in Brigade of Guards mode, using his officer's voice which demanded instant obedience.

'I'm afraid he's not available at present, sir,' said George Elliott.

They were in the reception area to the school, where she had been summoned by the receptionist on Perry Stevens's arrival.

'What do you mean not available?' Stevens harrumphed. 'He's on the premises, isn't he? I demand to see him. At once, Sergeant. At once.'

'Mr Stevens, I understand you've been informed about Pearl Bowen being taken to the General Hospital with suspected poisoning,' George Elliott began, seeking to emolliate him as they stood facing each other, surrounded by display boards filled with garish examples of children's painting. 'Since then there has been another incident. Mrs Hilton has been found in a collapsed state. She has just been taken to the General Hospital for tests. I'm afraid

182

that Chief Inspector Tallyforth is tied up with our investigation into these matters. It seems possible, maybe even probable, that they are connected to the poisoning of Hubert Stanton, the Registered Inspector.'

Perry Stevens sat back quickly on one of the plastic chairs in the reception area and patted his chest.

'Good grief, Sergeant, what is going on? Isn't it about time you policemen caught whoever is behind all of this nonsense, rather than wasting your time making dangerous and false allegations about my firm's complicity in some underhand financial dealings?' he said. 'And where on earth is Brian Pickevance? I was told he was ill. Is he too ill to be fetched in here to help sort this out? We can't leave that dinosaur de Courcy in charge here. Where is Pickevance?'

George Elliott blanched. Their strategy of keeping news about Pickevance's disappearance quiet was beginning to backfire on them. But she couldn't say anything without Tallyforth's say-so. And he'd made it quite clear, when the receptionist had phoned through to tell them about Perry Stevens's arrival, that he didn't want to see him.

'Sir, we are doing everything in our power to resolve all of this,' she answered, then added, lying, 'and Chief Inspector Tallyforth is trying to contact Mr Pickevance at this moment. That's why he can't see you just at present.'

'Good,' said Perry Stevens, stretching out his legs and checking the creases on his trousers. 'Then tell him I want to speak to Pickevance as soon as possible. And tell him that I've been in touch with his Chief Superintendent. I shall wait here in the meantime. But I have no intention of waiting long. I have a business to run and there's a Council Meeting this evening. I will not be kept longer than is necessary. Is that clear, Sergeant?'

She decided not to tackle him. After all, she had achieved what she had set out to achieve, which was to keep him out of Tallyforth's way for a short period.

'I'll inform my chief that you're here,' she said and nodded in his direction as she turned to walk down the corridor back towards the headteacher's office where Tallyforth still sat.

But Tallyforth was not alone as George Elliott re-entered the room. She recognised the short hair and the green track suit of the figure whose back was turned towards her. Tallyforth motioned to her to wait and listen.

'So you locked up the changing rooms and the sports hall entrance at about seven o'clock last Thursday, is that right?' he asked, swivelling slightly in the chair.

The auburn-haired Denise Hadlington, who stood opposite him on the other side of Pickevance's desk, nodded.

'Yes, it would have been about seven. The Under-fifteens had a match, which we won, against a school in Lichfield. I dropped some off them off on the way home but some live close to the school, so they came back with me and helped me unload the kit into the changing rooms. Then we all left about the same time,' she said.

Tallyforth paused and doodled on a piece of paper he had in front of him on the desk.

'And you have your own set of keys?' he asked.

'To the changing rooms, yes. And the sports hall.'

She flourished the set of keys in front of her.

'And you keep those with you?' he persisted. 'I mean, you take them home with you?'

'Yes,' she replied, looking round at George Elliott to see what she was doing.

George Elliott half-smiled back at her.

'And these are only keys to the sports hall and the changing rooms?' he tried again.

'Yes,' she said, turning back to face Tallyforth. 'Well, there's one to the corridor outside the sports hall as well.'

Tallyforth's eyes narrowed.

'Would that be the corridor that's linked to the science laboratories?' he asked.

'Yeah, that's right,' came the response. 'But I never use that. It was just on the set that Alf gave me. Alf Pugh. Left last year. Used to be head of boys' P.E. and Year 11. He had a set as well. Though I expect he'll have given his in when he left.'

Tallyforth smiled slightly but meaningfully at George Elliott, who had sat down on one of the armchairs at the side of the room.

'Could we just borrow those keys?' he asked, holding out his hand and taking then from her before she had chance to say no. 'Sergeant, would you go with Miss Hadlington and let her show you where each of these keys fits? I think we may be close to the answer to one part of this conundrum.'

As George Elliott got up to take the proffered keys from him and to accompany Denise Hadlington towards the sports hall area, the telephone suddenly rang. Tallyforth picked up the receiver, as the two women froze in mid-stride on their way to the door.

'Yes, yes, this is Chief Inspector Tallyforth. What can you tell me?'

He listened to the lengthy reply in silence, nodding his head occasionally and making an odd note on the paper in front of him.

'Thank you very much,' he said into the mouthpiece. 'Yes, I'll be in touch shortly.'

He put the phone back on its cradle.

'That was the General Hospital,' he announced. 'Mrs Hilton is all right. And she was poisoned. But it was paracetamol, not cyanide. Probably an overdose.'

Denise Hadlington looked questioningly at George Elliott, who in turn looked knowingly at Tallyforth.

'Jigsaw beginning to fit, sir?' she asked with a hint of a smile.

'I think so, Sergeant,' he said, sitting back and turning in the chair to stare out of the window. 'I think so indeed. You can let Mr Stevens know I'll see him now, while you're on your way.'

By five o'clock that Tuesday afternoon Tallyforth had had enough of Æthelfleda High School and its denizens. He had listened patiently to Perry Stevens's protestations, explanations and denunciations, which had included a lengthy explanation of the code of conduct of the Chartered Accountants' Association, an equally lengthy disquisition on the ethics required of someone involved in public life in the political sense accompanied by a listing of all his good works on behalf of the people of Tamworth, and had ended with details of his one-time service as Chairman of the Staffordshire Police Federation and as a Justice of the Peace. It would have been churlish for Tallyforth to have pointed out to him that such activity did not preclude Stevens from the possibility of corruption, indeed that the history of the world was full of examples of so-called pillars of the establishment who had fallen foul of the law.

But Tallyforth had desisted, because he was inwardly satisfied that the conclusion to their enquiries into the murder of Registered Inspector Hubert Stanton was near. And, furthermore, that Perry Stevens, though he might not be as scrupulously honest and upright as he was protesting, was not responsible nor even involved.

Tallyforth had also had to put up with the bleating of Norman de Courcy, whose demeanour had changed remarkably since he had been put in temporary charge of the school. Would Pearl Bowen be back soon? Could he phone Brian Pickevance about some timetable matter? What about sorting out the payment of salaries at the end of April? How could it be done? Who would do it now Alicia Hilton too was in hospital?

And finally Gideon Lashley had been to see him to complain that they had run out of loo paper for the school toilets and he needed to order some more but Mrs Hilton wasn't there to do it and unless something was done about it quickly they'd be in a right mess by the middle of the following week.

Tallyforth had been tempted to respond with a salacious comment but again desisted. His mood was still upbeat.

George Elliott walked beside him across the puddled school car park to where their two cars were parked. There had been a heavy rain storm just after lunch but it was not raining at that moment. She had already passed on to him the information he had expected about the keys.

'So, George,' he said with almost a tone of exultation. 'What's it to be tonight then? Balti? Pasta? Or can I treat you to a Chinese in town?'

'It's not sorted yet,' she replied, realising his good mood and his use again of her forename. 'We haven't arrested anyone yet. And Pickevance is still missing.'

Tallyforth scarcely broke his stride but smiled at her.

'But it will be soon,' he said. 'Sorted. By this evening. Mark my words.'

And as they reached their cars, another car swished through the school gates and into the car park. Seeing them, its driver pulled alongside and drew to a halt.

It was a white B.M.W. coupé

'Good afternoon, Chief Inspector. Afternoon, Sergeant.'

Brian Pickevance leaned out of the window, his curly hair and moustache looking greyer than when they had seen him last. He looked at them through his horn-rimmed glasses. His wife Sarah sat disconsolately next to him.

'I think we have a lot to talk about,' he said. 'Shall I follow you to the police station? Or do you want to talk here?'

Tallyforth's smile was forced. For this was the person whom they had been hunting for three days, who held the answers to a lot of questions, who one way or another was responsible for the murder of Hubert Stanton. Yes, they had a lot to talk about.

'I think the station would be best, sir,' he said grimly. 'Sergeant Elliott will go with you, if you don't mind.'

'Chief Inspector,' smiled Pickevance, 'I've returned to clear the air. I'm not about to disappear again, believe me.'

'Nevertheless, sir,' said Tallyforth. 'Just to be certain.'

And he ushered George Elliott into the back of the B.M.W. and climbed into his own Range Rover.

The tired-looking spider plants still drooped over the filing cabinets in the office in Tamworth Police Station that had become their base. Tallyforth moved the chairs in the room around so that he and George Elliott were sitting on the opposite side of the table from Brian Pickevance, who gazed at them almost in bemusement as they prepared to hear his story. He had wanted his wife Sarah to be present but Tallyforth had forbidden that, even though Pickevance had assured them that he had told her everything already.

Tallyforth, having got himself comfortably seated, looked across at the errant headteacher. Was this the end of the trail? Would he confess to it all?

'Mr Pickevance, may I remind you that you are not under arrest and that you are here quite voluntarily to help us with our enquiries?' he began. 'Perhaps you'd like to begin by explaining

187

where you have been for these past three days and quite why you disappeared at a time when you knew that the police were conducting an enquiry into the murder of Hubert Stanton, the OFSTED Registered Inspector who had been leading the inspection of your school.'

Pickevance looked down at his knees, re-arranged his glasses on the bridge of his nose, then looked back at Tallyforth.

'Chief Inspector, I have been under intense pressure for some time now,' he began. 'I guess that what has happened to me in the past few days is the equivalent of a mental breakdown. Until this morning, I just was not able to function properly. My mind was seething with the enormity of everything and I just didn't seem to be able to find a way through it all. I was like a fly caught in the middle of an enormous spider's web. I couldn't escape. The more I struggled in my mind, the more I seemed to become entangled in the mess I found myself in.'

'So what made you come to see us?' asked Tallyforth.

'Sarah,' Pickevance replied immediately. 'I finally managed to get home to Sarah and she made me come to see you. She thinks I'm mentally ill and need help but she said I needed to talk to you first. In order to sort everything out.'

Tallyforth sat back, saying nothing but watching like a hawk.

'Let me begin with where I have been for the past few days,' continued Pickevance. 'I have been staying in a guest house in Stamford. It's where my family come from, though my parents are both dead now and I was an only child. I felt this desperate need to get back to where I came from, where I was born and brought up, where my roots were if you like. I thought somehow there I would find a way of dealing with all these conflicting emotions that were racing through my body.'

Tallyforth caught George Elliott's glance out of the corner of his eye. He knew she was registering that the Stamford sighting had been accurate after all.

'Have you been in Stamford all that time?' queried George Elliott.

'Most of it, yes, Sergeant,' he answered. 'Well, generally, yes. Though I have driven around a bit. I find driving sometimes clears my head, though it didn't help on this occasion. And I tried to come home on a couple of occasions. In fact, I got as far as Burton-

188

on-Trent last night but I just couldn't get any further. I turned round and went back to Stamford. I still wasn't ready to face up to everything, I suppose.'

There was a silence which lasted for several seconds. Pickevance's eyes had moved back to his knees. Tallyforth and George Elliott waited.

'Then this morning, when I woke up, the fog that had seemed to surround me and stop me acting began gradually to clear,' Pickevance began again. 'It was as if the spider's web had been slackened if not quite broken. I phoned Sarah again and she told me I had to come back and talk. And I did. Hard as it was, I told her everything. And she's being totally loyal. But she made me come and see you and tell you as well. Because there's still a lot of confusion and there's still a lot of things I don't fully understand, though I'm beginning to see how and why what has happened has done so.'

He paused again and looked down at his knees. Clearly it was requiring a huge effort for him to do what he was doing. Perhaps his wife was right, thought George Elliott. Perhaps he was disturbed and mentally ill. He certainly wasn't the same person that they had first met at Æthelfleda High School on the Friday morning of the previous week.

'Would you like a drink?' asked Tallyforth, concerned that Pickevance was going to literally dry up. 'Tea? Coffee? Water?'

'No, I'm fine,' answered Pickevance, raising his head again. 'It's just..... No, really, I'm fine. Where was I?'

'You were telling us that your head began to clear this morning and that you drove back home,' prompted George Elliott.

'Yes, yes,' he said. Every word was costing him now, they could see. 'Chief Inspector, I have been the most God-awful fool. I married a wonderful woman who has given me four wonderful children and who has given me total support in my professional career. And I have broken my marriage vows. Not just once but twice. Are you married, Chief Inspector?'

He spoke as if George Elliott was not in the room. Tallyforth's mind filled with the days of his own marital break-up - the lying, the accusations, the recriminations, the pain. George Elliott looked from one face to the other of these two middle-aged men reflecting on the failures in their marriages.

'I was.'

There was another lengthy silence. George Elliott could almost trace the course of the invisible tears that were running down their faces.

'Is this about Pearl Bowen?' she asked, conscious of the silence but also of the need to shift things on.

'Yes,' Pickevance replied, looking now in her direction. 'You've spoken with her, I take it, Sergeant. The best deputy I've ever had. Much better than I was at the job. She'll be a superb head one day, mark my words.'

'But that's not what we're talking about, is it, sir?' she reminded him gently.

Pickevance slumped again.

'No, you're right, Sergeant, it's not,' he said.

'You were having an affair with her, weren't you? And you were planning to leave your wife to live with Pearl Bowen, weren't you, sir?' she asked.

'How did you....? Oh, I suppose Pearl told you,' he began again, his eyes cast down. 'Yes, it's true. Pearl and I had to spend a lot of time together professionally. She's a very attractive woman. Very. And she was keen to develop her professional career and to improve the school. She used to push me to attend all these conferences. And we became closer because of the time we spent away from home. And inevitably.....'

His voice tailed off.

'You said twice,' interjected Tallyforth, sitting up at the table and resting his chin on his hands. 'You said you broke your vows twice. Who would that be?'

Pickevance's face turned pale. He took off his glasses, fidgeted in his seat, put his glasses back on again.

'Don't you know, Chief Inspector?' he said at length. 'I suspect that's what all this is about, don't you?'

'You mean Alicia Hilton?' asked Tallyforth.

Pickevance nodded.

'After her husband left her, Alicia became a close family friend,' he explained. 'She used to bring the children round to our place at weekends. Then one weekend her car wouldn't start, so I fetched

190

the children then went back to try to repair it. It was the starter motor. Anyway I got oil all over my arms, had to have a shower and then.... We managed it for over two years. But then she wanted me to leave Sarah and I wouldn't. So I ended it. I don't think she ever forgave me.'

'But you were prepared to leave your wife for Pearl Bowen?' interjected George Elliott.

He looked at her. It was a look which conveyed the conflict that he had been going through in his mind for the past few days if not weeks.

'I thought I was,' he said. 'But I've come to realise these last few days that I wanted to stay with Sarah. And she's agreed to stand by me. Whatever happens now.'

'Did you put cyanide in Stanton's coffee?' asked Tallyforth suddenly.

'No, Chief Inspector, I didn't,' Pickevance replied quietly.

'But you knew your school was going to get a poor report. And you knew that there would be criticisms of the school's management, didn't you?'

'Yes,' he answered, still in a quiet tone. 'Hubert Stanton had informed me on the Thursday afternoon of the likely outcome of the inspection.'

'And that he knew of your affair with Pearl Bowen?' asked Tallyforth.

'Yes.'

'And about the fifty thousand pounds missing from the school's finances?'

'No! He never mentioned that. And I know nothing about that. Believe me, Chief Inspector, I was not aware that any money was missing. It certainly wasn't on Wednesday of last week when I last looked.'

His voice was becoming stronger now as the details of the previous week came back to him.

'You are a chemist by training, Mr Pickevance?' queried Tallyforth.

'Yes.'

'So you would have been aware of the effects of cyanide?'

'Chief Inspector, my hands are clean,' said Pickevance, stretching

191

out his hands palm upwards as if to physically demonstrate his innocence. 'I did not murder Stanton.'

'Even though you admit that you knew your school was facing huge problems as a result of the inspection? Even though your affair with your deputy was about to be made public? Even though you admit to a knowledge of chemistry which would certainly have acquainted you with the lethal effects of cyanide? Even though you were one of only three people who had a complete set of keys to the school's buildings?'

'Even though,' answered Pickevance.

'Did you know that Pearl Bowen and Alicia Hilton have both been admitted to Tamworth General Hospital today with suspected poisoning?' asked Tallyforth, his eyes watching Pickevance carefully for the reaction.

'What did you say, Chief Inspector?' Pickevance suddenly say bolt upright. 'So it wasn't her then? I thought it must have been her. But if she's been poisoned too! Who then? Who?'

Tallyforth smiled to himself and prepared his final dart.

'D'you mean Pearl Bowen, sir? Did you think she'd done it?' he asked.

'No, of course not,' came the sharp retort. 'No, I thought it was Alicia. A woman scorned and all that. And she'd become very friendly with that idiot Pugh, which was dangerous and a foolish thing for her to do, though obviously I was in no position to tell her that. But if she's been poisoned too, who on earth....? Are they all right?'

'Mr Pickevance,' Tallyforth said quietly. 'Pearl Bowen drank coffee which had been laced with cyanide. As Hubert Stanton did. Fortunately she was discovered in time for the hospital to pump her stomach clean. She'll be kept in overnight but she's basically okay. Just a bit whacked.'

'And Alicia?'

'She overdosed on paracetamol as far as we can tell,' replied Tallyforth. 'But again she's all right. Not enough to kill her. You thought it was her that murdered Stanton? Is that the real reason you disappeared?'

Pickevance held his head.

'Yes,' he said. 'I knew she'd spoken to Stanton. I'd seen Pugh's

192

letter in the *Tamworth Herald* when I got home on Friday afternoon. I knew they were trying to frame me. And I couldn't clear my name without Sarah finding out about everything. So I panicked.'

'So you ran.'

Tallyforth's curled lip revealed his feelings.

'Yes,' came the weak reply.

But there was no point pursuing him further. Brian Pickevance was a broken man. And they knew now who had killed Hubert Stanton.

NINETEEN

Alf Pugh was arrested at the bar of Tamworth Rugby Club, where he had gone for his regular Tuesday evening booze-up, begun in his days as a player when Tuesday evening was selection evening. He had shown no emotion when the two uniformed constables had entered the club premises and asked him to accompany them to the police station in Tamworth, merely asking if he could finish his pint of Murphy's.

By the time he was brought into the room in Tamworth Police Station where Tallyforth and George Elliott were waiting for him, however, he had begun to show signs of anxiety. His balding head gleamed in the harsh artificial lighting and his walrus moustache was looking distinctly droopy.

'Alfred Pugh,' began Tallyforth, looking up at the standing figure in front of him who was framed between the two constables, 'we have reason to believe that you were involved in the murder of Hubert Stanton, OFSTED Registered Inspector, responsible for leading the inspection of Æthelfleda High School, on the night of Thursday 25th April 1996. It would be easier for you if you told us everything. Is that clear?'

Alf Pugh nodded. A trickle of sweat ran down by his left ear.

'Good. Sit down,' ordered Tallyforth. 'Thank you, constables. You can leave now. I'll call you when I need you.'

The two uniformed constables went out of the room, leaving Alf Pugh facing Tallyforth and George Elliott. The harsh lights beat down on them. Outside there was the patter of rainfall and the distant noise of traffic.

'So?' queried Tallyforth, waiting for the other man to begin.

'I don't know where to begin,' came the reply.

'Try the beginning,' said Tallyforth.

Pugh sighed, adjusted his sitting position, and cleared his throat.

'I suppose it goes back to just about this time last year,' he began. 'That was when Pickevance got the Bowen woman to tell me that I was being made redundant. I was gutted. I'd worked in that school for fifteen years. Went there as head of boys' P.E. fifteen years ago. Used to have the best rugby teams in this part of the county. The under-sixteens won the Eastern Area league five years running. Had seven boys who played for the county and two of them got capped by England schoolboys. Made head of fifth year, as we used to call it, six years later. By the old headmaster. Never stood any nonsense. They knew where they stood with old Pugwash. No nonsense. Stay in line and you'd be all right. Step out of line and you got punished. Rules. You've got to have rules. And you've got to stick by them. In life just as in rugby. I told the kids that. They knew where they stood.'

Pugh's need for self-justification was a trait they were familiar with in their work. It usually preceded a confession. So they were patient. Tallyforth watched him closely, while George Elliott took notes.

'Then Pickevance arrived,' continued Pugh. 'And everything started to change. Ask de Courcy. Ask Jack Parry. Ask Al...... Ask anyone who was here then, they'll tell you. The old headmaster would support you completely. If you sent a kid to him for punishment, you could be sure the kid would be punished severely. With Pickevance, he used to just talk to them and tell them to be good next time. Used to come out of his office laughing their heads off. I've seen them. They'd come back into the changing rooms laughing about Pickisnose. That's what they called him. They didn't do that with the old headmaster. No respect. The school started going downhill. It's never really been the same since they banned the cane. Some kids just need it. And others need the deterrent. But we'd managed to keep the discipline good despite that. Till Pickevance arrived. After that, it went downhill fast.'

There was a pause as he collected his thoughts.

'Then Pearl Bowen told you that you were to be made redundant,' prompted Tallyforth. 'Tell us about that.'

'We'd been warned that there might be job losses,' Pugh recalled.

His forehead had begun to glisten again. 'Same across the country, wasn't it? But you never think it's going to be you. Personally, I thought if anyone went it would be some of the older folk. Like de Courcy or Jack Parry. They were close to retirement anyway. I just assumed..... Anyway, the first time we hear about it in detail is just before the Easter holidays when Pickevance announces at a staff meeting that it's likely we're going to have to lose up to five teachers by September. But you still never think it's going to be you. Took the under-fourteens on tour to Devon. As usual. Done it every year for the past fifteen. Different age group each year. It was the under-fourteens' turn last year. Then, first day back after the holiday, Pickevance announces that the job losses were definite, that he would be interested to hear from anyone interested in voluntary early retirement and that he was discussing a possible restructuring of staffing with the governors. It still never clicked. Even when the Bowen woman stuck a notice on the notice board about proposed changes to the pastoral system, with a head of upper school and a head of lower school instead of five year heads, I just assumed that some of the other year heads had asked to go or been offered other jobs. Some of them had talked about it. Then two days later, she calls me into her office and tells me that I'm to be made redundant. I couldn't believe it. After all I'd done for the kids of that school. Given half my life to that place I had.'

He was getting angry now and his anger showed in the colour of his cheeks. George Elliott guessed that, given his size, he probably suffered from high blood pressure, particularly when he was stressed.

'Didn't you get your union to support you?' she asked.

'Of course, but they're no good now. Especially with the Grant-maintained business. Though I'd been in favour of that, I have to admit. Because it brought in more money. Mr Stevens, he's the Chair of Governors and he's on the committee at the rugby club, he explained it to me at the club one night.'

'Didn't you ask him for support when you were told you were to be made redundant?' she asked again. 'Couldn't he have helped?'

A bitter expression came over Pugh's face.

'I tried him. Of course I tried him. Didn't really want to. Never believed in that sort of thing really. But the boys at the club told me I should. So I rang him and asked to talk to him. But he didn't want to know. Said it was out of his hands. Said the governors had discussed it and made their decision. Said he couldn't do anything even if he'd wanted to. Bastard!'

'Was that the reason you tried to implicate him in fraud?' asked Tallyforth, who had become impatient at this long-winded piece of soul-searching that they had allowed Pugh to indulge in. It was time, he felt, to bring him back to the present. Back to Stanton's murder.

Alf Pugh's face drained of all its colour.

'What do you mean?' he stuttered.

'Come on, Pugh,' said Tallyforth. 'You know exactly what I mean. You planted that story about the fifty thousand pounds missing from the school's books, didn't you? There never was any money missing, was there? You dreamed it all up and got Alicia Hilton to alter the figures on the computer so that it looked as if the money was missing when she was questioned by Hubert Stanton. That's right, isn't it? That way you were planning to get your revenge on Pickevance and on Stevens, weren't you?'

George Elliott looked across at Tallyforth in surprise. How long had he known about this? How had he worked it out? Or was he just guessing again?

Alf Pugh's chin had fallen on his chest. He gazed at the floor.

'And just to make sure that it became public knowledge you sent that fax to OFSTED and that letter to the *Tamworth Herald*,' Tallyforth continued. 'Yes? I notice you're not denying any of this.'

Pugh tried to speak.

'I didn't....' was all he could manage.

'And I suppose that story that Norman de Courcy heard about the sale of playing fields to McDonald's was planted by you as well. I'm sure Stevens isn't the only Conservative who drinks at Tamworth Rugby Club. Well?'

Alf Pugh's head nodded cursorily in agreement. George Elliott was amazed at the accuracy of Tallyforth's guesswork but she scribbled furiously to ensure that she had everything noted.

'What were your movements last Thursday evening?' pressed Tallyforth.

Alf Pugh was still wrestling with himself. His face revealed the mixture of emotions that were flowing through him.

'I was with Alicia all evening,' he said at last, so quietly that they had difficulty in hearing him.

'Do you still possess a set of keys belonging to Æthelfleda High School? Keys that open the changing rooms and the sports hall and give access to the science area?'

'Yes,' Pugh mumbled again. 'But I...... But we...... But she..... But we.....'

'It's no use protecting her, Pugh,' barked Tallyforth. 'You're in this together. Up to the eyeballs. Both of you. Give us your version of what happened.'

There was another long pause. George Elliott watched Tallyforth's gimlet-like gaze penetrate the cortex of Alf Pugh's brain, saw him squirm in its grip, then noted the slow movement of his chin from his chest as he raised his head again to look back. Pugh had composed himself again.

'He treated her like dirt,' he began, the distaste evident in the look on his face. 'Pretended he was supporting her after her husband left, then having it off with her whenever his wife's back was turned. And in his own home as well. And at school. In the stock cupboard. In his office. In her office. He couldn't keep his hands off her. And she couldn't refuse him because she needed the job. Left with two kids to bring up and hardly any maintenance from her ex-husband. And Pickevance kept promising her promotion and more money, as long as she kept quiet. As long as she gave in to him.'

'Is this what Mrs Hilton told you?' asked Tallyforth.

'Yes,' Pugh replied. 'We met up last autumn. By accident. In Sainsbury's. I've been on my own for some years now. Wife left me. Went back to her mother's. Didn't like the rugby club. Said she didn't see why I had to spend so much time there after I'd stopped playing. Anyway, Alicia and I were both shopping in Sainsbury's when we met. It was the term after I'd been made redundant. Still at a loose end. So we arranged to go for a meal and she told me all about Pickevance and the Bowen woman and their house in Lichfield and everything. When I asked her how she knew so much, she told me about him and her and how it had all happened and how he'd ended it when he'd got somebody else

198

in tow.'

'And that was when you decided to get your own back, was it?' asked Tallyforth, with a grim smile. 'Perfect partners in crime. You wanting revenge for being made redundant. Her wanting revenge for being rejected in love.'

Pugh nodded his head.

'We knew that the OFSTED inspection was our chance, yes,' he said. 'We planned to discredit Pickevance and show him up for what he really is.'

'And murdering Stanton - how did that fit in?' asked Tallyforth.

Pugh stiffened.

'That wasn't part of the plan. That was nothing to do with me. I was at home all night.'

'Are you saying that Alicia Hilton murdered Hubert Stanton, is that it?' pressed Tallyforth.

'I'm not saying any more. I've told you all I'm going to tell you. I want to see a solicitor. I have a right.'

'Yes, you have a right, Pugh,' said Tallyforth. 'But the public also has a right to be protected from people who engage in criminal activity. And you're an accessory to murder at the very least. If you won't tell us what happened last Thursday evening, we'll have to see what your lady-friend has to say. But don't think I've finished with you yet. Sergeant, get this man looked after downstairs, will you? We'll probably need to talk to him again later.'

George Elliott stood and moved round the table towards Alf Pugh, who didn't resist as she took his arm and led him to the door.

Though he'd seen it a thousand times and had steeled himself when it came, Tallyforth had never really learned how to handle a woman's tears. Something to do with his mother in his childhood, the police counsellor had explained some years previously when he had sought help. And he would probably never overcome that primitive reaction imprinted on him at such an early age. But he could know about it, could be prepared for it, could take steps to control it when it happened.

But he wasn't prepared for it with Alicia Hilton. Maybe she

reminded him too much of his mother.

She'd been escorted from the General Hospital, where the doctors had wanted her to stay overnight so that she could receive some counselling, for she had admitted by then that she had taken the overdose herself. Though she hadn't told them why, except that it was about a man. She was wearing the cream linen suit that she had had on in the school, though it was rather crumpled by now. Her face was even paler than ever as a result of what she had tried to do and the subsequent hospitalisation.

None of that had been a surprise to Tallyforth. But, after what they now knew about her and what she must know they knew, he had expected her to have dropped the simpering little lady act and to be quite cold. But the tears began almost as soon as she started talking.

'You just can't understand, Chief Inspector,' she began, wiping away the first sign of moisture from the corner of her right eye. 'You just don't know what it's like to love someone and then be thrown over. And not just once either. Yes, I loved my husband John, even though he was cruel to me, even though he used to hit me for overspending on the housekeeping, even though he never gave the children any of his time. But when he left me for another woman, my love for him disappeared overnight. I began to see him for what he really was and Brian Pickevance helped me on the road to recovery. He was kindness itself. And I came to depend on him. First of all, it was just the kindness and then I came to long to see him. And I'd make up reasons for going into his office just so that I could see that craggy face of his, that curling hair. And the first time we made love, it was sheer ecstasy. He'd come over to help repair my car and the children were with Sarah at their house. And he got rather oily so I told him to have a shower and I just went into the bathroom with a towel for him and it just suddenly happened. There on the bathroom floor. It was magic! Better than I'd ever known it.'

The tears were flowing down her face now and Tallyforth shifted in embarrassment in his seat. George Elliott looked on impassively. She was not as easily swayed.

'We were lovers for two years,' Alicia Hilton continued. 'He promised me that he would marry me but he said we must wait till the children were a bit older and a bit more independent. And I agreed. I worshipped him. I thought he was so wise, so sensible, so thoughtful. He used to bring me flowers. Every time he visited. No-one's ever done that before. I really believed he loved me as much as I loved him. And I was prepared to wait for him.'

'What about Sarah, his wife?' interposed George Elliott, seeing that Tallyforth was having difficulty coping with the flow of tears.

'I felt awful about that, of course,' came the reply. 'Sarah had been kind to me as well. She was my friend. And the children too. I loved them nearly as much as my own. But I was in love, Sergeant, and love is blind. All I could see was Brian and me living happily ever after. And then that trollop arrived.'

'You mean Pearl Bowen?' George Elliott asked.

'As soon as I saw her I knew she was trouble. All that make-up and that short skirt and her bosom sticking out. Even though it wasn't cheap stuff she was wearing, she couldn't fool me. I knew her type. I'd seen them before.' Her voice was bitter now as she recalled the arrival of Pearl Bowen. 'She was making eyes at him on the day of the interview while he was showing them all round the school. They came to my office and he introduced me to them. I could see her fluttering her eyelashes at him and I saw his response. He was taken in straightaway. So it was no surprise when she got the job. I'd have wagered pounds on it.'

'Were you still lovers then?'

'Yes,' Alicia Hilton sighed and the tears resumed their course. 'But not for much longer. She started working at the school and I could see her playing up to him, leaning over his desk and giggling. I even tried to warn him but he would have none of it. Said she was a thorough professional and that I was being silly. But I wasn't. I knew what was going on. I knew what she was up to. And then they started going off to weekend conferences together. I argued with him, pleaded with him, begged him not to. But he kept saying it was necessary because of changes in the education system. And then he came back from Malvern a year ago and I knew straightaway from his face that she'd hooked him. He couldn't look me in the eye. But I pressed him and pressed him until finally he admitted that they'd been to bed together. And I told him that it was over between us. I'd tried to hang on to John when he'd started playing around with another woman and I knew it didn't work. I had to get clear of Brian immediately. So he went. And we managed to avoid each other as much as possible at the school. I couldn't leave because of the children. I needed the money, you see. I'd never have got that kind of money anywhere else. And then I caught them at it. In his office. Right before my eyes!'

George Elliott looked at Tallyforth who had stopped shifting awkwardly.

'Was that when you decided to get your revenge?' he asked.

Alicia Hilton's tears redoubled in their intensity, forcing Tallyforth to look away again. There was a long and uncomfortable silence, broken only by the sound of her sobbing and George Elliott's impatient thrumming on the table with the fingers of her left hand.

'It was all Alf's idea,' Alicia Hilton began again at last. 'I'd been on my own for several months. I thought I was getting over it. Until I caught them at it in his office. It was the weekend after that when I was shopping in Sainsbury's and I bumped into Alf. I hadn't seen him since he left, though I knew he felt bitter about being made redundant. And we arranged to meet for a meal and, while we talked, it just sort of emerged, the idea that we could pay him back for what he'd done to us. And her as well.'

'That was the plan to make the OFSTED inspectors think that he had defrauded the school of money and to make them aware of the affair between Pickevance and Pearl Bowen?' queried George Elliott.

'Yes.'

'And to discredit Perry Stevens, the Chair of Governors?'

'That was down to Alf really. He felt let down by Mr Stevens over the redundancy business. You see, he's on the committee at the rugby club. Alf thought he would help him out but he didn't.'

'What about last Thursday evening, Mrs Hilton?' interjected Tallyforth. Tears or no tears, he had to get her to tell them what had happened.

Alicia Hilton's sobs echoed through the room. She took a paper tissue from her handbag and blew her nose.

'Stanton had found out what you were up to, hadn't he?' persisted Tallyforth.

George Elliott looked at him in surprise. How had he known

202

this?

Alicia Hilton sniffed and nodded. Then nodded and sniffed again.

'When he was interviewing me on the Thursday afternoon, he asked me if I knew about Brian and Pearl, so I told him. Then he asked me to show him the school's finances on the computer, so I did. Then he asked me if I knew anything about a fax that had been sent to OFSTED. I told him I didn't but he knew I was lying. I could tell by the way he smiled at me.'

'So you thought he knew that the alleged fraud was false too?'

'Yes,' she sniffed again. 'I just knew that we'd been found out. And I didn't know what to do. I was desperate when I got home. I just knew that the whole world was going to cave in on us on the Friday and not on him and her like we'd intended. We talked, Alf and me, for three hours. Then we went back to the school. It was after Gideon Lashley had gone to the pub - we know he's as regular as clockwork. Alf used his keys to get into the science area and steal the poison. And then I went up to the boardroom where Mr Stanton was working and explained that Mr Pickevance had asked me to check that everything was all right and could I make him some fresh coffee.'

Tallyforth looked at George Elliott meaningfully.

'What about the computer?' asked George Elliott. 'When did you tamper with that?'

'We came back later. We had to make it look as if.........'.

But her voice trailed off and Alicia Hilton was sobbing again. She was still sobbing when the uniformed constable whom Tallyforth had summoned by phone came to take her down to a cell.

Tallyforth stood up and stretched his arms above his head.

'And I said let grief be a falling leaf,' he said. 'Remember? Mitchell's band? That Van Morrison number? Plenty of grief here. Plenty of falling leaves. The old, old story.'

TWENTY

23rd June, 1996. It had been hot all day with temperatures approaching twenty degrees Celsius in the Birmingham area. Even at seven o'clock the sun's heat was still in the air and the atmosphere was sultry as they walked through the car park towards the main arena to find their seats.

Tallyforth had found his coolest clothes, a green cotton shirt and blue cotton trousers. George Elliott, who sat beside him in Block K towards the rear of the massive National Exhibition Centre, wore a pink and white seersucker shirt which hung loosely over a white cotton skirt. It was his first visit and sitting so far away from the stage was a novel experience for him, being used as he was to smaller venues to satisfy his musical tastes. He could understand, looking round, why so many people had hired or brought with them binoculars. He was wondering about hiring some himself but contented himself with the knowledge that what he had come for was more of a musical than a visual extravaganza.

'Is this going to be good?' he asked, turning towards her.

'Difficult to know,' she smiled back at him. 'He has been known to be a complete bastard. And you don't always know what he'll be like. People tell me it's a bit of a game to try to guess his mood from his facial expression.'

Tallyforth was a recent convert to the singing of Van 'The Man' Morrison. He was only one year older than the singer and he could identify with much of the personal reminiscing that Morrison sometimes indulged in, as well as that air of underlying sadness that he brought to his singing of the blues. Tonight Morrison was sharing the bill with the veteran American jazz and blues singer Ray Charles.

'Apparently he was dreadful in the concert he played last weekend in London.' she said. '*The Guardian* slated Van Morrison's set but said that Ray Charles was brilliant.'

'What about that bit in *The Observer* on Sunday about him making some reference to a story in one of the tabloids about him in a steamy sex scene with two naked women? Did you see that?' asked Tallyforth.

'They say he'd split from Michelle Rocca,' she answered. 'Maybe that's affecting his music. It could be one thing or the other tonight. We'll just have to see.'

'A good week to get the O.B.E. in, isn't it?' Tallyforth chuckled. 'Interesting times, as the old Chinese proverb has it!'

George Elliott was reading from the concert programme, while Tallyforth looked around him at the thousands of people still arriving and taking their seats. Because of the heat, many were licking ice reams or drinking beer or coke.

'There was a bit in my paper about Æthelfleda High School yesterday,' Tallyforth began again. 'Seems it's being closed down.'

'Because of the inspection? Or because of Stanton's murder?' she asked, looking up from her reading.

'Both,' he replied. 'Apparently after all the fuss, they got hardly any kids wanting to go there next year. And a lot of the older kids have transferred to other schools.'

'So Pugh and Hilton got their way then?' she asked grimly. 'Even though they've got long jail sentences to enjoy their success in! What about Pickevance?'

'He's retired. On medical grounds. Mental breakdown.'

'So who's been running the place? Pearl Bowen?' she asked, genuinely curious now as she recalled the interviews she had had with the deputy headteacher during the enquiry into Hubert Stanton's murder.

'No, she was moved sideways to another school,' Tallyforth answered. 'Norman de Courcy's been in charge. That's what the article was about. Because yesterday was the celebration of the Twelve Hundredth anniversary of Offa's death - the re-creation of the Boxing Day feast with all the staff dressed up as Mercian lords and ladies and the kids putting on various side shows and entertainments. De Courcy was quoted as saying that what had been planned for the celebration of Offa's death had become a wake to the death of Æthelfleda High School.'

'Sad really,' she said.

'Life is, George.'

Tallyforth looked at her as she bent over her programme again. Was it possible? he wondered.

But then the lights dimmed, the crowd's noise dwindled and the Van Morrison Big Band, which included Georgie Fame on the organ, Brian Kennedy on support vocals and Pee Wee Ellis on saxophone, came on stage and led into the singer's opening number.

Right from the defiant opening numbers from the *Too Long in Exile* period, through the poignant *Who Can I Turn to?* and the old favourite *Moondance* to his finale of *Have I Told You Lately that I Love You?*, Van Morrison was on top-class form. His voice roared through the huge stadium, holding his audience in thrall. Tallyforth marvelled at the voice - that roaring, shouting, whispering, angry, melodic, powerful voice, which seemed to contain and control every emotion he himself felt and yet which simultaneously challenged those same emotional states and went out to meet them head on.

For his encore, Van Morrison chose *That's Life* and *All Saint's Day*, before surprising his audience with a number from his back catalogue.

As the singer quietened down his band to allow him to give the full treatment to the melody, Tallyforth felt George Elliott's hand reach for his and squeeze it. He looked at her and she smiled up at him as Van the Man's lament roared through the still night air:

> *I saw the danger, yet I walked*
> *Along the enchanted way*
> *And I said let grief be a falling leaf*
> *At the dawning of the day.*